A PERFECT DOM

Club Perfect

Jade Belfry

EROTIC ROMANCE

Siren Publishing, Inc.
www.SirenPublishing.com

A SIREN PUBLISHING BOOK
IMPRINT: Erotic Romance

A PERFECT DOM
Copyright © 2014 by Keri Jade Ruddick

ISBN: 978-1-62741-380-0

First Printing: June 2014

Cover design by Harris Channing
All art and logo copyright © 2014 by Siren Publishing, Inc.

ALL RIGHTS RESERVED: This literary work may not be reproduced or transmitted in any form or by any means, including electronic or photographic reproduction, in whole or in part, without express written permission.

All characters and events in this book are fictitious. Any resemblance to actual persons living or dead is strictly coincidental.

Printed in the U.S.A.

PUBLISHER
Siren Publishing, Inc.
www.SirenPublishing.com

DEDICATION

For Channon and Dwayne.

You wouldn't be reading this book without the support of my mother, author Dale Cadeau. So glad we're taking this journey together.

Much love to my grandma, who always has a good book and a cup of tea by her side.

To my mister, John, for patience, support, and snuggles.

Last but not least, love to Linda, Jennifer, Michelle, Bassam, Kyle, Aileen, Dave, Julie, Bill, Wayne, Michael, Faye, Shannon, Kristy, Yvonne, Scott, Katee, and of course, Jax.

A PERFECT DOM

Club Perfect

JADE BELFRY
Copyright © 2014

Chapter One

"Come on, Baby Dom, I've got someone for you to meet."

The next person to call him Baby Dom was going to get punched. So what if that's what they called everyone who was new here. Sure, Vincent was new, but he didn't care about that rule, and he also didn't care that it was his best friend who called him that. He'd been on edge for weeks. His fists were clenched tight and itching to start something. *Just say it one more time…*

Shit. He tried to calm down. Of all the schemes that he had gotten himself caught up in, this was just about the craziest. That was saying a lot from the guy who had been a regular on the suspension roll all throughout high school. Vincent hoped that since he'd managed to charm his way into a diploma and survive graduation, that he'd be able to make it though a few weeks here. Hopefully.

The here was Club Perfect, a private BDSM club. That's right, a club devoted to the darker side of sex. He'd been told that it was a place of bondage, discipline, dominance, submission, sadism and masochism. Apparently there were thousands of clubs like this around the country, hidden in industrial areas or private residences. This one was conveniently located just two short exits off the freeway, but about a million miles away from his ordinary life.

He had expected it to smell. To be dank, dark and absolutely filthy. Instead it was just a normal night club—well, a much more naked version of a normal night club. It had a calm atmosphere, rich tapestry couches readily available and a well-stocked bar without any line. The club was even well lit. Vincent he had no trouble seeing all the members that his friend James wanted him to meet. Someone had put some serious bucks into this place. An advertiser might have easily billed it as a "conservative lounge for people over thirty." Except, in the fine print they would have to run a disclaimer that it was also a place for people who liked to undress in public and spank each other.

Was he one of those people? Not yet, but hopefully he could learn to be someone who got off on this kind of kink. If he was going to join this lifestyle, and he had no choice but to join, he had to jump in with both feet. He was a fighter, a scrapper in his youth, and stubborn to the bone. If he was going to commit to this, he couldn't do it half cocked. Especially not if he was going to get vengeance.

Ahem, revenge, not vengeance. He wasn't Batman. He wasn't obscenely wealthy, and he didn't have a special symbol beckoning him out into the night in the name of justice. Although his new clothes could be considered a type of costume, and this club, he supposed, could be considered a secret lair. It sure had a lot of tools and gadgets. Some even vibrated.

His revenge, not vengeance, would be against his ex-girlfriend, Catherine. She was the woman of his dreams, and she had dumped him exactly thirty-six days ago.

Catherine. Just thinking about her brought him to his knees. *Oh God. Get a grip.* It probably wasn't proper protocol for a dude to cry in a BDSM club—well unless it was crying out in pleasure. Vincent tried to focus, stuff it down, and get past his grief toward the ending of their relationship.

His sassy, beautiful girlfriend Catherine had left him. She had always kept him guessing, and apparently had saved her biggest surprise until the end. They had been together for just over three years. The almost 1200 days he had held her, been inside her and welcomed her into his home? Well, they mattered to him. They were some of the best days of his life. Anyone could see that they had a future together, and yet she had thrown it all away as if it meant nothing. As if he meant nothing to her. And it was all because of sex.

It would have been easier on his ego if she had been cold or cruel when she stomped on his heart and broke it to a million pieces. Instead she just seemed bored. Apparently she was totally uninterested in anything else he had to offer or in the life he worked so hard to build for them. She had dismissed him from their relationship with all the emotion and tact of a manager firing the incompetent fry clerk at your favourite fast food joint. "It's not you, it's me" would have been kind. Instead he was told that it was very much him. And specifically, he didn't measure up in the bedroom. Inches yes, domination, no. Instead of sweet romance, she wanted force for foreplay. She explained that she had been asking for it from him for a while in subtle ways and he had never taken the hint. So she had given up on him. Good-bye, Vincent, and good-bye, relationship.

Catherine was single now and so was he. She could do whatever she wanted with whomever she wanted. For all he knew, she could be using multiple partners to achieve multiple orgasms. She was probably having the time of her life. So why was he here, the new Baby Dom in residence at an underground sex club, with his best friend, sweating his balls off in leather pants?

Because he still loved her. His wounded pride had to take a backseat to that fact. Sad but true. So, she wanted him to be more dominant? Then that's what he would become. Simple as that. He would do whatever it took to get his girl back.

That was the plan, anyways.

It hadn't been a direct line from her bedside to this club. No, it had taken a while to figure out what to do. First he had moped. For days he just lain on the couch with his dog Gus and felt sorry for himself. He ate pizza for far too many nights in a row and ended up with a couple of cases of empties to return for refund. Emptying those beer bottles had helped bury his pain. Until the night he had drank one too many and had called up James for help. James was his best friend. James was cool. James was in charge. James was…well after that drunken conversation he quickly learned that James had the perfect solution to his problems, because James was something called a "Dom."

His friend revealed that several nights a week he came to this club wearing heavy boots, a tight black T-shirt and stupid leather pants. He also did something called "scenes" with a "Sub." A Sub was apparently a submissive person, or the yin to the Dom's yang, James had explained. It was the Dom's job to control the Sub and see to their pleasure and well-being. And if Vincent wanted to be a Dom, James could help him. Drunk Vincent had been an easy sell on the idea. Sober Vincent had his doubts. In the days that followed, much to Vincent's embarrassment, James had moved forward with the plan and had arranged a trial membership to this exclusive club.

James had also set him up with someone who taught people how to be dominant. A female Sub and trainer, who apparently was very good at her job. All Vincent had to do was attend some one-on-one classes, learn the lifestyle, get comfortable with a little slap and tickle and he'd become the man Catherine wanted him to be.

So that was why he was here now, dressed ridiculously, being blasted by loud music, and sidestepping freaks in every manner of dress or, um, position. Tonight was meet-the-teacher night, but James, the social butterfly, stopped to chat with other members every few minutes. The delay was both a blessing and a curse. A curse as Vincent was repeatedly introduced as the new Baby Dom in residence. A blessing because he got a chance to quietly observe the other club goers and try to get a feel of exactly what he was getting himself into.

Everything was openly displayed here in the club and no one seemed to care. Men and women together, two guys, two girls. Some even with three, four, or five partners. No one batted an eyelash, no matter the coupling. Every fantasy was on display and wrapped up in sweat and PVC leather. One group was using some weird fallen-over cross thing while an audience watched, enthralled. Vincent tried not to stare, it was just so bizarre to see people openly having sex. Other members were milling about the club, dancing or hanging out at the bar. Everyone seemed to be having a good time. Guess it must be just their idea of an interesting night out. *Honey, call the babysitter, we're gonna go watch some real-life porn tonight!*

James's conversation drew to a close and they moved further inside the club. Vincent dutifully followed him past the marble-topped private bar. James, who was usually pretty reserved and refused to socialize at work, was the life of the party here. Everyone knew him, and it appeared, respected him. The members sitting at the bar even put down their drinks in order to shake James's hand. Vincent realized just how comfortable James was in this club. He was in charge at work too, and liked well enough, but this was different. This was James fully in his element. He introduced Vincent to the drinkers. Again he called him a Baby Dom. While Vincent scowled, James smirked.

"Look, you don't have to be so happy about this."

James feigned innocence. "Vin, you're the one who came to me. I'm just glad to finally be introducing you to the lifestyle."

Finally? Wait, had James really thought that he would be interested in this stuff on his own? Without Catherine giving the death sentence to his sexual technique? Wow. Maybe James didn't know him as well as he thought. "Look, I'm just glad that you're not the one training me."

James's smile grew even larger. "A newbie could never handle my level of kink, Vin, that's why I'm not the trainer. Mia is."

Mia. She was the Sub who, James claimed, would mold him into the perfect dominant. She was a longtime friend of James's. That was basically the only information he had on the woman who would be his teacher. If nothing else, she would be an honest third party, who would point out what he was doing wrong sexually. If all went according to plan, she would teach him everything he needed to know about BDSM and becoming a Dom. He would be back in Catherine's bed in no time.

Mia. It was a pretty name. Feminine. Although, you couldn't tell from a name alone if someone was nineteen or ninety. Vincent felt very anxious about the meeting and wished that James had coughed up more details about her. He was excited to get this plan started, but also felt awkward and nervous like this was a first date. He hadn't gotten a kiss from Catherine on the first date. In fact, it had gone so poorly he had thought that she would never want to see him again. Luckily she had called the next day to offer him a second chance. Hopefully she would give him a third chance and they could put this all behind them.

He'd probably have to have sex with Mia. Ugh. Vincent's stomach rolled. Not that he didn't like sex, he had just never cheated on a girlfriend before. How was he supposed to touch another woman when his girlfriend—ex-girlfriend—was only thirty-six days in his past? If he really loved Catherine, shouldn't he stay monogamous to her?

Wait, she had left *him*. She could be out doing God-knows-who. Before they had arrived, James had kindly reminded him that he was single now, and not dead. He was a human being with clear needs. Plus, plain and simple, this was research. Even the best mechanic doesn't know what's wrong with a car without taking it for a ride around the block, right?

Besides he might not even be attracted to Mia. She could be hideous. What kind of woman would make a career out of being a sexual submissive? She must be a little off to just offer herself up to someone, sight unseen. Was she just that obsessed with sex? Maybe.

A thousand other thoughts rolled through his head about how terrible Mia could turn out to be. His excitement died down and his nerves took centre stage.

"Can we grab a drink first?" Vincent had a crumbled-up twenty stashed in his boot. Of course there wouldn't be pockets in these ridiculous pants.

"No alcohol in the training room," James growled. "And quit stalling."

Vincent was about to protest that he hadn't been stalling—hey he wasn't the one who was stopping to talk every two seconds like he was some King of Kinksville—but James was already walking away, towards the back of the club. Did this place never end? It hadn't looked half this big from the street.

In fact it hadn't looked like much at all. The building that housed the club looked like just any other older anonymous office building in the industrial area of town. The street housed a coffee shop, a small dive bar, and office after office where people went to work day in and day out. Yet this particular building housed a secret that most would never find out.

Walking in, Vincent had discovered that the lobby was guarded by some meathead-looking ex-military guy who carried a concealed weapon. Too bad he hadn't bothered to conceal his contempt. It was clear that he didn't want to take your ID and run it through their database. He didn't want to let you though the darkly tinted double door behind him. Lucky for him, if you were a member, even on trial like Vincent was, the meathead had no choice but to let you in. And when those doors had opened, Vincent stepped into another world.

Vincent had the same fish-out-of-water feeling now. Walking down a hallway and reaching a particular doorway, James abruptly stopped. Vincent, distracted by the club atmosphere and still fiddling with his revealing garb, almost walked smack right into him. The main room of the club was far behind them. The thumping music was at a more tolerable level now.

James chuckled at Vincent's distraction in a kind way. His sympathetic look told Vincent that he had once been there too, new and unsure and about to experience something completely different. "Are you ready?"

Suddenly, Vincent felt lightheaded, like being at the top of a roller coaster right before the car speeds down the first loopy loop on the track. Shit. Was this training really what he wanted? "Maybe I should just go home."

James cocked an arrogant eyebrow, and any kindness instantly evaporated. "Fine."

"Fine? You're cool with that? I can just go?"

"Vin, if you leave here, you will never get Catherine back. Which I am perfectly fine with, because she's a bitch."

"Don't say that."

James gave him a look that dared Vincent to argue with him. There had never been any love lost between James and his ex. "Look, are we doing this or not? I had to call in a favour to get you this particular trainer. At least meet her before you decide to tuck your tail between your legs and run."

"Fine, yeah, okay I guess." Vincent cleared his throat and wiped his damp nervous palms on his pants. He couldn't remember the last time he had been this nervous. This was more than first date nervous. There was so much more riding on this.

James sighed. "You guess *what?*"

"I guess we'll do this then. I'll meet her."

James smiled and put a hand on Vincent's shoulder like a big brother. "Don't worry, Vin, It will be fine. Mia's used to inexperienced guys."

"I'm not a fucking virgin," Vincent snapped and shrugged off James's hand.

"Sure, sure you're not." James shook his head and chuckled. "But you're here because you're a virgin to *this* kind of experience. Just calm down a little, or else you'll spook her."

"I thought she was a pro."

For a brief second James's cool and collected façade slipped. "She's not a pro, she's a human being. Remember that." James looked him in the eyes and for a minute, Vincent thought maybe his friend was having second thoughts. Maybe he would need his fists after all. Then James's anger cleared. "Look, I'm only bringing you here because you're my friend and a good guy who could really benefit from this training."

Vincent nodded, not sure which of them James was trying to reassure with his explanation. Then, with a final nod, James went back to being regular old James. His smile was cocky as he swiped the key card to unlock the door.

Vincent expected the door, heavy wrought iron and antique, to groan and slowly swing open to reveal a medieval castle. Instead it opened silently. James stepped through the doorway, gesturing for him to follow. "Welcome to the dungeon."

Vincent took a deep breath and walked into the room. For a dungeon, it was pretty damn bright. It was much brighter than the rest of the club. It took a full minute for Vincent's eyes to adjust to the glare. Vincent shielded his eyes with one hand and tried to make out the shapes in the room. It was a large room. He'd had to duck his head for his six-four frame to get through the doorway, but here the high ceilings gave him lots of room to stand tall.

Where to look first? Vincent's eyes were drawn from one foreign object to another as James shut and locked the door behind them. It was almost silent in this room and was a little cold. The stone that covered the walls and floors helped the dungeon live up to its name. Other than that, it was more of a storage room then a training room. Built into the stone walls were hooks and shelves that held a variety of different instruments and devices. At various points around the room, equipment stations were set up. At one end of the room was another weird fallen-over cross.

While Vincent was still trying to get his bearings, James strode across the room like he owned it. He wrapped his arms around a petite female. His hug must have been a tight one. She squealed, catching Vincent's attention.

She was a little thing, maybe five foot or a bit more. She was a little too lean, but her body was toned. And she looked really nervous, maybe even more nervous than Vincent was. She was young. Mid-twenties, maybe? He hadn't expected that. That made him at least a half dozen years older than her. Would it be strange getting lessons from someone younger than him? He hoped that she would still be as knowledgeable and committed to the lessons as he needed her to be. His stomach took another nosedive with fresh worries.

Wait, James said that he had specifically picked her for Vincent. He trusted his friend. Maybe a young woman was what he needed to teach an old guy like him new tricks.

Man, she had a ton of hair. Her thick raven-black waves were pinned back from her face but the back flowed freely to her waist. That hair would look great spread out on a pillow or grasped in his fist as he…

Whoa, slow down there. At least speak to the girl before you start imagining her in bed! Wow, well the whole hope he had earlier of not being attracted to his teacher went completely out the window. This should be a very interesting semester.

James still held Mia. James wasn't usually an affectionate person, so seeing him holding a woman he was obviously fond of was…not normal. He held her and whispered in her ear. She smiled. After one last small hug, he released her. Then they both looked over at Vincent expectantly.

"Come on, Baby Dom, time to meet your teacher."

Vincent snarled at his friend, and that stupid nickname. When he turned to Mia, he saw that she was taken aback by his aggression. She actually took a step away as he approached, a flash of fear in her big brown eyes.

Shit. So much for not starting off on the wrong foot. He needed to check his attitude. His big size would have probably been enough to frighten her already. He didn't want her to think he was some macho asshole too...even if maybe that was the way he was acting to cover up his feelings of inadequacy.

He took a deep breath and tried to calm down. Maybe even smile. "I'm Vincent." He extended his hand to her to shake, but instead she just nodded to him. Her fear was still tangible in the air and she regarded him very carefully.

Awkward silence.

James sighed. "Oh God, you two can just relax. Mia, this is Vincent. He's a gentle giant who can act like a prick occasionally, but is completely harmless." Vincent fought to rein in any reaction and stay calm. "Vincent, this is Mia. She will be your Sub to train on. Be nice to her. She's perfect for you."

"Now I'm perfect, James?" Mia's weak smile at James's words was a step in the right direction. She seemed, like Vincent was, to be trying to calm her nerves. Her voice was bigger than he had expected from this slight girl. Her tone was rich, high, and a little nasally, but sweet.

"I said you were perfect to train him, not perfect in general," James teased.

She chuckled. "Thanks for the clarification."

There was a pause, where she seemed to be making up her mind about something. Then she took a deep breath and approached Vincent. She held out her small hand for him to shake. Carefully he took it in the rough mitt of his palm. Her skin was very pale against his, but warm. After he finished shaking and released her hand, she stayed still in place, observing him.

"James said that you two work together."

Vincent nodded. "Yeah, the same place but not really together." The company they worked for dealt in international goods. While Vincent was the warehouse supervisor, James was the head of the shipping department.

"And you're friends?" Mia raised an eyebrow.

"Yup." Vincent wasn't exactly sure why he was getting the third degree from Mia, but he wasn't biting. She had no reason to doubt who he was or his desire to become a Dom.

Mia took a step back, suddenly unsure. Shit, he she was just making small talk. He needed to relax. Vincent had the distinct feeling that if he didn't start opening up soon and answering her questions, their training together would be over before it even began.

He cleared his throat. "Ah, James and I actually met years before we ever worked together."

"Oh?"

"That's right." James nodded, encouragingly. "Vin was dating my inept former secretary."

"Catherine?" Mia asked. James must have told her some things about him ahead of time.

"Yes. But she only worked for him briefly. We met at an office party. I was working a construction site at the time and came as her date."

"And I wanted to meet the asshole who was dumb enough to date such an airhead."

Vincent shot James a warning look. "Except James found out that we actually have a lot in common. He suggested I apply to the warehouse and I've worked my way up to my current position. I stayed even after Catherine was asked to leave."

"When was this?"

"Three of four years…?" James guessed.

"It's odd that I've never heard of you until now." Mia looked back and forth between the men for an explanation.

"I've never heard of you either, Mia. Not until I confessed my little problem to our friend here."

James chuckled sheepishly. "You know I keep my personal life and business life separate. There was no need for either of you to know about each other until now."

Mia shook her head. "It makes me wonder what else you're hiding, James."

"Have you checked his closets for skeletons lately?" Vincent joked.

She laughed. "I doubt many would fit in there between the designer suits and fetish wear." As soon as the words were out of her mouth, Vincent was reminded of the fetish clothes he currently wore, that James had assured him was normal Dom attire. Unfortunately both his T-shirt and leather pants were skin tight and left little to the imagination. And his trainer was very openly checking him out at the moment. He took the opportunity to do the same. When in Rome, right? Just like earlier when he was squinting around the room, he didn't know what to look at first. Her freckles, maybe? Perhaps her pixie nose? She had a very classic look, with a slight exotic hint to her features. She had a classic prettiness that was very appealing. She wore a purple corset and a short grey skirt. Both revealed that she had a nice body, even though her hips and breasts were a little smaller than what he was used to. Overall he had to admit she was pretty damn hot.

He was pleasantly surprised when he saw that she had tattoos. So there was a wild side to the teacher! First he saw red *X*s on both of her wrists. Next he spotted what looked like some sort of portrait on her legs mostly hidden by her skirt. He didn't have any body art himself, but hers didn't turn him off. In fact they made her more interesting. Despite the tats, she still looked like a nice, ordinary girl. Probably too nice to be in a place like this. If he saw her outside of here, would he buy her a drink? Sure. That was a no-brainer. Would he have the balls to ask her out? He'd like to think so, even though she was obviously out of his league.

He wondered what else James had told her, and what preconceptions she had about him. Would she think him weak or lacking in masculinity because he wasn't naturally dominant? What kind of man needed someone to teach them about being in control? He probably didn't look like the kind of guys she usually trained. Although he appeared strong on the outside, he had learned thirty-six days ago that he was fragile as glass on the inside. He needed someone to help him get back everything he had lost. If he was truthful with himself, he would admit that more than just an ex-girlfriend was at stake here. Was Mia the one who could help him feel like a man again? Was James right? Was she perfect for the job?

Vincent realized, embarrassedly enough, that he had spoken that last thought out loud. James laughed. Mia did too, with only a slight hesitation. She was clearly still nervous. Her smile highlighted her small red mouth. "In case you're wondering, James tells everyone that I'm the perfect trainer. He's good for the ego."

"Do I lie?" The two shared a private look. There was an easy, obvious affection between them. Vincent wondered exactly how well they knew each other. He almost growled when he thought of the two of them together. Oh man, he had just met her and he couldn't possibly be possessive of her already. It was none of his business if they were more than friends. "Stop worrying," James commanded softly. At first Vincent thought he was saying it to him, but when Mia started to visibly relax he knew that the command was for her benefit alone.

Mia cleared her throat, and nodded to herself. "I'm sorry, Vincent. It's been a while since I trained anyone. I'm a little out of practice."

"That's okay, I've never been trained before." This brought about more shared laughter between Mia and James. *Wow, great.* He sounded like a fool.

James cleared his throat. "So I've decided on a test to make this all a little more interesting."

Vincent rolled his eyes. "Geeze, James, I don't even know if I'm going to like this yet and already I have to take a test?"

James was smug. "Oh you'll like *this* test all right, but it's not going to be given today. It will be at the end of your training."

"A final exam?" Mia asked, raising an eyebrow. Oh, so this test was a surprise to her, too.

"Yes. You have, let's say...eight weeks from now to prepare."

"That's quick." Mia frowned. She didn't seem pleased. Why would James spring this on her? He wasn't her first Dom to train, so why create a new element now? Was it just for him? What kind of shit was James pulling? Vincent crossed his arms over his big chest and his look matched Mia's.

"It'll be more than enough time." James's voice was firm. There would be no arguing with him. It made Vincent want to roll his eyes again. To him, eight weeks seemed like way too long, but whatever. If he wanted a final exam from him, fine. He would learn what he needed, get Catherine back and then get on with his life.

James backed toward the door. "Go ahead and get started. Have fun. I'm going to leave you for a while."

"You can stay if you want, James." Mia's voice sounded strained. They shared another look. James shook his head but smiled, sending her some nonverbal reassurance. It was like James had just vouched for him. Man, he owed his friend a hell of a lot if this crazy scheme actually worked.

"No. You'll be fine without me. I have some business to take care of. Feel free to join me later if you think you're ready." He winked at Vin and left them. The heavy door closed with a click.

Alone with Mia, Vincent's nervousness tripled. What did they do now? Talk? Have sex? He tried not to show how panicked he felt.

Mia smiled softly. It hit him then that she had probably done this introduction many times before. Shit. He didn't want to think of how many times a man like himself had stood before her and she shared her knowledge and her body with them. Was she always this jumpy at first?

"Do you prefer Vincent or Vin? I know James calls you Vin…"

"Vincent is good."

She smiled and took a deep breath. "Okay then. Vincent. Why don't you tell me why you're here?"

She didn't know? "I thought James…"

"James did tell me, but I want to hear it in your own words, okay?"

Vincent tried to relax. It was still difficult to put his shame into words. "My girlfriend Catherine broke up with me. She said that I wasn't man enough in the bedroom for her."

Mia nodded her head. "So you're looking to become more dominant?"

"Um, yeah, I guess so."

"And Catherine will be your Sub?"

Vincent nodded. "Yes, if she'll have me back. If she hasn't already moved on. I understand we're broken up right now and we're both free to do what we please, but I hope if I learn to show this side of myself she'll…"

"…Want you back?"

"Yeah," he sighed. "That sounds pretty pathetic, doesn't it?"

Mia shook her head. "Would it help if I told you that you're not the first guy to have this problem?"

His head snapped up, hope in his eyes. "I'm not?"

"Far from it."

"It just feels so humiliating, so devastating to be told that you suck in bed. Men are supposed to be good at sex. It's in our genes." Vincent shifted from one foot to another. It was hard to admit the truth, but if this was training was going to work, he supposed he may as well be honest.

"Vincent, you have to stop judging yourself. We all have different motivations for what we do. I can understand yours completely. You're struggling with your need to please her." She shook her head. "I actually think it's kind of sweet that you love her so much. Not everyone would go to the lengths that you're going to."

"Thanks."

Mia smiled. "Vincent, do you know what it means to be a Dom?"

"Sure." He bluffed.

She smiled sweetly, totally not buying his act. "There are many different kinds of dominants. Let's get the basics down first. Anything more you can learn as you go. First, Baby Dom…"

Vincent growled. "I'd prefer you not call me that."

"I can understand that. But you have to earn your titles here. That way we can figure out how our training will go."

"Yes, but aren't submissives supposed to respect the wishes of their Dom?"

There was a flash of something in her eyes. He couldn't tell if it was anger or pride. It was gone in a second, but an edge crept into her voice. "Absolutely, but I'm your teacher, not your submissive. Respect needs to be earned. As I was saying, first, a Baby Dom is a Dom in training and new to the scene, as you are. I assume you're reacting negatively because James called you a Baby Dom out on the club floor in front of the other members. Clear communication is important so that misunderstandings don't arise later. James called you by that title to both tell the other members that you are new, and to prepare them for any questions you may have. It was not meant as an insult."

She paused to allow her words time to sink in. It all made sense now. Fuck, he had acted like a thug for no reason. She must have thought he was a Neanderthal. What else had he been wrong about? *Time to park your expectations at the door and enjoy the ride, buddy.*

He uncrossed his arms and tried to open his mind as she continued. "A Dom or a Sir is a fully-trained dominant. A top is a

Dom without a Sub, or bottom. A bedroom Dom is in control only in the bedroom or 'sexual situations.'" Her eyes twinkled. Was that her favourite place to be dominated? Very nice. "A sexual sadist is in charge of sex and the administration of pain. A dungeon Dom is in control of punishment and rarely includes sex in the play. A slave holder is in charge twenty-four-seven and finally, a Master is a full-time committed Dom that has been accepted by the Sub. Usually a contract is required to bind them, and the Sub is collared." She paused again, and her smile returned. "That's a brief summary of some of the types of Doms out there. Some overlap and titles can change regionally, but most are universal."

"I didn't know it was so complex."

"Yeah, it's an entirely different world." Truer words were never spoken. "So, Vincent, what kind of Dom do you think you are?"

"I don't know. I just want to be the perfect Dom."

"There's no such thing as a perfect dominant, Vincent. And there's no perfect submissive either, so don't expect it." She laughed. "Sub, bottom, slut, slave. It's all just terminology, but let's pick a place to start from and see where it takes us. What do you think Catherine means when she says that you need to be more dominant?"

He took a deep breath and tried to think of what he wanted, and what he hoped Catherine would want. Catherine didn't say that she had a problem with him outside of the bedroom, so he decided to just stick to the reason why he was here and leave those other types of Doms to the people who were really interested in this stuff. "Bedroom Dom."

"Okay." His words drew another sweet smile from his teacher.

"So I would control everything in the bedroom? No questions asked?"

"To a certain extent, yes. Being a Dom isn't just about being in control. Although yes, most do normally crave a certain amount of control within themselves and their environment. It could be through organization or by controlling certain situations." She smiled sympathetically. "You'll understand it all in time. Don't get overwhelmed with the details now."

"So is there a bedroom around here?" He looked around the dungeon. Nope, no bed. He'd have to improvise. "And what do I do first?" He reached for the zipper of his tight leather pants, anxious to have them off and start training. He stopped when he saw that Mia was just watching him and making no move to undress. He blushed. Maybe he had this all wrong.

"The first thing you do is calm down. We're not quite ready for that part yet, Vincent. Don't try to rush your training."

"Fine." He zipped himself up, then crossed his arms over his chest again and waited. He tried to look tough again to cover his embarrassment. And he pretended he didn't see Mia quickly check out his arm muscles. *Good work, teach.* So maybe she was just as attracted to him as he was to her. Sweet.

"Let's sit for a moment," she suggested and gestured to the leather sofa along one back wall. It was black with thick lines and had a similarly designed coffee table in front. Both looked a little out of place and too modern for the dungeon. She followed him as he crossed the room and took a seat.

They both sat stiffly on the sofa. The expensive leather was comfortable enough, but they were both still a little on edge.

"Let's take this a step back. How good are you at giving orders and communicating clearly?"

He shrugged. "I'm okay. I assign tasks to guys at work daily, manage manpower, that sort of thing."

"Good. Then this exercise should be easy." She slid a pack of cards onto the table. They were the cheap plastic kind, with navy blue writing on the box. There was nothing special about them, you could get a pack like this for a buck anywhere.

"You want to play a card game?"

She had a mischievous glint in her eye that was pretty cute. "Do I? You decide. Tell me what to do."

This exercise seemed a little bizarre, but okay, he would play her game. "Spread the cards out on the table."

She shifted closer so that she could reach the table easily. She looked at the pack of cards for a moment, and then made a show of trying to spread the pack across the table's surface. Her movements were exaggerated. There was no mistaking her meaning. There was no spreading the deck without taking them out of the container first.

Vincent's tough act vanished. He chuckled. "Okay, fine. Please open the pack and take the cards out."

Mia smiled and did as he instructed. She slid the pack of cards out of the box and into her hand.

"And now spread the cards out on the table." Again, she did exactly as he asked, fanning the cards.

"Do you see how things work better when you give clear specific instructions?" He nodded. "That's what I meant earlier about clear communication. It's important."

"Okay I get it."

"Good. Now what?"

Still with the cards? Okay fine, keep playing along. "Please put the cards in order." She gave him a blank look. "Start with the aces and then... No, turn over each card, look at what value it is and then put it in a pile depending on its value. Count the ace for one, and go up to the king for thirteen. Put them in a nice stack."

"Excellent." She grinned as she started to sort the cards. She flipped the cards over with relish and quickly put them in order. Her long fingers were very agile and she completed the task quickly and easily. When finished she looked at him for approval. "All done, Vincent."

"Uh, thanks, good job."

She glowed under his praise. He found it a little odd. Why should she care about pleasing him? "See Vincent, imagine this was a scene...a scene is an encounter between a Dom and a Sub. It starts with the Sub recognizing that the Dom is in charge. Just like I did when I put the cards on the table and turned to you for instruction. Then the Dom decides how the scene will go and gives instruction to the Sub. The instructions are the tools of the scene. Then once the scene is completed the Dom gives praise to reward and appreciate their Sub. You did beautifully."

"Thanks." Score! He only hoped he remembered all of the steps she mentioned. "Do you do this card thing with everyone?"

"Nope, I just thought of this with the cards a few days ago. I've taught this particular lesson a bunch of different ways before. One time I had a Baby Dom walk me through cooking a spaghetti dinner. That was interesting…and messy." She smiled, remembering. "Of course I was also naked the whole time because the first thing he ordered…"

"…was for you to lose the clothes?"

Mia blushed and nodded.

"I'll try to remember that for next time," Vincent teased. He was loosening up and he liked it when she blushed. Yeah, he was flirting a little. No harm in that.

"Always be specific when telling a Sub what you want them to do. Never assume anything. Once you have a relationship established with someone, of course, you don't have to be this literal, but until then it helps to negotiate first or give directions ahead of time. That way there's no confusion in the heat of the moment."

"Okay, I'll try to remember that."

She picked up the cards and carefully put each card back into their original package. "So now what?"

"Do you know how to play hearts?"

Mia's look told him that was the wrong answer. "Is that really what you want to do?"

"Nope, I hate playing cards." He looked around the room. "Man, this is a weird place with all kinds of weird stuff."

"Would you like a tour? I could explain what each piece of equipment is for."

Vincent was relieved. "Thanks, I was worried that I'd have to figure all of this out for myself."

"No problem."

He stood up and adjusted his pants. They were sticky when they heated up. He couldn't wait to have them off. Then he noticed that Mia hadn't moved. Was he supposed to still be giving her specific directions?

Instead she just looked up at him and held out her hand. She looked a little timid, unsure, but once his hand touched hers, her smile deepened. He gently helped her to her feet. But when standing, she didn't let go of him. He hesitated, but when his eyes met hers, she nodded encouragingly. "This is how we start, Vincent. Connection is very important." Her hand felt warm and smooth. He was sure it was just his imagination, but her touch felt a little electric. He hoped that his tough callused hands weren't too rough for her.

"Might as well start as we mean to go on." The old saying was past his lips before Vincent realized what he was saying. Instantly he looked embarrassed. "Sorry, that's just something my grandma used to say." No matter if he was going off to school or on a first date, she'd always remind him that it was best to start a new task as if you had the intentions to go the distance. He smiled at the memory. It seemed appropriate for the moment, even though a dungeon was not the most appropriate place to think about his dear old granny.

"Mia, you lead the way."

"Sure." She kept her smile and her steps were light and bouncy as if today was her first day at school, instead of his first day in her classroom.

And what a classroom it was! No blackboard or desks but plenty of other equipment that Mia was more than happy to introduce him to. "This is the exercise area," she said, pausing beside a weird double bench. Without letting go of his hand, she gently kneeled on the lower part of the bench and leaned over the top part, demonstrating how it was used. It was just high enough that her heels couldn't touch the floor. He supposed that was to make the Sub feel more vulnerable. The position placed her ass high in the air and on display. Peeking out from her skirt he could see the top of her stockings and her garters. Old-fashioned but hot as hell. Yeah he liked what he saw, and he liked this piece of equipment. "This is a spanking bench. Some Doms tie their Subs here and punish them. Or, other times they use spanking as a reward to their Sub for a job well done."

"Really? I don't see how spanking someone would be a reward *for them*."

Her eyes twinkled. "You will in time." He helped her climb down off of the bench.

There was plenty of equipment, but she bypassed most of it. He supposed she was giving him the highlights, or else just pointing out her personal favourites. Next she led him toward the large wooden cross on its side, stationed against one wall. As he got closer he realized that it wasn't a cross at all, but rather a wooden *X* with cuffs at each end. Mia walked right up to it and stroked the worn brown wood fondly before she turned and put her back to it. She held her free arm high as if really restrained against the dark wood. "This is a Saint Andrew's cross. A Dom can restrain their Sub here, again for punishment with a whip or flogger, or else decide to use it for oral or fucking as a reward." She licked her lips, a little lost in the moment. "There are many possibilities with this one."

Vincent nodded, thinking of a few himself. She had an ease around this equipment that he wish he felt. "It seems like everything is used for both pleasure and discipline?"

She eagerly nodded. "Yeah, that's exactly it. Discipline can be pleasure, Vincent." He nodded too, trying to comprehend. The thought was bizarre. He had never found punishment to be fun, but whatever floats your boat, he decided.

The next piece of equipment looked like an ordinary table, but had restraints at the corners. She surprised him by jumping up on the table and lying down. This time, instead of extending her arms, she extended her legs as far as her skirt would let her, her feet dangling over the end. "This is the rack. Here you can use stocks or ropes to restrain the arms and legs, or even a spreader bar to add some weight." A few of the things she spoke of Vincent didn't understand, but he didn't care. He was watching her on the table. He could see the tops of her stockings again and had a full view of her legs. This might be the hottest piece of equipment yet.

Mia caught him admiring her body, and he blushed. Mia didn't seem to mind. She smiled and moved her legs slightly to give him a better view up her skirt. "This is one of my favourite pieces of equipment. Do you like it?"

"Uh huh."

Her smile grew. After a minute or so more, he reluctantly helped her down off the table. Beside the rack was a shelf holding gags and ropes. She walked down the line, her free hand touching some, straightening others. "I've stocked the rooms with just about every length, gauge and texture of rope." She paused, trying to judge his reaction. "Have you tied anyone up before Vincent?"

"Yeah, Catherine, once."

"Did you like tying her up?"

"It was okay." The word okay danced in the air. Okay. It sounded more like a question then an affirmation. "She had read about it somewhere and asked me to use her panty hose to tie her to the headboard." He shrugged. He didn't want to offer any more details. Yes, it had been okay. He didn't like or dislike it. Catherine seemed to have enjoyed it, though. His guess was that she was disappointed that he hadn't liked it enough to make it a regular part of their lovemaking.

"If it was just okay than you weren't doing it right," Mia joked lightly.

Vincent recoiled as if struck. Who was she to say shit like that to him? Actually she sounded just like Catherine and he didn't need any more of that. God, he really hoped this wasn't what training with Mia was going to be like. "It seemed to get the job done at the time." His words were chipped and defensive.

Mia raised a beautifully sculpted eyebrow and, to her credit, didn't react or comment on his misplaced anger. "What about spanking? Have you ever spanked Catherine?"

"No, never."

"What about oral?"

"Of course."

"Do you like giving or getting?"

"Both."

"Good. The best Doms understand the need to receive kindness and give kindness as well."

Mia turned to walk again and he let her hand slip from his. He didn't need her leading him around like a dog. When she paused in front of a wall of hooks, he folded his arms across his chest. The hooks held every sort of instrument from riding crop to wood cane. "Have you ever hit Catherine before?"

"No, of course not." He spat his words like venom. He could never hit a woman. The idea was repulsive to him.

Mia sighed. "Vincent. Remember, discipline can be pleasure, and pain can be pleasure. Do you understand that?" He nodded, but was still smarting from her earlier comment.

She held out her hand to him again and waited. Vincent just looked at it. She sighed again and her posture and tone softened. "Vincent, I'm sorry I hurt your feelings. I know you're sensitive about Catherine, but I need you to listen to me, and answer my questions honestly. Please remember that I'm here to help you. This is a judgment-free zone. What I said earlier wasn't a slight against you, it was just me indicating something that we need to train on. Okay?"

Vincent looked up into her big brown eyes that were pleading with him. Shit. She was trying to be nice and he had acted like a caveman. Again. Yeah his pride was still smarting over being dumped, but being defensive wasn't going to help him here. Mia was not the enemy. It was Catherine that had criticized him, not Mia. Mia was kind. She was already teaching him things, and trying to get him to loosen up while she introduced him to her world. And he was being an ass.

He took a deep breath. He rolled his shoulders and tried to let go of the tension he felt. "Okay. I'm sorry I got mad at you."

Mia nodded in forgiveness. She held out her hand and he took it in his again.

Without further comment on the matter, the tour resumed. Next she opened a long cabinet. "This is where we keep the smaller, more personal tools." Vincent stepped closer and saw an array of different instruments inside of the drawer. "This is the dildo drawer, below that are vibrators, and in the next cabinet are plugs and probes. The cabinets at the end hold the electrical stimulation wands and cattle prods. They are probably more advanced than you're looking for but we can try them later on if you'd like." The ease with which she comfortably rattled off the different types of extreme sexual toys was a little shocking.

"Nah, that's okay. I don't really need to see any more."

She stopped abruptly. She looked rather serious and Vincent feared that he had offended her by declining. She regarded him for a full minute before her features softened. "You know, it's okay to be nervous or uncomfortable. Meeting someone and talking about sex for the first time should be a little awkward. It will get better, just try to trust me, okay?" She smiled weakly.

"Okay. I'll try." Was that strike two for Vincent? Man he was messing this up every step of the way. "Please continue the tour."

She opened a few more drawers and let her hands run over the toys contained within. She seemed rather fond of the instruments. To Vincent, many of the things looked alien or medical, things he could never imagine giving pleasure. Some he couldn't even picture the logistics of how to use them. Did they come with an instruction manual?

There were a few he did recognize. A few months before the end, before even the panty hose incident, he had found several erotic instruments hidden around her apartment. Now he wondered if they were really as "hidden" as he thought, or if they were hints or clues left by Catherine for him. Should those things have been the first big indicator that he wasn't pleasing his girlfriend?

Vincent tried to keep his mind on the task at hand and listen to Mia as she explained many of the pieces to him. Her tone was soft and patient, but he knew, and she probably did too, that she would have to explain all of this to him again at another time. Already he was feeling overwhelmed. Mia noticed.

"Let's go sit on the couch for a minute."

They returned to the sofa and sat down again, still holding hands. "I'm sorry, Vincent. Like I said, I'm a little out of practice. Confession time, I had to take a break for a while and this is my first day back here." She looked down at her lap when she said that. He did too and saw her hand holding onto his so tight she had almost gone white knuckled. Odd. She had worked so hard to put him at ease, maybe it was his time to return the favour.

"That's okay, remember it's my first day, too." Vincent joked lightly.

Mia's head jerked up in surprise. Her following laugh was natural. He liked the way her eyes sparkled. "I like you, Vincent. James said that I would."

"Well, I like you too, Mia." Vincent internally felt like fist pumping. Day one and he had already won over the teacher. Hopefully he would win over Catherine again this easily. Right then he felt confident. He could do this. James was right, this would work.

"Vincent, do you know what BDSM is?"

"Uh yeah, it's why I'm here."

Her voice was as soft as her skin. "No, do you *really* know what it is?"

He gulped in a deep breath. "I think so."

"Just try to relax. It's okay if you don't know. BDSM is a lot of things. Sometimes it's sex or role playing, sometimes discipline, but not always. And people have a million different fetishes that they bring into how they play. Beyond that, BDSM is about trust. I know we don't know each other yet and we're still working to earn each other's trust. That's the hard part, but it will come in time. Everything else is just play heightened by that exchange of that trust. Does any of this make sense to you?"

"Sorta."

Her smile deepened. "I'm sorry, in the past I've mostly trained people who have been to the club before or at least had some experience in the lifestyle. It's actually refreshing to look at BDSM through fresh eyes."

"I'm glad *you* think so." Vincent smiled too. "So what do we do now?"

Mia thought for a moment. "Well, we could go watch an exhibition scene in the main room."

"That sounds like fun." Vincent was definitely interested.

"Okay, but I want you to think about what you see and ask me questions about anything you don't understand. I have to warn you, public scenes are performed by the more experienced people in the lifestyle and what you see will be a very advanced demonstration. You may have seen something like it on the Internet but seeing it live is totally different, more intense."

"Fine." What she said sounded good. Watching a scene in action would probably help him with what he was supposed to do as a Dom.

"Come on, Baby Dom, let's go see the show." She stuck her tongue out, kidding him.

After she carefully shut the door and locked the room with her key card, he followed his teacher back down the hallway into the music and the darkness of the main room. The club had filled up considerably. Instead of small groups of people talking, there was now just one large group filling most of the club.

"Does it always get this busy?" he shouted to her over the music.

"Tonight's a special occasion," he thought he heard Mia shout back. James hadn't mentioned it as a special day. Maybe it was their kinky Christmas or something. He smiled at the thought.

Together they walked back past the bar. Now he was the one who held onto her hand tightly as not to lose her in the crowd. Where was James? Was he still taking care of "business"? Vincent didn't see his friend as he let Mia pull them through the crowd although he did spot some of the people James had introduced him to earlier. He didn't remember any of their names and he was glad that Mia didn't stop to talk or shout at them.

People seemed to recognize Mia, but didn't approach her. In fact it was more than that, people appeared to be going out of their way to give her space. Maybe it had something to do with Dom/Sub respect or something.

Mia didn't see any of this. He noticed that as she led them, her eyes were cast down to the floor. She must be very familiar with the club to know the way without looking where she was going. Odd, but it seemed she wasn't the only one who had a strange fascination with the floor. Was this more of this respect thing or some kind of protocol? Should he do the same? In the end he decided to just keep his eyes on Mia and try to keep pace as she headed toward a new part of the club.

This area hadn't been on James's tour. Approaching the far wall, the floor opened up a bit. In front of them were a row of four alcoves cut into the wall. Each had thick red velvet curtains closed across them, like the kind you'd see in old theatres. A section of benches were arranged in neat rows in front, providing an area for an audience to sit.

It was a busy place and most of the benches were already full. Vincent thought they would have to stand for the show, but people moved for them without being asked. Soon he and Mia had a front-row seat.

While they sat, Mia continued to hold his hand. She also scooted closer to him on the bench so that her thigh was against his. He still felt a little out of place and he had to admit that her touch was a comfort. She kept her eyes down and didn't speak with anyone. What was her story? If she worked here as long as she claimed, she should have friends here. James was Mister Popularity compared to her.

The curtain opened slowly and the crowd fell silent. The atmosphere was almost giddy. This was why the club was packed. This was what they were here for. Mia squeezed his hand, even she was excited.

A spotlight snapped on illuminating the stage and revealing the scene. A woman, a very naked woman, stood centre stage. Her arms were bound with rope and painfully stretched far above her head and hanging from an industrial hook. Like a grotesque ballerina mid-dance, her toes barely touched the floor.

At the right of the stage, the lights revealed a man. He wore the Dom uniform of black on black. His back faced the crowd as he hunched over a table of devices. Every few seconds he held up an instrument for the crowd to see. A blindfold, a cane, a paddle. Next he wielded a whip. He smacked it across his palm and the crowd gasped and jumped. Then they applauded in glee!

The man held up his hand for quiet. When the crowd was settled again, he finished sorting the tools he needed for this show.

"Scenes aren't usually this theatrical," Mia whispered. "But the crowd loves it when he really puts on a show."

Vincent was about to ask who 'he' was, but the man saved him the trouble by turning around. The man was James.

James proudly held up a bag of ordinary dollar-store wooden clothespins. They didn't look like anything special to Vincent, but the crowd *oohed* and *aahed* as if they were the most precious diamonds. He picked up a few other tools and slung the whip across his shoulders.

James approached the hanging woman slowly. His steps tapped out a rhythm as he crossed the stage. When he reached her, he checked her ropes to ensure that they weren't tight enough to cut off circulation. Then he gently, almost lovingly, caressed her face and hair. Her eyes focused only on him. He said some words for her ears only, and she nodded. It reminded Vincent of the care that James had taken with Mia earlier and how he whispered secret words of guidance to comfort her as well. The effect was the same here, and the woman on stage stopped struggling against her bonds.

He took his time touching her body. His hands roamed down her arms and across her chest. He cupped her large breasts in his hands, feeling their weight. Then he gently plucked at her nipples, until they were hard. She mewed like a pleased cat with each fondle.

Letting go of her, James walked around the stage to stand in front of her. Her eyes followed his every move. Violently he thrust his hand between her legs. Her body reared back, surprised by the sudden touch. James kept his hand in place, massaging her. Gradually her surprise was replaced by pleasure.

James smiled. "Very good, pet."

Pet? What an odd term. If a Baby Dom was a new dominant, what was a pet? An experienced Sub? He made a mental note to ask Mia later. That wasn't the only question Vincent had. They started to pile up in his brain. For example, who was this woman to James? He couldn't remember his friend ever having an actual girlfriend. Was a pet a girlfriend? Was a pet just a Sub?

Vincent snapped out of his thoughts when Mia leaned in toward him. "Can you imagine your girlfriend like this? Tied up and begging for you?" she whispered in his ear. Vincent shook his head. He couldn't imagine it, but this is what Catherine had said she wanted. The question now was, could he become the man that she begged for, instead of the man she left and pushed aside with insults and put-downs? He shook his head to clear it. He couldn't be held back by those negative thoughts now. If he was going to become the Dom he wanted to be, he needed to pay attention.

Mia squeezed his hand. She seemed to know that he needed an extra pull to remain in the moment. Had she ever been in a scene like this? Had his teacher ever found her way up onto the stage, and stood naked and bound in front of a club full of people? Had she moaned and begged for release? And had James been the Dom to put her up on the hook?

Vincent tried to concentrate on every move James made. He wished he had brought a notepad with him to take notes. There was something very appealing about being the man on stage and in charge of the show. He could understand why James liked it. He seemed to be in his element currently. There was no mistaking that James was a Dom and that he was very, very good at being in control. The attention of both the woman and the audience was focused on his every move.

The next thing James did was affix the crude wooden clothespins to the woman's nipples. The woman squirmed a little, as the pin bit into the tender flesh, but her arousal was evident with the further flushing of her skin and another soft moan. James continued with the pins, placing them in two long parallel lines down her stomach. She gasped and squirmed. Vincent had missed it at first, but there was a tiny string that attached each one together except for the ones on her nipples. They were connected so that every movement was reflected in the combined movement of every pin. The woman's breath was ragged with pain.

With his free hand, James retrieved a vibrator from the table. He twisted it on and a loud hum filled the air. He let it touch against her legs and thighs, teasing her. When it grew too much for her to bear, her legs parted and he showed mercy by holding the vibrator to her clit. Her head fell back and her loud moan echoed across the alcove.

Vincent chanced a glance around the audience and many other members were openly touching themselves or their Subs. Beside him, Mia stiffened. Her breathing was shallow and heavy. She looked to be almost as aroused as the woman on stage.

"What is your safe word, pet?" James shouted to his Sub in order to be clearly heard by all over the noise of the vibrator and the crowd.

"Red, Sir."

"Very good, red is the club safe word and you may use it." James picked up the end of the string that was attached to the pins and gently tugged it, pulling it taut. "Pet, do you wish to use your safe word now?"

"No, no, Sir." Her voice shook with arousal. It was clear that she was seconds away from orgasm.

"Good." And with one quick pull of the string, the pins were yanked off of her body.

Fuck! That must have hurt! The pain showing on the woman's face was indescribable. The Sub swayed in her bondage and let loose a low terrible cry. The pins still on her nipples bounced with the movement.

Vincent was reeling. Pain. And then another emotion crossed her face. Release. She looked like she had come, even with the extreme pain James had just given her.

That didn't make any sense to Vincent.

Beside him, Mia squeezed his hand. She obviously meant to encourage or comfort him with the gesture. Did she get off on this kind of thing? He focused on her and, sure enough, he could feel that Mia's breathing had quickened. Her eyes never left the scene.

Returning his attention to the stage, he saw that red welts were forming on the poor woman's skin where the pins had been ripped off. She shuddered as James tenderly ran his hands over the marks. Ugh, Vincent couldn't imagine how much pain she must still be in. James whispered to her again privately and the woman nodded enthusiastically. It was clear that she wanted more pain and he was eager to give it to her.

He slowly unwrapped the whip from around his shoulders. He curled the leather ends around his hands and tested the strength of the weapon. The sinister tool looked to be very strong and very dangerous. Shit. What was James going to do next to that poor woman?

James had no expression on his face as he returned to his Sub's side. He didn't look like Vincent's friend anymore. This guy was cold and calculating. "Fifty lashes. Count them off, pet."

"Yes, Sir." Calmly he raised the whip in his hand and snapped it through the arm to hit her hard in the crotch. She jerked back when the leather contacted her skin.

"One." She gasped.

James mechanically pulled back his arm and the whip hit her for a second time. Again the woman jerked back in pain.

"Two."

Again James hit.

"Three." And he kept on hitting her, each time the lashes fell faster against her body. She could barely count off the lashes and had no time to recover from the last hit before the whip hit her skin again. The leather burned her skin red, over her chest, stomach, legs. The woman struggled but continued to count off her punishment and never said the word red.

As the intensity of the strikes increased, so did the woman's screams. "Please, Sir," she cried. James did not stop. Now no part of her body was safe from the lashes. Her cries became frantic. James was either so focused on his task that he couldn't, or didn't want to hear her.

If no one was going to go to the woman's rescue, Vincent would. He was seconds away from getting up and jumping up onto the stage, when James wheeled around to face him. He must have seen the movement out of the corner of his eye. The look James gave him was hard and unforgiving.

"Pet, what is your safe word?" James's words came out fast and angry, his eyes staying glued to Vincent. This part of the scene was clearly unscripted and purely for Vincent's benefit.

"Red," she answered, her breathing laboured.

"Do you wish to stop the scene?"

"No, Sir."

Without another word, James turned back to the woman and resumed the whipping. Her eyes were glassy and removed, while James's were hard steel. Did you have to be mean to be a Dom? Vincent tried to remember Mia's words that pain was pleasure, but it was impossible now to see any pleasure in this scene. Submitting yourself to this kind of domination was insane.

A burning feeling began in the pit of Vincent's stomach. He had achieved many things in his life—had a good job, bought a nice house, went to college. And yet he had never before felt so out of place. He didn't belong here. So what if his girlfriend had left him? If she wanted someone to beat her, it wasn't going to be him. He could never be that cruel.

Vincent stood, Mia's hand falling out of his due to the abrupt movement. "I'm sorry," he heard himself say, apologizing to no one in particular. His only goal now was to get the hell out of this place. He heard his name being called as he pushed through the main doors to the outside. He didn't stop until he was in his car. Soon he was flying down the freeway toward his house. Then he focused on getting inside and locking the door. Only when that was done did he let himself start to process what he had seen.

The James on stage was not the friend he had known for years. He couldn't be! None of it made sense. Not his friend's split personality, nor the reaction of the crowd, nor Mia's obvious arousal from watching. Catherine couldn't want him to be that kind of monster. He was certain of that.

That was it. It was over. Thank God. He never had to go back to that club.

He had a beer and tried to stop shaking.

Later he tried to sleep, but the sound of the whip hitting flesh haunted him throughout the night until he finally fell asleep, exhausted.

Chapter Two

It had been a hell of a morning. A bunch of his employees had called in sick. Another had made a stupid mistake and Vincent had been tougher on him then he should have.

God, it had been almost a full week and he was still off his game.

He felt wrecked. And James had caused it all. His friend had brought him into that terrible place and had actually thought he would get off on it, like the other members did. His friend had handed him Mia to train on, in hope that he would become the same kind of monster. *No thanks, buddy.* Even if that's really what Catherine wanted him to be, and he doubted it, he could never be a person that hurt women for fun. Case closed. *Fuck that.*

Except it wasn't so easy to close that door. Not when every day he had to get up and go to work at the same warehouse James worked at. That was a problem. James had helped get him the job years ago, and Vincent had worked hard there to reach his position. He liked his job and he was good at it, most days.

Sometime between Monday and Wednesday, Vincent had made the decision to start looking for a new job, pronto. Until then he would just do his best to avoid James and go on living his life as if everything were normal. He could pretend that there wasn't a secret club on the other side of town that catered to sadists.

Thursday he was grumpy, because he was tired from still not sleeping well. By now his dreams had changed and Mia was the woman on the stage and he was the sadist. Great. He left work early, and almost ran into James in the parking lot. Luckily he managed to avoid him and drive away before James could flag him down.

Vincent remembered the voice that had called out his name as he had left the club. It wasn't James's voice. That bothered him more than he would have liked. James had let him go, but Mia had been the one calling out for him to stay.

Today was Friday and he was almost free. Thank God. He felt like he was at the end of his rope. He had only planned to grab a quick bite to eat in the cafeteria before heading back to the warehouse floor. Four more hours to go and this day and the week would be over. He would go running first thing tomorrow morning, and try to get back in his zone. He liked running. Just him and the pavement. Running was great for heavy thinking and ironing out problems. That was the perfect plan. Just get through this day and then he could fix his head.

He didn't see James, until the guy sat down in the seat beside him. *Crap.*

James's Dom outfit had been replaced by a casual suit. Not everyone at the warehouse wore a suit—Vincent sure as hell didn't—but on James it worked. It had looked natural on him, that is, until Vincent had learned of his preference for black leather.

For a while neither of them spoke. Vincent tried to pretend to be super interested in his meal but he didn't feel like eating anymore. He decided to get up and throw the rest of his sandwich away. Yes, that's what he needed to do. Just get up and get out of there. Get away from this freak.

He was starting to stand, when James spoke. "So what part made you leave, Vin?"

Vincent groaned internally and sat back down. Who was he kidding? Avoiding the problem wasn't helping. Maybe it would be best to just get it all out. He chanced a look around the cafeteria. Good, no one was looking at them or trying to listen in. This wasn't the best time or place for this discussion but it would have to do. He just hoped he wouldn't end up having to punch James at work. Things like that could really ruin a reputation.

"Vin, you said you had tied up Catherine before, and experimented with other things. So what was it, what was so bad that you *had* to leave?"

Vincent cleared his throat. If he said what was on his mind, there would be no going back from this. He tried to steel his anger the best he could. Time to let go of everything that had been building up inside of him since Saturday. Time to wipe that arrogant look off that prick's face.

"You're a monster."

James laughed. "Sometimes."

Vincent was incredulous. How dare he joke about this? "You hurt that woman."

"That woman, Terry, is an experienced Sub. It wasn't our first time playing together. Before the scene on Saturday, we discussed what we were going to do. Every move I made was carefully negotiated and agreed to."

"How could anyone want *that*?" Vincent growled.

"How could she agree to touching, stimulation, advanced punishment? Submissives find pleasure in different things. It's our job to figure out what they need and give it to them."

"It's your job to be a monster? So you use that to justify beating someone?" Vincent worked hard to keep his voice down when he felt like screaming at James.

James sighed. "Vin, I was joking about being a monster. I didn't beat her and never would. The rules of BDSM are always the same. Safe, sane and consensual. A scene is a well-orchestrated power exchange to bring both parties pleasure. It's not rape, not abuse, and it's certainly not a crime. If Terry, my Sub for the night, hadn't wanted to be there on stage with me, she wouldn't be. She needs to be dominated. Just like Mia needs it, just like Catherine thinks she needs it. Terry craved that level of pain so I gave it to her."

"She craves pain? Listen to what you're saying."

"It's true, Vin. And don't be deceived by the whip. Its bark is far worse than its bite."

Vincent thought about that for a moment. "But you're not telling me why they want this. Why would they give up power and choose to be controlled by someone else?"

James laughed. "Vin, my man, the Sub *always* has the power. They can stop the scene any time they want. It's called a safe word. Each Sub has their own word that they pick to use when the scene gets too intense. Or they can use the club word, Red."

"It looked intense enough on Saturday."

James chuckled. "True, but remember she never used her safe word the entire time we were on stage. It was an advanced scene, what some call Porno BDSM. I just wish that you had stayed to see the end."

"So I could see you beat on her some more?"

James smiled like a man who knew a secret, and leaned in closer. "No, so you could see her come again, see how much she enjoyed the scene. And so you could learn about aftercare. During a scene there are a lot of endorphins released. Aftercare is when the Dom and Sub are most vulnerable. Gently the Sub comes out of whatever subspace or headspace she's mentally gone into during the scene."

"Did you fuck her?"

"Not this time, but Terry and I have had sex before. Aftercare is a completely different kind of intimacy. I carried her off the stage because aftercare is just for her privately. Usually I find a nice corner, with a chair or a sofa and I sit there holding them until all of the adrenaline is gone from both of us and the Sub feels safe again. It's nice. Aftercare is as important as the scene itself. Terry and I are not together, but I care about her enough to make sure she is not left alone or frightened after a scene. If I just walked away then yes, I would be the monster you seem to think you saw Friday night."

"So you beat them, then you cuddle them?"

"Don't cheapen it, Vin. Aftercare is another privilege that the Sub gives their Dom."

Vincent's mind was reeling again. So much so that he wasn't quite sure what he believed any more. James had been hurting that woman, hadn't he? Could Vincent have been mistaken in what he had seen?

He tried to think about everything James had just said. Some of it made sense to him. This aftercare stuff seemed to be the opposite of what he had witnessed Saturday. That part sounded good. Like a way to make sure the Sub is okay afterwards and show them some kindness. That certainly appealed to him. But did that make beating on a person okay? Vincent was so confused.

And the James he was today was no different than the friend he had known for years. Could he trust what he said to be true?

James sighed. "Vin, just think about it. Was there anything about the scene you liked?"

Vincent thought for a long moment. He reviewed the scene in his head as he had a million times before. This time he tried to distance himself at the bit of horror he still felt about the beating. The thing that stood out most was the reaction of the woman who had been sitting beside him and who had held his hand, Mia. He had been too overwhelmed by the scene to properly understand her response. Her breath had quickened, her body had relaxed and act of holding his hand now seemed very intimate. If he had allowed himself to feel on Saturday instead of reacting, he would have felt how watching the scene was a form of foreplay.

"I liked how it made Mia feel. I could tell she was turned on. Every time your Sub cried out, she squeezed my hand. I guess maybe she was letting me know that's what she wanted, or that's what she would want me to do to her?"

"And?"

"And even though I didn't like what was happening on stage, I liked being there with her," Vincent admitted.

A huge smile spread across his friend's face. "Right on! Remember that, it's the key to everything." James sat back in his chair, satisfied. "So I'll see you at the club Saturday night?"

Vincent's head jerked up to look James in the eye. "Are you kidding me? After what happened last Saturday? No way. I could never go back to that place."

"Don't you want Catherine back? Don't you want to prove to her that you can be a Dom?"

"Yeah. I mean—I don't know. I just don't think I can do that type of stuff or be like that."

"Just give it another try."

"I don't know if I can," Vincent said softly. His anger was slowly dissipating. Mia had warned him that he might not be prepared to witness the scene. Looks like she was right.

Vincent leaned back in his chair, more confused than ever.

"Remember why you wanted to become a Dom. To do that, you have to put aside your judgments, Vin, and go back in with an open mind."

Vincent didn't think that it was possible to have an open mind anymore. He was about to tell James this, but was distracted by several of his coworkers coming into the room and toward their table.

"Hi, James, Vincent," Eve, a strikingly tall brunette with glasses, called out as she approached. Her friend Allison followed a step behind. Eve was an administrative assistant in another department. Eve was shy but once you got to know her, she was always fun to talk to. Also, she was seriously into James. He liked to look at her but Vincent knew that his friend would never take it beyond that, not with someone from work. Did Eve know that James was into whips and chains? Was she into the lifestyle too?

"Have you talked to Catherine lately?" Allison asked Vincent. The thin blonde was a truck dispatcher. She was usually lighthearted and sweet. Lately, though, that sunny outlook had disappeared. She and James had recently been up for the same promotion. James had won it, making him her boss and leaving Allison bitter.

Her question was odd. Allison and Eve were both good friends with Catherine. They probably knew all about their breakup. There was no reason why he would have spoken to Catherine.

"Nope." Today seemed to be the day for uncomfortable conversations. He hoped the women hadn't accidently overheard any of his conversation with James. He didn't need them reporting back to his ex on the activities Saturday night at the club.

"We haven't heard from her either."

Vincent's head snapped back. He couldn't remember a week passing when the girls didn't talk at least a few times or go out for drinks together after work. It wasn't surprising that Catherine wouldn't have called him, but her best friends? That was very unusual. "Not at all?" Both women shook their heads no. "Oh. Okay, I'll tell you if I hear from her."

"Thanks." Allison looked like she was considering saying more, but decided not to. The two girls shared a look before leaving.

Vincent groaned as the two women walked away. That was all he needed, more drama from Catherine. The look they shared before leaving had been as clear as if they had spoken their thoughts aloud. They didn't want to say it, but they both thought that Catherine must have met someone and taken off with him. She had done that in the past—hell, when she and Vincent had first gotten together they had only surfaced for food and water. If Catherine wasn't available to answer her phone, that meant she wasn't available to him anymore. She had moved on.

Shit, there was the grief again. The possibilities of winning her back just changed from slim to none.

James patted him on the back. "I told you Catherine was a bitch."

Vincent nodded. He couldn't argue that.

"Time to get back to work." James sighed and stood up. "Vin, will you at least meet me for a coffee tomorrow night? There's a little place beside the club. It's pretty discreet and we can talk more then?"

Vincent felt himself continue to nod. Fine. A coffee was just a coffee. It didn't mean that he had changed his mind. He wasn't going back to the club again, ever.

They stood and walked out of the cafeteria in silence. Vincent was tossing the rest of his lunch away when Andrew, a warehouse forklift operator pushed through the double doors into the cafeteria and almost right into James. He shot a raging look their way before stalking past them further into the room.

"What's his problem?"

James sighed. "That is untrained testosterone without an outlet."

"Like a Dom without a Mia?"

His friend winked. "Something like that."

* * * *

Great.

James had lied to him. Vincent knew it as soon as he walked into the small coffee shop. He knew that he had lied, because James wasn't waiting at a table for him. Mia was.

That prick had planned this.

He was pissed off by his friend's manipulation, but Mia's smile won him over. Instead of leaving and heading back home, he found himself moving toward her and taking a seat at her table. What the hell, he had nothing to lose and no other plans. There were worse things in the world then being tricked into having coffee with a pretty woman.

"Hello, Vincent." Her voice betrayed her nerves. Why should she feel nervous again to talk to him? Shit, had she been fired from the club because he left? He would feel bad, if that was the case. He liked her. Odd, he barely knew her but he liked her.

Although she was nervous, otherwise she didn't look the worse for wear. Her makeup was a little lighter than it had been the week before, and her hair was tied back. She wore a long red coat that covered most of her from neck to toe. He wondered if she was hiding another pencil skirt and corset under her coat. He shook his head. He hadn't even been here five minutes and already he was wondering what she was wearing. Or letting his mind wander to think about what she wasn't wearing under that coat.

He felt a little embarrassed and awkward. "Mia, I'm sorry about last Friday, I…"

"Don't worry, Vincent. I'm used to Alpha Males. They have mood swings worse than any woman." She chuckled. "I've been a trainer for a long time. It's not the first time I've been walked out on." She took a sip of her tea. She seemed lighthearted about the whole thing, but there was still an edge. Maybe this was a mistake. Damn James and his bullshit.

Vincent was trying to think of something to say, how to apologize and make her understand how he felt. He was out of his element here and he didn't like it.

She put down her cup, her hand shaking only a little. "You know, a lot of people don't believe that you can train Doms. They say that you are either born dominant or you're not. I don't believe that. Not everyone is so aware of what they can become until they're shown." Although the café was nearly empty, she kept her voice low and discreet so that only he could hear her words. "Others say that any training of a Dom is really just constant topping from the bottom. Again, not true. You can't hold a person's hand all the time. You give a person the tools to succeed and then they either do or they don't." She paused, taking a moment to look into his eyes. Her big brown beauties were swimming with emotion. "I think you can succeed at this, Vincent."

"Why?" His shoulders slumped at the question. Why did Mia think that he could become dominant when Catherine, who previously was supposed to be his partner and the love of his life, didn't think that he had the same potential?

"Because I see that you crave control and have a lot to give to another person. You've just never been allowed to be dominant before."

He thought about that for a moment. Was that true? He didn't think of himself as a control freak. Yet being in charge at work did make him feel important. Did that necessarily make him a dominant? The other part of what she said he agreed with fully. Catherine had always tried to change him and never just allowed him the freedom to love her the way he wanted.

Wait, is that really what he felt or had Mia put those thoughts in his head for him with her rhetoric? Was she manipulating him just as much as James had?

"What's in it for you?"

She was a little taken aback by the question. "Do you mean, does James pay me for training you? No he doesn't, and I assure you that I wouldn't need the money, even if he did. This is a little unusual for me too, Vincent. I don't usually beg men to let me train them, but I feel that I owe this to James, and I guess a certain amount, that I owe it to you too. I feel for you. I understand wanting to be wanted, and coming up short."

He shook his head. So much confusion and he was being difficult again for no reason. Mia had only ever been kind and honest with him.

"Vincent do you remember what you promised me last week?"

He shook his head no. "I'm sorry, I don't remember, it's been a long week."

"That's okay." She smiled. "You promised me to ask me any questions you may have and give me a chance to explain."

"I'm sorry, but I couldn't keep that promise. It was just so much…"

"Too much." Mia reached across the table and patted his hand. "That was my fault. You weren't ready. If you don't know the meaning behind the acts I can imagine it can be quite barbaric. But believe me, the Sub agreed to every single thing that was done to her."

Vincent nodded and it looked like what she was saying was finally starting to have an effect. "That's what James said as well. But everything is so confusing."

"You can ask me whatever you want, I don't mind. I will answer as honestly as possible and admit it if I don't know the answer."

Okay, he could work with that. Vincent took a deep breath. "What's it like?"

"What's *what* like?"

"Being a Sub?" There. The question that most intrigued him.

Mia took a deep breath. Her surprise showed. "Well, I'm sure I could describe to you what it physically feels like, or even mentally what headspace a Sub goes into during a scene, but I think what you really mean to ask is, why would anyone be willing to be the bottom in such a top-heavy relationship? Why I do it, why Terry needs it and why Catherine wants it."

"Exactly!"

"That's a very good question, Vincent. I don't think anyone's ever asked me that before. Okay, my brother asked me something like that once, but that's another discussion for another day. People submit for a variety of reasons. Maybe because they are in charge in other aspects of their lives and just want to let go. Or perhaps because they had an experience once that they liked and are now trying to replicate. It's hard to say. It's like asking someone why they prefer baseball to football. Some people are taught the lifestyle and others are born into it, just like some people are born left handed, some right. I was definitely born to be a Sub, and you definitely weren't."

"I was also born a stutterer, but I grew out of it."

She laughed, "I'm sorry, I guess it's true, some people do 'grow out' of being a Sub or a Dom. They bury it down deep inside themselves or try to ignore it and go about their daily lives and prefer to live a lie."

"But not you?"

"Nope. I'm in control at work and every day I make important decisions. It's nice to give up control and let someone else make decisions for me."

"You work outside the club?"

"The club isn't work for me, Vincent, it's all pleasure."

He sighed. "So there's no way of knowing really what it's like unless you're a Sub yourself?"

"If we had more time or if you were interested in being a Sub trainer you would find out. A good Sub trainer experiences every single part of being a Sub so that they know what they put their partners through."

"Does that mean that because you're a Dom trainer, that you have experience being a Dom?"

"Maybe." Her eyes sparkled mischievously. He wanted to ask more, but he didn't want to get off track with his first question. Although, he did allow himself a second to think of Mia trading her soft skirt and stockings for the tight leather and whip of a Dom. Then he remembered her in the dungeon, stretched out on the rack showing him the proper position to be tied. So hot. Yes, he liked her as a Sub much better.

She laughed. Damn it, he had spoken his thoughts out loud again. Mia sure had a way of getting him to let his guard down…and a way of making him embarrassed. He was glad that her laughter was kind. "I'm glad, Vincent. In case you're wondering I'm no switch. I don't do both top and bottom, I'm a Sub through and through, but with…"

"…experience?"

She nodded. "Yes. A good way to put it. Next question."

Vincent thought for a moment. "Why do you perform scenes? Why go to all the trouble with the gadgets and tools? Why drag it out? If the goal is just getting someone off, why not just do it?"

Her eyes lit up and she leaned toward him. "Have you ever made out with a girl…"

"Plenty of times."

She laughed. "Nice, your Alpha Male comes out again. As I was saying, have you ever made out with a girl for so long that you were hot and sweaty? Fumbling kiss after kiss? Clothes barely on, hands stealing a touch or a caress, trying to work their way to where it's warm and wet?"

"And my dick was so hard I thought I'd die?" He chuckled. Yeah, he could easily think of a times like that. In his car with his date after prom. With his first girlfriend on the couch at her parents' house when they were supposed to be studying. After his second date with Catherine.

"Yes, but you keep drawing it out because it just made it so much sweeter when you finally got down to slipping inside her?"

"Yeah, yeah I know that feeling." Those were good times, when foreplay was the destination instead of just rushing straight into sex.

"A scene is like the best foreplay ever. That's why we don't rush straight to orgasm. We like drawing out the pleasure so that when you come it's more intense. And when you add a little bite of pain with your pleasure it can focus your senses and keep you deliciously in the moment. How much pain is entirely subjective. Some Subs need just a little pain—nipple clamps or a light spanking. Others need varying degrees of pain in order to feel free. Think of it as extreme foreplay. Giving up control is freeing, putting your pleasure is someone else's hands can be the best feeling in the word if it's someone you trust." She said the last word as if it was holy.

"Trust is the key?"

"Absolutely. It goes hand in hand with honestly, respect, kindness. Those are the graces of the safe, sane, consensual BDSM pledge."

Mia tried to keep her tone light, but Vincent could tell there was something else there beneath the surface.

"Trust is the big one for you though. You haven't always trusted your partner?"

She shook her head sadly. "You have it wrong. I have always trusted." She shrugged. "Even when I shouldn't have."

"Did someone at the club hurt you? Was it James?"

"Not at the club, no. There are security guards and always other members around. Subs are protected." She looked away. He barely heard her say under her breath, "They are precious."

"During the scene James looked like he was hurting Terry."

She took a sip of her tea and thought about it for a moment. "I guess it could seem that way. She wasn't hurt, though. It was just the level of kink she needed. Did you notice that he tested the whip on his own hand first to know what amount of strength to use when he whipped her?"

Vincent nodded, remembering. He had seen James do that, but thought that it was just part of the theatrics.

"He's played with Terry before so he knew what level of intensity she needed to get her hot. He didn't seriously injure her. I doubt she had a single bruise the next morning."

"But she was screaming."

"Have you never made a girl scream in release, Vincent?" Mia teased. "Some girls moan during a scene or during sex, some talk, and some scream. It just depends on the person and the level of stimulation. Do you think that you can understand any of this?"

"Maybe. It makes more sense when you explain it." Vincent sat back in his chair, a weight lifted off of his shoulders.

"Any other questions?"

"Why did he call her *pet*? Is that a different kind of Sub?"

"Nope, it's just a term of affection, like sweetheart. Some people call their Subs 'slave,' 'bottom,' 'love.'" She shrugged. "It's just a nickname. Anything else?"

Only one last question came to mind that he felt he had to ask now. "Do you think I'm an idiot for reacting the way I did last week?"

"Not at all. You reacted honestly. Next time, talk to me instead of just leaving."

Her eyes were a little sad and the edge was back to her voice. He felt like a tool for offending her. "I'm sorry."

"It's okay. It's part of our journey together and your first lesson. Now is it my turn to ask you a few questions."

Vincent smiled. She deserved the same respect she had given him. "You can ask me anything."

"Good." She took another sip of her tea. "You do have natural Dom tendencies. Are you only looking to become a Dom because your ex-girlfriend wanted you to be one, or do you yourself want to awaken your dominant nature to enrich your life?"

Vincent didn't immediately answer. A week ago he would have said that he was doing this just to get Catherine back and nothing else. That's what James's understanding had been from the beginning. But now he felt a little mixed up. He still felt off about the scene, but…there was something else intriguing about the lifestyle. He hadn't really admitted it yet, but Mia was right. He liked the control it offered him. Maybe he could see himself in the BDSM lifestyle.

He made up his mind. It was quite possible that all hope was lost with Catherine. He had to push past his anger and hurt at being dumped. He had to make a decision for himself. If he continued to explore the lifestyle, the only reason would be because he himself wanted it and nothing else.

He took a deep breath. He had made his choice. "A week ago I probably would have said that I was only doing this for her, but now I think I want to do this for myself."

"Good." He realized he was starting to like this little pixie before him. Maybe after he was fully trained they could keep in touch. Maybe if Catherine didn't want him back, Mia would help him find a pet of his own.

Bells sounded over the door as a couple came into the coffee shop. Vincent didn't recognize them, but Mia waved to them and they waved back. He was glad that they went to the counter to order and didn't try to join them. He had to admit that he was finding this conversation fascinating.

"James told me that you would be confused but that your true tendencies would shine through. You would think that I would be the natural people reader, but James is amazing. He can spot a Dom, a Sub, a sadist, a brat, a tourist…anything, as soon as he meets someone, he can tell if they are a Dom or a Sub. He says it's because he's been a little bit of everything at one time or another."

"James was a Sub?"

"Yes." She nodded. "Before he realized that he needed control and that he needed someone at his feet to make him feel whole."

"I've never thought of James as anything less than being in control."

She chuckled. "That's because he has the self-control needed to be a truly great Dom. Do you have that self-control, or have you just never been challenged?" Her eyes sparkled at the question and he knew that she asked it out of curiosity, and not as an insult.

"I don't know."

"Me neither. First you have to learn to control yourself before you can control anyone else." She took another sip of her tea and Vincent wished that the café served something stronger than fucking tea. Why couldn't James have suggested they meet at the bar next door? Mia leaned toward him. "James told me that you liked that you could tell how I was affected by his scene."

Oh man, it was embarrassing that she knew. "Shit. Is nothing sacred?"

"It's okay, I need to know these things. Listening and observation are very important. That's how you get to know your Sub. Do you want to train with me tonight?" When he hesitated, she frowned. "You live inside your head a lot, don't you? I'm guessing that you eat lunch alone, you live alone. Other guys would just go sleep with a bunch of women to gain experience, but you're the type of guy that trains for it. I'm going to need you to live in the moment and just experience freely. Can you do that for me?"

Vincent sighed and tried to do as she asked and let go, wipe the slate clean. "I can try."

"Stop thinking so much, Vincent. Don't put yourself in a prison because of other people's thoughts and ideas of what is right. You have the gift of freedom to learn how to do sexually what you always wanted to do." Her brown eyes met his. "Will you come to the club now and let me give you control?"

He wanted to scream yes. He didn't care that he wasn't dressed right. He didn't care that the members might think of him as a fool for running out last week. There was something so honest, so attractive in her offering herself to him. He wanted to throw off all of his baggage with a great roar and just let go.

But still he hesitated.

"Trust me," she whispered.

"Trust is key?"

"Absolutely."

Mia stood. This was it. Say good-bye or go forward. Either he trusted her and went to the club and trained with her tonight or he left. A decision to make with two possible outcomes. He had already admitted to himself that he wanted to learn more about the lifestyle, so why not continue to let her train him? It was the only way to find out if he was ready to be a Dom after all.

Then she held out her hand to him. His body reacted and made the choice for him. His body wanted to feel the electric warmth of her hand again. His body wanted that connection.

So he reached out and took her hand.

She smiled a brilliantly large smile. Her face lit up like sunshine after the rain.

He smiled too.

Holding onto her tightly, he led her out of the café. Together they hurried across the road, mindful of the late evening traffic. Anyone who saw them would think that they were just another young couple, perhaps going out to see a movie or out to have dinner. They looked like average normal people. Not a Baby Dom and his teacher, about to enter back into the world of kink and dark pleasure.

* * * *

She unlocked the dungeon room with a key card and he followed her inside. It looked exactly the same way it had when they were last in the room last week. Exactly.

"No one else uses this room?"

"Nope." Mia flicked on the main overhead light. "James reserves it just for me. When I took a break from teaching, James kept it empty, waiting for me to come back." An emotion crossed her face that Vincent couldn't quite read. "You're my first Dom to train since…" Her voice broke as it trailed off.

He didn't push her to finish her sentence. He remembered what she had said. She had trusted someone and they had hurt her. It probably would have taken a great deal of courage to return to this place. Hopefully, in her own time, she would tell him more about what had happened to her.

He stood awkwardly as Mia unbelted her coat, slipped it off of her shoulder and hung it on a hook by the door. Although Vincent wasn't dressed for the club, Mia certainly was. Gone was the corset. In its place was a black PVC minidress that laced up the front and over her cleavage with dark red ribbon. The material was skin-tight and showed off her body beautifully as she bent to unzip her stiletto boots. There was no question Mia was stunning and sexy as hell. She caught him watching her. "So where were we?" Mia asked, laughter in her eyes. She enjoyed his open admiration.

"I think we were watching a scene and I was running away with my tail between my legs."

"Ah yes, how could I forget?" she joked as she came back to him and took both of his hands in hers. Bootless, the top of her head didn't even reach his shoulders. "Time for a few questions."

"I thought we did that last Friday. Hell, didn't we just do that out in the café?"

"These are scene questions. This is how we negotiate and how we begin. Okay?"

He nodded.

"How many people have you been with?"

"A few."

Mia sighed. "Vincent, you have to trust me. I'm really glad that you agreed to come here with me but please, you have to try." Trust, that's the key. He had opened up so much already, what did he have to lose?

"Eight or nine, maybe?" He shrugged.

"What do you mean eight or nine? Which one is it?"

"It depends on what you count. Oral, um, vaginal…." Vincent trailed off sheepishly.

Mia laughed. "It all counts, Vincent. Okay, we'll go with nine, maybe more. Now, what do you fantasize about?"

"I don't really have any fantasies."

"So when you're alone jerking off you don't think about anything?"

"I don't know." He shifted from one foot to the other. "What does it matter what I fantasize about? Isn't BDSM about making the Sub's fantasies come true?"

"What you want, what the Dom wants, is as important as what your Sub wants. You have to align your desires with your Sub's and not the other way around. How can you control something or properly administer it, if you abhor it? Safe, sane and consensual goes for

Doms too." That made sense. "Close your eyes, please. Let's do a little visualization."

He closed his eyes and sighed. Mia chuckled. If his eyes weren't closed he probably would have seen her rolling her eyes. "Stick with it, Vincent. Picture yourself in bed with your girlfriend. What's your favourite thing to do?"

"Oral. I like going down on her."

"Good. Tell me what it's like when it's just the two of you together and you're between her thighs licking her. What do you like most about it?" Vincent wondered if Mia's eyes were closed too. Her breath seemed a little shallow. Was this talk turning her on? She seemed so sexual, so easy to arouse.

Vincent thought for a moment. He let himself imagine himself there, remembered the last time he had been with Catherine and had gone down on her. "I like it because I know immediately when I do something she likes. Because she can't hide what's she's feeling from me, her body won't let her."

"And how does that make you feel?"

"Good, powerful." And he did, even now there was a pull in his groin. He liked being powerful.

"There you go, there's the Dom. Would you like to play with me, Vincent?" He nodded. "Then open your eyes." He blinked at the light.

"And before you start a scene you should always ask your Sub what their hard limits are."

"Um, what's a hard limit?"

A smile played at her lips and he was too inexperienced to know if she was joking or not. "A hard limit is something that I don't want to do or can't do. Physically or sexually." He couldn't help but blush, thinking of the many possibilities. "For now, just tell me what you desire and we'll try it. I'm a little nervous about being restrained with chains, but other than that try whatever you'd like. If you want to try something with me that you've always wanted to but were too afraid to ask for, do it. Even something your ex-girlfriend said no to. I told you before that this is a no judgment zone."

"What's your safe word?"

Mia frowned. "I don't have one."

"I thought all Subs had a safe word."

"I've never needed one before, here in the club." She paused. "A safe word is a way out. It's a way to stop the scene when things get too intense. We'll be communicating at all times during our play so we should be okay. Some Doms forbid their subs to speak unless spoken to, but for our training purposes we need to be able to talk freely and ask any questions that come to mind, okay?"

"Do I get a safe word?"

She laughed. "No, Doms do not get a safe word. They control the action and can stop any time they like." She paused. "Is there anything else you need to know?"

"How long have you been doing this?" It was an impulsive question and as soon as he said it he regretted it. It seemed a little rude, but he couldn't call the words back to his mouth.

"I've been here since I was nineteen, I'm twenty-six now." Although her tone was light, he thought her response was a little too quick, a little too rehearsed. "Anything else?"

"Nope."

"Good, then let's get started on your lesson." She stood and started unlacing the red ribbon from her dress. It was a delicate procedure, and the agile movement of her hands had Vincent fascinated. He watched as the ribbon was pulled out through every loop, loosening the material that fit her so tightly, slowly revealing her body. "Enjoy it, Vincent, this will probably be the last time you see me clothed. Next time you come here I will greet you in slave position." Sure enough, soon she was pulling off the remnants of her dress, revealing her full naked body.

He felt a little awkward, but she seemed to expect him to look at her. It was hard not to leer like a teenager. Man, she had a great body.

She had small breasts, a healthy round ass, toned arms and killer legs. Her pale creamy skin housed a few scars and a couple more tattoos, but nothing that diminished her beauty in any way.

She folded her clothes and put them in a neat pile on the floor. Then she slowly knelt at his feet. She sat back on her feet and opened her knees. Then she placed her hands on the top of her thighs and turned them over so her palms were facing upward. It looked like a yoga move.

"This is slave position," she said, and cast her eyes down to the floor.

Vincent didn't know what to do. He waited for her to speak and teach him what came next.

As he stood there, he took the opportunity to further explore her body with his eyes. When she had undressed she had also freed her long hair to fall down over her shoulders. Shoulders that were marked with a trails of light brown freckles. Obviously she wasn't a fan of tanning as her creamy skin would attest. His eyes left her shoulders, and feeling like a voyeur, they moved quickly over her breasts. Not too big and not too small, but exactly the kind he liked, with large areolas. Her nipples were pierced with small barbells. The jewelry was too dainty to see through her clothes but the piercings framed the tips while helping to keep them hard. Her stomach was soft but her hips were slight. He snuck a look at her pussy. He could just barely see it through the frame of her thighs.

He felt his cock tightening. She was nowhere near his usual type—Catherine could almost be considered her opposite—but that was good. If anything about her reminded him of Catherine, it would distract him from his training. It was great, actually, he could focus and be in the presence of an absolute stunner. Lucky guy.

Although he must admit that the Mia kneeling at his feet looked little like the one he had sat across from in the café. In minutes, under his gaze, she had transformed from instructor to…submissive?

The minutes passed and Mia stayed as still as a statue. Vincent began to feel like she was waiting for him and he had missed his cue. Oh shit. Was he supposed to get naked? Was he supposed to sit with her?

He wasn't self-conscious about his body and had no problem undressing. He wasn't the kind of guy who spent hours at the gym, but he loved to get out and run, especially by the lakeshore. When he was younger he spent most of his time on a basketball court. Although he wasn't that athletic now, his body was still toned and strong. Without hesitation he unzipped his jeans and pushed them down over his hips, causing his half-hard dick to happily spring free.

At the sound of his pants hitting the floor, Mia looked up at him. Her long black hair had fallen into her eyes, but still he could see the flash of arousal there. Nice, she was attracted to him. Awesome.

She smiled at him mischievously. "Nice cock."

"Um, thank you?"

She raised one perfectly manicured eyebrow. "Are you going to fuck me, Vincent?"

"Ah…is that what you want?"

"Generally Doms do not get naked unless they're ready to have sex, sometimes not even then."

"Oh."

"Remaining clothed makes the Subs feel more vulnerable and reinforces the power balance. Although I certainly don't mind the preview." He followed her gaze as she admired his half-naked body.

Feeling like a fool he picked up his clothes and quickly and carefully stuffed his dick back into his pants. Clothed again, he stood there feeling stupid, not knowing what to do next but sure as hell not wanting to make another misstep. Shit, maybe he wasn't some Alpha male stud after all.

She sighed. "Vincent, what do you want to do to me?" Mia's voice was soft. Gone was any feeling of reprimand.

"I just feel so awkward. I don't know what to do." God he sounded like a pussy admitting that.

After a silent moment passed, Mia sighed. "I keep forgetting you're so new to this."

She stood. The movement was fluid and graceful, as if it was the most natural position in the world for her to have been in and quickly get out of. She walked over to Vincent and took his hand, making a connection between them again. "Being intimate with someone new is always a little awkward. It's okay to be nervous."

"James wasn't nervous during his scene."

"No, but don't worry, I've seen James nervous plenty of times. He wasn't always so comfortable in the role of a Dom. Don't compare yourself to him. Just be yourself." She looked up into his eyes. "Vincent, I think you should start by kissing me."

"Okay."

A kiss he could do. She stood on her toes and angled her mouth toward his. She reminded him of Terry, onstage waiting for James to give her pleasure. Vincent took a deep breath and moved his head down so it wouldn't be as much of a strain for her.

He went in for the kiss, but stopped.

He wasn't sure why he hesitated. It's not like it was the first time he had ever kissed a woman. He'd been kissing girls since he was fourteen. It was one of his favourite things. In his reckless youth he had kissed quite a few strangers—not that Mia was exactly a stranger anymore. She was his teacher and she was a beautiful woman. He wanted to kiss her. She had asked him to kiss her. So he should just man up and do it already.

Vincent took a step toward her. His nervousness rolled off of him in waves. It made his every movement a bit jerky. His hands shook as he reached out for her. *Why was he feeling so awkward?* Mia wasn't going to would push him away or deny him like Catherine had. With Mia he had a pre-approved relationship, negotiated down to the even the finest point on paper. A contract was something the club demanded of members entering into a training agreement and he had signed it eagerly. Of all of the physical acts mentioned on paper, a kiss was just about the most chaste activity listed. There was no way she wouldn't kiss him back.

Still he hesitated. In the moment his senses felt heightened. He could smell her faint perfume and hear her deep intake of breath as she prepared for their first romantic touch. He could even feel the heat in the air between them. Time slowed and he watched her eyes blink and then close tight, waiting for him to kiss her. That was his undoing. She closed her eyes and everything seemed right. She'd probably been kissed hundreds of times, and yet she still closed her eyes for his kiss.

He touched his lips to hers.

His mouth was shy, not pressing too much or demanding too much of her. He was gentle and light. A sweet kiss. First kisses usually are. Sometimes they are slow and fumbling and end as quickly as they begin. Mia's kiss was dark and electric. He could tell that kissing her would be different from the very moment their lips first touched. She tasted of her tea and something else distinctly her. It was nice, but he rushed through their first touch before his spinning mind caught up with him. This restrained kiss was good, but it wasn't great. It wasn't a real kiss. It certainly wasn't what they were here for.

He was a good son, sure. He had proper manners and treated everyone with respect. But those manners were getting in the way here. He was holding himself back. If he was going to do this, he needed to let go.

He pulled back just a second to take a quick breath before he returned to kiss her again. The second pass of his lips started almost the same as the first. He had some doubt. Would he be able to pull this off and actually become a Dom?

Then her felt her move. Her arms found their way blindly across his shoulders and brushed into his short hair. She pulled him closer, letting him know that he had her permission to go further. That was the last push he needed.

With a growl that surprised them both, he took control of her lips and kissed her more forcefully, capturing her mouth and making it his. Her lips against his felt good and sweet, yet at the same time purely sensual, like tasting warm caramel in the middle of soft dark chocolate.

He dipped his head even lower to deepen the kiss further. His movements mimicked hers. His hands were drawn to her hair too, and in his haste to bring her closer he pulled at the strands. That little bite of pain encouraged her. She kissed him back with an intensity that almost knocked the breath out of him. Her response was raw and primal.

She moaned and Vincent took the opportunity to push his tongue into her mouth. In response her tongue danced over his, tasting him and beckoning him to continue to claim her further.

Taking her up on the offer, he pushed his body fully up against hers. She staggered back for a second and then moved back toward him like a moth drawn to a flame. He could feel her breasts rubbing against his bare chest. Then her bare hips against his jeans. She was right, it was a turn-on knowing that she was fully naked and vulnerable while he was not. Every part of her that was soft was matched up with the parts of him that were hard and ready. He forgot all about being embarrassed about his body's reaction when she melted against him. There were other parts of their flesh that demanded attention.

He let his hands leave her hair and travel down his shoulders and arms. As his fingers traveled over her smooth skin he felt a multitude of tiny electrical shocks. It was a little jarring, but it felt right. This was like no other kiss.

He pulled his lips away a fraction. His breath was ragged. "This feels amazing."

"I know." She panted. "What do you want to do now, Vincent?" She panted. "Do whatever feels natural to you."

He could have kissed her all night, but he knew he had a decision to make to move forward his training. It was time for intimacy. Again he hesitated. She had given him free rein over her body. She was available for him to try, taste, and experiment with. Neither of them was a virgin, yet Vincent understood now that he was inexperienced in this kind of sex. Every fantasy he had was plain, boring even. He couldn't guess what she expected of him. He just didn't want to disappoint her.

Ugh. What did Mia tell him to do? Get out of his head and live in the moment. He had to remember that he was in control here. For years he had waited for the woman to give him signs of what he should do or how far he should go. That part of his sex life was over. He had to trust himself and trust Mia.

He tried to focus as his hands twitched, desperate to touch her. Yes, that's a good place to start. "I want to touch your breasts."

"Do it." She moaned.

His hand moved as if it had a mind of its own, his palm curling around the soft mound of her left breast. Close up he could see she had freckles here too. They were like beauty marks on her beautiful skin. His thumb stroked over the nipple. What would it be like to kiss those sweet rosy buds?

Vincent's hand was replaced by his willing mouth. His rough tongue lapped out across the soft side of her breast before finding and playing against the tight peak of her nipple. He sucked each one into his mouth in turn, pulling the nipples into peaks. Her skin tasted clean yet spicy, like cinnamon.

"Try this." At her words, he stopped his worship of her breasts to receive the metal chain she held up. It was the set of nipple clamps that he had seen earlier in the cabinet. She must have picked it up when she went she hung up her coat and hidden it in her pile of clothes. Vincent took the clamps from her and examined the jewelry.

Both ends of the intricately woven steel chain had an adjustable clamp. He took one between his thumb and first finger and saw how the mechanism worked and how tight the clamp was. As he tested it, her breathing changed in anticipation.

"Like this." Her voice was throaty and deep. She took the clamp back from him and showed him how to place it over her nipple, being mindful of her piercing, and then let it go. It squeezed her nipple tightly. It looked like it might hurt but the moan that escape's Mia's lips proved that it gave her far more pleasure than pain. Carefully he took the other clamp and slid it the way she had shown him over her other hungry nipple. The short chain pulled her breasts together slightly and brought blood to the surface of her nipples. The jewelry looked amazing on her. Gingerly Vincent touched his tongue to each distended nipple. Yes, the clamps he liked. His cock was at full attention as he licked and sucked her pinched peaks.

His hand touched the taut tight skin of her stomach. He slid it down her body inch by inch. She hissed at the feel of his skin moving over hers. Her hand found his and pushed it down the length of her torso. She let go of him as his fingers found her mound. And an inch later, they probed inside her folds and found her clit. His mouth never left her breasts as his finger teased her clit and then slid easily inside of her. She was incredibly wet, and again he felt powerful. It was amazing to see such proof of her arousal.

He was aroused too. He wanted more.

His greedy mouth left her nipples and followed the same path that previously their hands had taken down her body. He was hungry and there was nothing else he wanted to do more than taste her.

Kneeling, he used his wet fingers to pull her hips toward his face and further open her legs for him. He wanted to see what his meal looked like before he ate it. Her lips were nice and rosy like her nipples but already wet and glistening with her cream. God, she looked good. He had to admit that Mia didn't look like any teacher he had ever had. The woman's body was built for pleasure. He smiled at the thought, and saw that she was smiling too. This time he didn't care if he had spoken out loud, it was the truth.

She nodded for him to continue. With a deep breath, he moved her forward. She was inches away from his tongue and he couldn't wait to have a taste. His lips kissed her mound—so nicely bare—and his tongue found her plump clit as easily as his fingers had minutes before. The swollen sensitive flesh rolled easily beneath his tongue. He licked her entire slit and then his fingers found their place inside her again. They plunged in and out of her, matching the pace he set with his tongue. He couldn't wait to get her off. He licked and sucked at a frantic pace. He wanted her to come fast just for him.

Mia's hips threatened to buckle under the attention. The chain between her nipples swayed as her body shook. She couldn't disguise the ragged edge to her breath. Already she was close.

Vincent added another finger inside of her and increased the pace of his stroke. He kept working her, licking and sucking and fucking her with his fingers. He pulled her clit between his lips and suckled hard on the tiny button.

"Oh God," she moaned. Her head was thrown back, and her eyes squeezed tightly closed. Her face was flushed with excitement. Her lips parted as if her moans forced them to remain open wide. Yeah, there was no doubt that his attention was having a big effect on her.

It was having a big effect on him too. He could feel the blood rushing through his body. It pooled at the base of his cock where it caused his shaft to thicken and grow. He would have loved to take her hands and place them inside of his pants, making her jerk him off until he came in the palm of her hand. The only reason he stopped himself was because this lesson was about the Sub. He was here to pleasure her. He could look after himself later at home, fisting his dick while thinking of how her creamy juice had filled his mouth.

He always enjoyed tasting a woman. It was one thing he had been told he was good at. Catherine had certainly never complained. He prided himself of technique, skill, and the ability to bring a woman to orgasm with his tongue.

Except, even as overheated as she seemed to be, Mia wasn't coming. Any other woman he had been with would be moaning and gripping his hair by now, as they tumbled into ecstasy. Mia had all the signs of an impending orgasm, but was holding back for some reason. His cock wilted and he tried to figure out what he was doing wrong. He increased the intensity of his tongue on her sensitive nub and scissored his fingers inside of her.

Finally she put a hand to his head, to get his attention. "May I, Sir?" She panted. "May I come?"

"Yes!" He yelled against her clit.

Then he felt it bubble on his fingers and then on his tongue. Her muscles contacted, and her body folded into orgasm. He kept licking as she came hard. He almost laughed because it felt like she had been waiting for him to give her permission to come. Fuck, that's exactly what happened! She had been waiting, suffering, and he hadn't known that she had waited for him to tell her to orgasm. He couldn't imagine someone having the power over him to choose when he came. But as much as he was sorry that he had made her wait so long, he really liked that Mia had given him that control.

God he felt powerful. He licked her wetness off of his lips. He felt high, he felt strong. So was this what being a Dom was like? If so, sign him up for full membership!

As the last tremors shook her body, Vincent sat back on his knees. There were so many rules to learn about BDSM. James swore the only way to learn how to be a Dom was through experience. Thank God he had Mia. He still felt bad though. This was a fairly calm instance but it could have been a lot worse if they were in a scene and he didn't know what command he was supposed to give or what he was supposed to do. Like now. What did he do now?

Aftercare. That is what James called it, right?

He stood. Mia had her eyes still closed but a sweet smile played on her lips. It was the smile of a woman who had just come. She looked truly beautiful. There was something intense, yet extremely vulnerable about her.

She swayed slightly.

Vincent caught her. He bent at the knees and picked Mia up in his arms. She opened her eyes in surprise but said nothing. He looked for a comfortable place for them to sit and unwind. Ah yes, the couch.

He sat down slowly and carefully cradled her in his lap. He wrapped his arms around her and instinctively pulled her head against his chest. He felt like his heart was beating a mile a minute. She must have been able to hear the wild beat though his skin. He was a mix of emotions at the moment.

He needed to try and focus. Aftercare time was for the Sub, James had said.

Vincent lightly stroked her long dark hair. The strands were like silk under his fingers. After a few minutes she looked up at him. She looked young and vulnerable. "Who told you to do this?"

"James."

"Oh, so you're seeing a new teacher now?" She was still a little out of breath from her orgasm. Her voice sounded husky and sexy as hell. "You know, a scene doesn't have to stop just because the Sub comes."

"But…" He paused, not knowing the right words. "But you took a while to get into it."

Mia threw her head back and laughed. "That's called orgasm withhold and control. Something new to learn. I've been a Sub a long time. I'm used to only coming when told to do so." She shrugged. "Make no mistake, I was into it. And I've been aroused since the second we stepped into the club. Actually before that, when we were talking about making out." Her eyes sparkled. "It's been awhile since I was good and kissed." She was pleased and therefore, he felt pleased. This was a big step forward toward achieving his goal of being a Dom.

"So how was your first taste of being in control?"

"I liked it."

"Good, I'm glad."

"Did you like it?"

She thought for a moment. "Yes, very much so. I especially liked when you decided to give in to your instincts and go for it. Your expression at that moment said it all. And of course it's always nice to get oral."

He grinned. "I guess that's my version of bringing the teacher an apple."

She laughed, deep and throaty. "That was a really nice apple." She leaned in and kissed him. This wasn't part of the lesson. She was going off book with him. Instead of questioning it, Vincent leaned into it, pulling her body taut against his as he added to her sweet kiss. He knew she could taste herself in his tongue.

He felt like the teenage version of himself that she had evoked the memory of earlier. He liked this, holding her, kissing her. His cock was back straining and ready for a release that wouldn't be granted tonight. The Mia in his arms was not nervous or hesitant. This Mia must be what her own teenage self was like, long before she traded lessons for her livelihood. He brushed the hair away from her face. Her makeup was mussed, her lips swollen and her face flushed. Yet she was absolutely stunning.

"No," she said. "No I'm not." She blushed and struggled to sit up. The magic of the moment broken by him speaking his thoughts out loud again. He wouldn't take it back, she did look stunning to him. The prettiest he had ever seen her.

"What was your first time like?" An impulsive question, asked to keep her with him and to keep her talking. He didn't want the magic of the night to be gone.

She laughed. "Vincent, I haven't been a virgin for a long time. I hardly remember it now."

"No, I mean your first time trying BDSM."

She didn't answer right away. In fact she moved herself further away from him.

"It's okay, you don't have to answer that."

She looked up at him and her smile was pained. "No, it's just that how I found out about BDSM is my private story, I'm sorry." Her words, though spoken softly, felt like a slap to the face. He had just had his tongue shoved into her private bits and yet she didn't trust him with a simple personal story?

As if sensing his feelings and his negative self-talk, Mia put a hand on his chest. "But I can tell about the first time I realized I was submissive."

"Okay. Tell me that."

"When I was about seventeen I met someone in the lifestyle. It felt like a date, except he already had a wife." Her smile returned, this time a little more warm as she recounted the memory. "This man wasn't my usual type…he wasn't like the boys I dated at school or the jerk I lost my virginity to. And, for good reason, he was almost twenty-five years older than me or any of those inexperienced boys. He was very tall and fair, his hair was all white and he had the reddest lips…I pay good money for lipsticks that vibrant. He was also charming and had the driest wit…and his attraction to me was evident. I'm not sure how it happened, but one time we found ourselves alone. Without discussing it, we started to fool around. He ordered me to give him a blow job. He was a little forceful because he wanted it so badly. And for some reason I wanted to please him, so I did it. I sucked him off and loved it. I even got off on it. He didn't even need to touch me and I came. Up to that point it was the single hottest thing I had ever done. Sure I had sex before, but this was different.

He took my phone number and sometimes he would call me. I could usually tell by the sound of his voice that he was masturbating. He would talk about his fantasies and call me a dirty girl. Again, I don't know why but I liked it. Soon the phone calls weren't enough and he asked to see me again. He picked me up in his old pickup truck and I sucked him off in a public parking lot. Next time it was the back of a school yard. Then at his own home. I did whatever he said. He would only let me give him oral, nothing else. Sometimes he would tie my hands and spank me or show off my breasts. He loved breasts." She laughed, he assumed recalling her private memories with this man.

"Did you feel bad that he had a wife?" Vincent tried to keep the judgment out of his tone.

"Vincent, she knew! He had left his first wife because she couldn't be open to his lifestyle and had newly married this second one who was in the scene. He had a huge sexual appetite and even being a newlywed didn't stop him. The difference with this wife was that he would tell her every detail of what we did together. You have to open your mind, Vincent. There are people who like to share their partners. Hell, there's entire towns made up of ménage families that are healthy and happy. But yeah, back then it was outside the norm for me. Maybe he and I got off a little on our bizarre triangle."

"Did meeting his wife make you feel guilty for what you did?

"Hell no!" She giggled. "His wife was much closer to my age and sexy as hell. Long red hair, beautiful eyes, and a hell of a rack!" Mia's eyes danced in pleasure. It was clear that this was a fond memory. "The first night he allowed me to meet her, I watched him fuck her and then I was allowed to make both of them come with my mouth. It was beautiful. She had partners of her own on the side, but when the two of them were together it was if no one else existed. The love between them was clear. My one wish is that someday I'll experience a love like that."

"And being with them is what made you want to get tied up full time?"

His question was lighthearted and meant to make her laugh. Instead it gave her pause as she struggled for an answer. "This wasn't a straight line to it, no. And I don't like to be tied up, not anymore. You have to remember that BDSM really isn't that different from regular sex and intimacy. It's all about making someone else feel good, and surrendering yourself so that in return you feel good. It's simple. Nothing else is more pure."

She smiled. "Besides, it was his son who really led me astray." She stood up and offered her hand to Vincent. "I'm sorry, but I think we're done for tonight. Will you come back next week?" He nodded and her smile grew. Vincent took her hand and stood, unable to hide that his cock was still hard. She looked at his bulge and then winked at him.

"Good work tonight, Vincent." She gave him a quick kiss then walked away to retrieve her clothes. He laughed when he saw the chain and clamps still swinging from her nipples.

Chapter Three

Friday night his cell phone rang just as he was getting home. It was crammed down deep in his jacket pocket. To answer it meant either dropping the pizza delivery box, or sacrificing to the floor his keys and the book he had just bought. It wasn't a hard decision. The keys and bestselling suspense novel crashed to the floor, causing Gus to start barking.

Only a handful of people had his cell number. Work, of course, but it had been a smooth week without any trouble. They shouldn't have a reason to call him. Then there was his Mom or his sister Jennifer. It was midday out on the coast, and they both should be at work, so if they were calling it wasn't for a friendly chat. The only other person that had the number was Catherine. Catherine!

Having finally extracted the phone, Vincent looked at the call display. He didn't recognize the number. Strange. Immediately his anxiety amped up and he punched the answer button.

"Hello?" He tried to keep his voice calm.

"Vincent?" The voice on the other end was female, hesitant, and a little unsure. It was impossible to tell more than that from her tone as Gus was still barking his head off. Calm down buddy.

"Yes? Who is this?"

"It's Mia. I hope you don't mind, James gave me your number."

"Mia?" He was a little stunned. "Of course. It's fine." James. He had forgotten James on the list. James had his cell number and had obviously thought nothing of giving it to Mia without asking first. Although Vincent probably should have given it to her himself, just in case there was a change in schedule and she had to cancel a lesson.

Wait, was that what she was doing now, cancelling tomorrow's lesson? Shit.

If she was, he would be very disappointed. Two weeks ago he couldn't imagine going back to the club, never mind actually looking forward to spending his Saturday night there. But it was what it was. He wanted to go back there, and he wanted to see her. And if possible, maybe make her come again. Maybe even make himself come with her.

"Is everything okay?"

"Yes. I called because I was wondering if you had plans for dinner tonight. I thought it might be nice to talk in a neutral space before we see each other again tomorrow night at the club."

The surprises just kept on coming. Looks like the pizza and his book would have to wait.

"Sure, we could meet at the burger place on Main, does that work?"

Mia paused then chuckled slightly. "That's not what I had in mind, but I guess it'll work."

"Meet there in twenty?"

"Sure, see you there."

* * * *

In retrospect it was probably the absolute worst place ever to suggest they have dinner. Although in all fairness, he felt it was at least fifty percent her fault. She could have suggested someplace else on the phone. She could have confessed when they met in the parking lot on the way in. Or maybe even made a comment when they were picking out their own red-and-white leather booth complete with sticky retro Formica table top. No, she waited until the waitress arrived to voice her conflict.

Vincent was shocked. "You don't eat meat?"

"Nope."

"Like, never?

She laughed. "Not ever."

The nametag-less waitress looked back and forth between them, eager to take their order and return to the kitchen.

"Do you have veggie burgers?"

"I can check with the cook and see what he has."

"Or a salad maybe?"

The waitress wrote something on her order pad. "I'll see what we can put together."

"Great."

"And you?" The waitress turned to Vincent, who was poring over the menu and chewing his lip nervously.

He looked up to Mia apologetically. "I'm going to get a burger." She shrugged and he turned back to the waitress. "I'll have a double burger with bacon. And a poutine. And a root beer." Vincent handed the waitress back the menu. This place was a favourite he had discovered shortly after moving into the area. It hadn't changed much in the last few years, and he was glad. The place wasn't fancy and didn't invest in gimmicks or things like good customer service. They just made damn fine burgers.

Awkwardly they sat opposite each other in a booth with ripped vinyl seats. Mia looked a little out of place in her business clothes. She wore a soft, pale-pink sweater and a long grey pencil skirt with matching grey high heels. Her hair was up in a twist and her makeup was much more conservative than usual. Obviously she was expecting a different restaurant, or maybe she had just come from work. Work. He tried to imagine what line of work she was in. Office job, maybe? She sure would make one hell of a sexy secretary. He imagined her being chased around her desk by her boss. That was a nice fantasy. Maybe next time at the club they could act it out together.

They sat in silence and watched the other people in the restaurant. There were some families eating together and a few couples out on dates. By them was a man, sitting eating all alone. That would have been Vincent, here or at home, if she hadn't called.

"Thanks for suggesting this."

"Sure." She smiled sweetly.

Her smile vanished when their food arrived. She looked dismally at her tiny overcooked veggie burger and sad excuse for a salad. She looked so sad, Vincent almost laughed.

"I'm sorry." He looked at his burger guiltily.

"Don't worry about it, Vincent. No judgment, remember?" She pushed away her plate and searched around in her purse. She retrieved a protein bar to snack on.

"I thought the no-judgment thing was just in the club."

She shook her head, unwrapping the bar. "No, with me it's everywhere. I'm just not a person who cares too deeply about superficial things. Especially after some of the things I've done in my life."

"Good, because I'm going to eat this burger and enjoy it." He picked up his burger and took a big bite out of it for emphasis.

She laughed. "Go ahead, carnivore. I have a friend that would have a field day protesting you." She bit into her bar, pretending to use just as much gusto.

He grinned and she grinned back. "I'm glad you called me."

"I won't lie to you, James suggested it."

"Wow." What should he say to that? Should he be thanking his friend or cursing him for forcing Mia to hang out with him?

"Yeah. Don't take that as an insult. I'm glad I'm here. I just don't—I mean, I go from work to home to the club. I have no other interests, no hobbies, nothing for myself. Well, beyond what I eat. There, I just made a decision that matches my ethics. I can control what I eat. Everything else…"

"Is out of control?" He finished the thought for her.

"Is out of *my* control," she corrected. "James has helped me with that though, and I'm slowly getting better at controlling the rest of my life."

Vincent put down his burger and wiped his hands on his napkin. "He controls you?"

"No, the opposite. He helps me to make my own choices." She shrugged. "Although he's not my Dom, he's my best friend and he wants me to be happy."

Vincent leaned back in the booth. Maybe he could help her too. He had an idea. "How about for the rest of the night, you can make all the choices. Where we go, what we do. Everything is up to you."

She didn't smile. "A few months ago that would have been overwhelming to me."

"Okay, forget it then."

"No. I want to try it. Thank you."

She stared off into space for a minute. She was doing some heavy thinking. She bit her lip.

"You know, I never do this."

"What, go to burger joints?"

She smiled. "No. And I never do dates. I usually meet men at the club only. In fact I don't know if I've ever been on a nice, normal date."

"This is a date?"

She winked at him. "What else did you think it was, Vin?"

He slowly took a sip of his soda. "Two people getting together to get to know each other better?"

She raised an eyebrow. "Sounds pretty much like a date to me."

"Okay, okay." He chuckled. "So James set us up on a date?"

"I guess in a roundabout way."

Vincent took another bite of his burger. He felt a little shy now that he knew they were on an official date. He probably should have dressed better. He should have made a mix CD for his car and picked her up. Maybe even brought her flowers. He was out of practice with the whole dating thing.

And how did it go dating a beautiful BDSM-lifestyle girl? Did that mean that he was expected to act as her Dom tonight? Did that mean she kissed on the first date, or maybe more? Would he get to experiment more or maybe have a repeat of last week? Yeah, he wouldn't mind tasting her sweet flesh again.

Shit, now he had a hard-on in his favourite burger joint.

Her smile was coy. 'What are you thinking about?"

Shit. If he said what he was thinking, would she be charmed or would she be creeped out? Just because she had declared their meal a date didn't mean that he had a season's pass to her body. They weren't in the club now.

He had James to thank again for getting him into another mess. *James. Say something about James.*

"I can't believe that James was a Sub once."

Mia nodded but crinkled up her nose. "Maybe I shouldn't have told you that."

He shrugged. "It shows another side of the guy."

"Yeah." She took a sip of the water the restaurant had supplied. "Is there another side to you, Vincent? Tell me something about you."

"Like what?"

"Like where do you come from, where did you grow up?"

Vincent picked up his fork and poked at his poutine. Where to start? How could he boil down his life into a few sentences? He cleared his throat and decided that the best place to start was from the beginning. "I was born and raised out west, in British Columbia. My family has a home in a little town named Sechelt that's part of an area called the Sunshine coast. People call it one of the most beautiful places on earth and I wouldn't argue with that. My great-grandfather ended up settling in the area when he went west chasing logging jobs. He never intended to stay. He took a job at a saw mill, and met my great-grandmother and settled in."

"That's romantic."

Vincent nodded, agreeing. "My whole family is still there, what's left of it anyways. When I was just starting second grade my sister Jennifer was born. My Mom says that she learned how to fight with me even before she learned to walk."

"Are you two close now?"

Vincent nodded. "Yeah, we talk often."

"That's nice. I wish I was closer with my brother Lee." She finished the last bite of her bar. "So what made you leave the most beautiful place on earth?"

"I dropped out of college and moved here for a girl."

"Catherine?"

"Oh no, a different girl, Sarah." He forked up more of his fries. "I guess I've always been the follower. I thought she was the one and that I loved her. But really I was just young and dumb."

"A lot of people do foolish things when they think they're in love."

"Is that so?" Vincent thought about that while he took a sip of his soda. "Well, my teacher, what foolish things have you done before for love?"

Mia shook her head. "Oh no, I didn't mean me. I don't think I've ever been in love. I'm just not the type. Anyways, this is about you. What did you study in college?"

"Fundamentals of Architecture. I liked the program well enough, but I liked the girl better. I packed my car and drove across country without sleeping. I left everything behind except for my suitcase and my dog."

Mia watched him fork in another mouthful of gooey fries and shuttered. "Do you miss your family?"

He nodded and took a deep breath. "Yeah. A lot. I lost my Dad last year."

"Oh no, I'm so sorry." Mia reached across the table, her hand touching his. Her eyes shined with tears and emotion. "My mother passed away just after I graduated high school. It's been so long and yet I still imagine that I'll walk into my parents' house and she'll be there." Mia took a deep breath. "I try to avoid going home as much as possible because every time it feels like the hurt of losing her is brand new again."

The emotion in her voice shook him. He and his father had never been close and hadn't spoken much in the years leading up to his death. Mia obviously had been close to her mother. She cleared her throat and took her hand back. She tried to regain her cheerful composure. "So, is there anything else you miss about BC?"

He thought about the question for a minute and pushed away his almost empty plate. He'd rather hold Mia's hand than eat. "Yeah I miss the water. My grandparents' house was on the beach and I'd visit them every summer. Even just the sound of the tide is comforting to me now."

He could almost pinpoint the exact moment that Mia had the idea. She blurted it out immediately, excited. "We're pretty close to the lakeshore here. Do you want to go walk down on the docks with me?"

"Uh huh." He nodded eagerly, trying not to laugh and losing the battle. Mia just shook her head at him and smiled. While she grabbed her purse, he paid for the meal. He was in such a good mood he left the waitress a very nice tip.

They quickly discovered that it was a little chilly out for the early summer night. He was fine, he didn't mind the wind, but he made sure Mia put on his jacket to keep warm. She looked cute, so tiny in his coat. She had to roll up the sleeves to get a hand free to hold onto Vincent as they walked.

A fair amount of people were still enjoying the beautiful view down on the Port Credit docks. The pier was a little piece of paradise so close to the city. It wasn't a busy waterway so they had an unobstructed view of the lake. Mia seemed to be enjoying it as much as he was. As they crossed onto another lower dock, she held onto him tightly so that she didn't trip on the well-worn boards.

"It's really nice out here."

Mia nodded. "It's one of my favourite places to come."

When the sun started to set they watched the sky blush with peach and pink hues before turning dark red to usher in the twilight. It was evenings like this that made Vincent miss summer nights back home. His grandparents' place wasn't decked out the same way this pier was, but it was still fairly impressive. Vincent had spent countless nights out on their dock, clowning around with his sister Jennifer in the water. Sometimes fishing or going out in his own little tin boat, a thirteenth birthday present from his folks that still ran halfway decent.

When he was younger and had nothing to do, his favourite thing was to sit out watching the sun go down. When the night would come, he would lie on his back out on their long dock and lose himself staring up at the stars. Infinite darkness and promise shining down at him from a thousand miles away. Here you could hardly see the stars. Back home, they were all you could see.

Catherine, who hated anything outside of the city core, would never have been content in that life. Hell, this pier was minutes away from her apartment and yet he knew that she had never been here. She was not the girl who would ever agree to a simple quiet after-dinner walk by the water. She needed more action to be happy. Vincent shook his head. More action. That could be Catherine's personal motto. It had always made him a little sad that she was never interested in his life back west. He couldn't imagine ever taking her back home with him, even for a visit.

Mia was different. Yes that was an understatement. She was perfectly happy to stand by his side and watch the sun set with him.

"My dad used to have a boat."

"Yeah?"

"He probably still owns it and just stores it somewhere. My mom and I used to wear bikinis and sit out on the front deck while my brother and my dad drove it around the harbor." She smiled, remembering the memory. "I used to get such a dark tan."

"That's hard to believe." He peeked over her shoulder. She had let the lapels of his jacket come apart and he could see an expanse of creamy white cleavage exposed through the neck of her sweater. Her pale skin didn't show a trace of a tan now.

Vincent took a chance and wrapped his arms around her. He told himself that it was because the temperature continued to dip and he wanted to warm her up. In reality he just wanted to touch her. Mia didn't seem to mind, she relaxed into his arms and allowed herself to be held. Together they stood like that and watched the last of the boats mooring for the night.

"I think they rent boats here. We could take one out some time."

"I'd like that."

Mia laid her head on his shoulder. Vincent realized how late it was getting. He should be tired. Hell, he was tired a few hours ago before she called, but he felt energized now. And he really didn't want the date to end.

"What should we do now?"

Mia thought for a long moment. "I don't know. What do you want to do?"

"We could hang out at my place for a while and watch a movie if you want. It's not far from here."

"Okay." Mia turned in his arms and hugged him. He was a little surprised, but he liked it. He held her tightly and reluctantly let go when she looked up and smiled at him.

For the walk back to the parking lot to their cars, he took her hand again. It just felt good to keep touching her.

The quiet of the lakeshore was a contrast to the noise of his house. When you live with a dog, you live with a built-in alarm system. Gus was on duty protecting the house when they arrived. His barking increased when he spotted Mia.

"You don't get many visitors?" she shouted over Gus's greeting.

"No, sorry."

He shouldn't have bothered to apologize. By the time he had shut and locked the door, Mia had started to tame the beast. She had crouched down and was lightly scratching the boxer's ears. Gus still let out the occasional woof, but was quickly calming down and becoming charmed by their guest.

"You have a way with animals."

"Some of them," she said with a wink.

He flipped on the lights and she looked around the room as she continued petting Gus. The front door opened into the kitchen. He was glad that he had stored his pizza in the fridge before leaving. His new book sat abandoned on the island. Otherwise the place was neat and tidy. It was a small house, but fit him perfectly. He had bought it a few years back. Back then it had needed a hell of a lot, much more than a fresh coat of paint to make it comfortable, and he had put some serious work into fixing it up. He was proud of what he had accomplished and happy to call it his home.

"Come on, I'll give you the fifty-cent tour."

"I think I can find two quarters in my purse." They laughed and she followed him out into the living room. Gus padded silently beside them and then took a seat by the window to chew on an old piece of rawhide. His living room was tidy and small, but comfortable. Sure, he had all the typical guy stuff. Obscenely big TV, leather recliners, video game system, worn out coffee table that had seen many a bottle of beer on its surface. He also had a huge bookcase filled with dog-eared novels along with an impressive collection of art-house and foreign-language DVDs.

Mia took her time looking around the room and uncovering this layer of his private self. She had been right of course, when at the café she had guessed that he didn't get many visitors. He had told himself that it was because he wanted it that way. Truth was, besides James he didn't have any friends. And James was definitely not the type of guy to just hang out at someone's house. Catherine had preferred her place to his so they had spent all of their time together there. As he watched

Mia taking his favourite books down off the shelf, looking at the covers and reading the back descriptions, he was happy to have this visitor in his space. He didn't have to worry about her thinking any of his things were lame. She simply accepted them as what they were and didn't read anymore into it.

Although she did make a face when she looked through his DVD collection.

"Do you like kung fu movies?" he asked eagerly.

She shrugged. "They're okay."

"Then you're not watching the right ones," he joked. "After the tour I have a great one to watch that I think you'll like."

"Sure, whatever you want, Vincent."

"No, remember, whatever *you* want."

She giggled. "Okay, fine."

When she finished thoroughly inspecting that room, he moved on to show the spare bedroom that he had converted into an office. To call it an office was probably too kind, it was more of a place to keep his laptop and check his email. It was nothing exciting, basically a plain empty room. Mia raised an eyebrow in question.

"I'm not much of a decorator."

"I can see that."

The last place he showed her was his bedroom. He didn't mean to save it for last, although it was more polite to wait than making it the first place he showed her. She followed along behind him up the stairs.

The door was closed tight—to keep out a dog that loved to chew his socks—and stuck a little with the humidity. Vincent popped it open and flipped on the light. He prayed that he had remembered to make his bed and that he hadn't left his underwear on the floor or used tissues or anything else equally embarrassing.

He had spent a little more time in decorating this space. Sure, the entire house was his, but he had always found his bedroom to be his true sanctuary. The walls were a deep, rich navy blue. His curtains, comforter and pillows were all plain white cotton. The bed itself was the real show piece. Mia appeared to be as drawn to it as he had been. "This is beautiful."

"Thanks. I bought it a few years ago when Jennifer visited. She dragged me all over town looking for furniture and we found this in a dusty antique shop. I loved the lines and the craftsmanship. I probably looked at it an hour before I decided that I had to have it."

"I think you made the right choice." Mia sat gingerly on the edge of the mattress. It bounced a little under even her slight weight. He liked a nice soft bed to sleep on.

She smiled and padded the space beside her, motioning for him to sit. When he was seated, she opened her mouth and then closed it. She looked like she wanted to say something but had thought better of it.

Slowly she began unfastening the buttons of her pink cardigan. She didn't look at him and although he was surprised, he didn't say anything. It probably would have been polite to ask her if this was what she wanted to do, and remind her that there was no obligation, nor was this his intention for showing her his bedroom. But he had told her that she could make the decisions tonight. And if this was her choice, he would not deny her.

When the last button on her sweater was freed, she slipped it over her shoulders, revealing her dark-grey lace bra. It was beautiful and far more delicate then he would expect of her lingerie. She unzipped her skirt and pulled it down her legs. He hadn't known that he was holding his breath until she let it fall to the floor.

His breath came out a little stronger than he would have liked when he saw that she wasn't just wearing that beautiful bra, but an entire matched set of bra, panties, and garters. Her stockings reached midthigh and framed her legs nicely. Mia looked great naked, but now, here in his room and in her lingerie, she looked impossibly beautiful.

She looked up and caught him staring at her body. "Say something, Vincent."

"You look lovely."

"Thank you."

He cleared his throat and tried to control himself. There was nothing he wanted to do more than touch her. As hard as it was, he had to remember Mia was in charge. "Are you going to teach me something new?"

"This isn't a scene, Vincent." She smiled sweetly. She looked a little flushed like she had last time in her room at the club. She turned and crawled further up on the bed. He was powerless but to follow her as she moved across the sheets.

She proved this wasn't a scene by making the first move. She kissed him. This time he swore he could taste the sea shore on her lips. Her mouth was both electric and delicious. When her tongue touched his, he couldn't help but moan. He hands found her ebony hair and held her to him as he continued to drinking her in.

Her hands found the edge of his shirt and they broke their kiss only long enough for her to pull it over his head. Her hands explored his torso and his lightly haired chest and firm stomach. He would never have washboard abs or monster arms, but his job kept him very fit. It was the only benefit of hand-loading freight that he had ever found.

Those hands of hers pushed him down on the bed. He felt the brushing of her breasts against him as she leaned over him. She broke the kiss to move her lips from his mouth to his neck and then down over his shoulder to his chests and nipples.

"My nipples aren't sensitive."

"Then you're doing it wrong." She lightly laughed and kept licking and sucking at his nipples and then down over the muscles of his belly. Her hands found the bulge in his pants and rubbed over it. The pressure of her hands rubbing the stiff denim against his cock was an incredible combination. She licked her lips. Man, he could just imagine how good those lips would feel on him.

"What do you want me to do, Vincent?"

"Whatever you want."

"No it's whatever *you* want." She rubbed his bulge harder. "Take charge, tell me what to do. Do you want me to suck your dick, Vincent?" He nodded. "Then say, please, Mia, suck my big fat dick."

"Suck my dick, please."

She gave him a look that was pure sin. "Thank you, Sir." She stopped rubbing him and started sliding down his zipper with her teeth, and he thought he might pass out with how impossibly hard his cock was. She pulled roughly on his jeans and boxers until his cock sprang free.

She looked him in the eye as she ran her hand down his length. The feeling was amazingly erotic. Her dark-chocolate eyes told him how clearly aroused she herself was and how much she wanted him. Her hands stroked him, moistened by the pre-cum that wept from his tip. It was amazing, but it was nothing compared to the erotic show she gave him as she stopped stroking and slowly slipped her tight lips over the purple crown of his cock. His healthy girth stretched her lips as she slid down to take as much of him into her moist mouth as possible. She showed off her ability by almost making it down to his balls without gagging or breaking eye contact. Oh God. There was nothing hotter than this woman taking all of him into her mouth.

After stilling a second and keeping his cock in her throat as long as possible, she swirled her tongue around the length of his shaft as she moved her mouth back up to the tip again. He saw that tongue of hers as it licked over the crown again. Going back down on him, she increased the suction of her erotic kiss, and the speed on which her lips came back up. He held back her hair to keep it out of the way and not to block the view. She pulled off his dick for a moment to catch her breath.

"I like having your dick in my mouth, Vincent."

And what a skilled mouth it was. She quickly went back down on him. It was clear that she enjoyed blowing him. It was so hot how into it she was and how she even moaned on his cock. He loved this different Mia who let him know how she was feeling and how much she loved having his cock in her mouth. The bed swayed as she moved her hips in time to the motion with her mouth. He couldn't stop himself from helping to guide her movement with his hands on her shoulders, her head.

"Oh God," he groaned.

Her lips and tongue played with the fold of skin on the underside of his cock where his foreskin had once been. It felt amazing and created a distinct tingle in his balls. Shit, he was close. He tried to signal to her that he was about to come, but she just shook her head and kept licking and sliding her lips over him. She even used her teeth a little this time.

"Fuck!" She didn't stop when he started coming. She took his salty shots to the throat and sucked the jizz out of him. It felt like he came for minutes as he emptied his balls into her pretty mouth. His liquid squeezed out of her mouth as she slid up his shaft one last time. It felt amazing and it looked so fucking hot. The effect worked to keep him hard and craving being inside of her.

He thought she had the same idea when she straddled him. Instead she used her hard-working and much-appreciated hands to pull him into a seated position. He wrapped his arms around her to hold himself up. He felt a little lightheaded and dizzy still from the recent orgasm.

Instead of fucking him, she kissed him. He could taste himself in her mouth and didn't care. It was pretty sexy having a woman service you and then taste of you.

"Thank you."

She ducked her head shyly. "You don't have to thank me, Vincent. I really wanted to do that."

He laughed. "Well I liked it. And I think it's my turn now." Vincent flipped her over onto her back. Surprised, Mia yelped. She tried to move as Vincent pulled her bra straps down over her arms.

His intention was to remove her bra altogether, but she looked pretty hot with the straps pinning her arms to her sides, immobile.

"Stop, stop," Mia begged and instantly he released her. She sat up and pulled her straps back up. She tried her best to catch her breath. He could see the panic in her eyes.

He gave her a moment before he reached out and gently rubbed her shoulders. "What was that?"

"Nothing. I have panic attacks sometimes." Although she said it was nothing he didn't believe her. He had witnessed her fear firsthand.

"Do you have them only when you're restrained? You had said that may be a limit for you."

Mia nodded quickly before crawling to the edge of the bed and stepping down onto the plush carpet.

"I should go."

"You could stay." He patted the mattress beside him like she had done before. "Big comfortable bed. Big hard man."

She laughed and her eyes sparkled like diamonds. "No, Vincent. I'll see you tomorrow at the club. Let this be motivation for our next lesson." She avoided looking at him while she searched the floor for her discarded clothes.

He, too, stood, and pulled up his boxers and zipped up his jeans as she dressed. Damn if her ass did look great both naked and in that figure-hugging skirt. He would love to strip that skirt back off of her and spread her lovely legs to bury his cock inside her wetness. Fuck her hard and command her to come. That would be perfect. So why was she leaving? Why did the night have to end like this? More than anything he didn't want her to leave,

"Sub, you will stay the night here." His voice was firm and steady.

Mia froze in place. When she turned to look at him, it was not out of anger, but with a sad, tragic mask of regret. "I can't," she whispered.

Vincent nodded. Whatever had scared her in the past must be bad. When they were both finished dressing, he led her back downstairs and to the front door. Gus was fast asleep, chew toy forgotten.

Mia tried to smile and failed. "You still owe me that kung fu movie, Vincent."

"I'll show it to you whenever you want." He tried to joke but wasn't fully able to be lighthearted.

"Goodnight, Vincent." She gave him one last quick kiss then walked out the door toward her car. He watched her the entire way. Safely inside, car started and driver buckled in tight, she waved and then drove away.

Back inside, door locked, Vincent stumbled back upstairs to his bedroom. He collapsed back onto the bed as if he had run a marathon. Instead it was just the thoughts inside his head that were churning a mile a minute. He could still smell her perfume and feel how warm her body had been while covering his. He didn't have to strain to recall how husky her voice had sounded. And that she said that she liked him. If he wasn't careful, he would end up really, really liking her.

He tried not to let the amazing parts of the evening be erased by images of the pain on her face or her scared whisper as she was running from him. There was something broken inside of her that he didn't know if he could fix.

He was in too deep now not to try.

Chapter Four

He listened to the phone ring once. *Pick up please.*
A second ring. *Come on, come on.*
A third ring.
A click. "Hello?" He said, hoping she was there.
Another click and the answering machine kicked in. "This is Catherine, leave a message," rang out her cheerful voice, spiced with her slight British accent.
Beep.
Vincent hung up. He probably shouldn't be calling his ex while another woman owned his thoughts.

After too few hours of sleep, he had watched the dawn with a cup of coffee in hand on his back deck. He hated himself a little. Maybe it was a mistake to go out with Mia last night. He definitely shouldn't have asked her to stay over or pushed her so hard. What was he thinking?

Mia was supposed to be his teacher, and he felt like he had used her a little. Maybe she had felt the same way and that's why she had left so suddenly. She had obviously been turned on, and he hadn't done anything to give her release. Isn't that what a Dom would do? Oh man. He was failing miserably at his new role. Maybe he didn't have the natural tendencies everyone said he had.

And what about their date? That part was great, especially when they were down at the pier. The part where he came in her mouth was good too. The part where he ordered her to stay and she still left, well that was bad.

He felt so mixed up. He had new feelings that he had never felt before. And of course some old ones popped up again too. Somewhere in the dark of night her "I can't" had become less about her and more about him. He could have done more, been more. He could have made himself be someone that she couldn't have said no to.

He felt inadequate again. So what did he do? He had called Catherine, the first woman who had made him feel that way and who had motivated this whole crazy quest. It was so early she was probably sleeping. Catherine was many things, but an early riser she was not. He didn't even know what he would have said had she picked up the phone. Something like, "I'm sorry but I feel a little lost…" Great, that would win a bunch of brownie points with his ex-girlfriend for sure.

Maybe he just needed to hear her voice. Hell, she could even yell at him for all he cared. He just needed to hear her voice and remember why he was putting himself out there and training to be a Dom. It was because of her, and because as he was, he wasn't enough. Did her opinion still matter to him? The lines between what he thought he knew and what he was discovering were blurring.

If she wasn't asleep then she either didn't want to talk to him, or she wasn't home. If she wasn't home, she was with someone. But who? Did she have someone teaching her how to be a Submissive? He thought about trying to get in touch with Eve or Allison to see if they had heard from Catherine yet. Then he decided against it quickly. He wasn't her boyfriend anymore, so he didn't have a right to know where she was.

So instead he wondered where Mia was. Had she called James on her drive home to tell him about what happened? Maybe instead of going home she had gone to the club. They were open last night. Maybe she had found someone else to give her comfort and spend the night with.

He was driving himself crazy. He wasn't Mia's boyfriend either. He had no more right to information on her then he did with Catherine. He had to get his head straight.

So Vincent did the only thing he knew would help him. He laced up his shoes and went for a run. Being out pounding the pavement always helped him think. But today, he ran mile after mile and didn't find a single answer. All he knew was that no matter what had or hadn't happened the night before, he wanted to see Mia again.

Mia was nothing like Catherine. Well, of course they had a shared interest in BDSM. That was where the similarities stopped. Mia was kind, and open. She was willing to try things and not judge him. Maybe he should remember that. Yes, commanding her to stay was a mistake that crossed all kinds of invisible boundaries in the teacher-student relationship. Although to be fair, she had made the first move and asked him out. She had said that she liked him first.

He smiled. *I guess we're both breaking rules here.*

What would James do in this situation? He would probably take whatever he wanted and not give up until he got exactly what he needed. Time to be more like James, more like a Dom.

His leathers were still uncomfortably tight as he pulled them on. This time he felt more comfortable in this skin, and a little less like he was putting on a costume. The black T-shirt was pulled over his head and the heavy boots strapped on. They were all part of a uniform for the man Vincent wanted to be, needed to be, would soon be.

He tamped down his excitement and tried to remain expressionless as he pulled open the door to the club. This would be his first time going inside alone. He probably should be feeling more nervous. Instead it was his excitement and determination that motivated each step.

"ID," the bouncer demanded.

Vincent wondered vaguely if the meathead was a Dom too, as he dug out his driver's license, stored in his boot. The bouncer looked at the card carefully and typed some keys on his computer. Details of his trial membership were displayed on the screen. Satisfied that Vincent was allowed entry, the bouncer pushed a button under the desk. The button unlocked and opened the double doors that lead into the club. Taking his ID card back, Vincent gave the man a curt nod in thanks. Then he took a deep breath and entered the main room.

Although the club had only just opened for the night, the party was already in full swing. Bodies filled the floor and the music was thumping at full volume. Vincent stopped just inside the door to take a full look around the place.

He spotted some of the people he had been introduced to by James a few weeks before. Members, he assumed. He wondered how many seemingly regular people filled their weekends this way. They could be respected businessmen, even doctors or lawyers, but here they were the people in fetish wear that didn't care that most of their bodies were on display. Hell, some were even fully nude. He chuckled. Now that was something he couldn't imagine himself feeling comfortable doing. Mia, though, would probably not think twice about being naked and on display.

Regardless of what they were wearing, or not wearing, people were clearly having a good time. Some were dancing, while others sat lounging around a bar area. He didn't see many single people, unlike a usual bar. Here it seemed that almost everyone was matched up with a partner or two, three, or more. Some sat together as equals while others showed their Dom/Sub role openly in the club by having their Sub kneel at their feet. Some Subs were tied up. He even saw one Sub that had a long chain attached to their collar. The other end was held tightly by the person who must be their Master.

He hadn't noticed collars on the Subs the first time he was here, but he did see a lot of them tonight. Some looked like dog collars but others were quite fancy and he saw one flashing in the lights as if it was made of gold and diamonds. He made a mental note to ask Mia about their meaning. It seemed his list of questions was growing second by second.

A number of scenes were also going on around him. Instead of being contained in the alcove theatre, they were spread out in the room with some of the same equipment Mia had in her dungeon. The people performing scenes came in all shapes in sizes and orientations. He spotted one scene in particular that was drawing a lot of attention. A crowd was gathered around a Sub restrained on the sideways cross thing Mia had showed him—St. Andrew's? St. Anthony's? He had forgotten which one the kinky saint was. A tall, lanky brunette male was bound by both his hands and feet and was facing away from the room. His head was thrown back in pleasure as his female Master—wait, would that be a Mistress because the Dom was female? Another question for Mia—stood behind him, her body twisted and turning with each throw of her whip. He grunted each time the lash hit his flesh.

The scene was intense and raw and primal. He should have been taken aback and disgusted, as he had when he watched James whip Terry. Now, with more knowledge, he was able to watch objectively and see the true nature of scene. The Mistress closely monitored her Sub as she whipped him. She spoke to him lovingly during the entire time to gauge his level of arousal. The thick brown whip sailed through the air time and again, making a loud snap as it lashed against her Sub's naked body. Her throws stopped when she saw that her Sub was close to ejaculating. She stepped forward and wrapped her arms around him and held him as he came. When his orgasm had finished, his Mistress tenderly released the ropes and helped him down off of the cross. She tenderly rubbed her Sub's wrists and ankles to bring back blood flow after being bound for so long. Then she rewarded him with kisses. He was much bigger than she was, but still she wrapped her arms around him to give him comfort. Their affection was clear. The crowd dispersed as the Mistress led her Sub away to receive further aftercare in private.

Although the scene had been intense, none of it was gratuitous or violent. It wasn't just because the female was in charge in this situation. Vincent started to understand the difference between a true scene and what James had done on stage. Porno BDSM, his friend had called it, just action with little emotion. He felt a little embarrassed the way he had reacted to James's scene. He wished he could go back to that night and start again on a different foot. He should have stayed and watched the scene in full instead of running out of the club like a fool. Now Vincent was more determined than ever to do as Mia instructed and leave his judgments at the door.

The scene he had just watched also helped him to realize that he only wanted to be the Dom, never the Sub.

Walking further into the club, Vincent was surprised to see James's Sub from his first night, Terry, sitting on the lap of a big Latino guy. She looked none the worse for wear and didn't have any lingering marks from her scene with James. And she looked pretty happy to be with this other man. James had said that they weren't together. Was she this guy's Sub? Did James just have her "on loan" for the night to scene? Possibly, he supposed. There seemed to be all kinds of relationships and arrangements in this place. Safe, sane, consensual Mia had said was their motto, and so as long as the people involved were okay with it, Vincent decided he was okay with it too. This was a judgment-free zone.

"See, she's fine." He hadn't heard him approach, but now James stood beside Vincent, his eyes also on Terry. "You came back on your own. I'm impressed."

"I couldn't stay away," Vincent joked. James laughed and patted him on the shoulder. James looked none the worse for wear either. Vincent decided he liked this side of James. He was still confident and controlling, but he was also a hell of a lot more relaxed and just more real.

"Did Mia call you last night?"

"Yeah, yeah she did." The corners of Vincent's mouth curled up.

"Good for you, Vin. Although I probably should tell you that I heard all about it from Mia this morning."

"Everything?"

"Yup. Right up to the part where she had a panic attack and did the 50-yard dash to her car."

"I guess that means that running away isn't normal for her?"

James shook his head. "Nothing is normal for her. Mia doesn't date. Like many of us she doesn't have much of a life outside of the club. These people are her friends and family. Which is great until one of them hurts you. No matter what, Vin, she needs you. Be patient with her and promise me you'll keep her safe."

Vincent nodded. "Of course."

"You need to push, make her see that she can move forward as a Sub. Go to her. She needs to submit and forget herself for a while." He took a key card out of his pocket and handed it to him. "This card will get you into the dungeon. She's there and she's waiting for you."

"Thanks." Vincent took the card, but stayed for a few moments. Everyone around him in the club looked so happy and relaxed. It was pretty cool. Vincent couldn't help but smile. He wanted to be that happy too.

When he was ready, he gave James a nod and started the walk across the club to his class room. James nodded back and then disappeared off into the crowd. Was there a Sub somewhere waiting for his friend? Vincent hoped so. Everyone deserved to be happy. If even James could only find happiness for as long as it took to orgasm, it was at least something. Maybe one day he would find a meaningful connection and look as forward to seeing her as Vincent was excited to see Mia now.

Outside the door to her private dungeon, he took a moment to prepare himself. He stretched and cracked his neck, a nervous habit. He took a deep breath, then swiped the key card and opened the door.

This time James hadn't lied to him. Mia was there and she was indeed waiting for him. He could hear her breathing as he walked into the darkened room. When his eyes adjusted he saw that candles were lit, and placed on the supply cabinet. They gave off an earthy aroma, like sage. The flickering light just barely revealed Mia. She was kneeling fully nude in the middle of the room as she had the Saturday before. Knees apart, hands upright on thighs, eyes down.

She had been waiting for him. He had taken too much time watching the scene in the main room. He was a little late for their lesson. He hated to think how long she had been kneeling there for him. He hadn't expected that.

Vincent cleared his dry throat, and walked across the room to stand before her.

"Hi."

"Good evening, Sir." She looked up and smiled, glad to see him. There seemed to be no ill lingering effects from last night. Her long ebony hair was tied up away from her face in a ponytail. She looked like she didn't have any makeup on. It suited her. He could see a few freckles dotting the bridge of her nose. Very cute. "Are you ready for tonight's lesson?" she asked.

As soon as the question left her lips, his lingering feelings of guilt from last night vanished. This was Mia, a Sub, and he would learn to be her Dom. No, not her Dom, but a Dom, he corrected himself. Still, there was no reason to be nervous or have second thoughts. She knelt before him with trust. That trust made him feel strong and ready to be in control. "Are you ready to submit to me, Sub?"

She smiled, sure. "Absolutely, Sir."

"Sir? I like that."

"I bet. What do you want to do to me, Sir?"

His mind ran through the possibilities, like a kid in a candy store. It was all up to him to decide. He could do whatever he wanted and she would be there along for the ride, guiding him and teaching him. He felt the thought strangely erotic.

"Can you stand up, please, Mia?" As soon as he spoke the command, she quickly and efficiently did as he asked. She stood before him, arms at her sides, eyes down. This must be another slave pose or position, like the kneeling one. He frowned. He didn't like that she wasn't looking him in the eye.

"Mia, look at me." At her name, she looked up and her eyes met his as he had asked. "That's better. I like you looking at me."

"High protocol in the BDSM world means that a Sub doesn't speak until spoken to and doesn't look anyone in the eye. It's part of discipline, yes, but also part of keeping the Sub in the moment, ready to experience everything fully without distraction."

"I think we'll skip high protocol if that's okay with you."

"Some parts of it you may like more, like your Sub sitting on the floor at your feet or only eating from your hand," she offered.

"Maybe we can try that later, but for now I want your eyes on me." She nodded and smiled. That was much better. Her brown eyes were warm and friendly. They always showed so much emotion. He liked that. Her eyes would tell him if she liked what he was doing and if he was doing the right things. Observation was part of this, she had said, and communication too. Although she hadn't said it, he knew that desire was a huge part of the Dom/Sub relationship as well. And right now, he desired to kiss her.

He walked closer to her and saw the surprise in her eyes as he cupped her face. Without working into it, he pressed his lips to hers and kissed her hard and deep. He felt her slight reaction to something and he pulled away, quickly opening her eyes to observe her. After separating, she licked her lips.

"You're an amazing kisser."

"Thanks."

The desire in her voice encouraged him. He took a step back. Now what?

"What's tonight's lesson?"

She smiled. "We keep getting to know each other and push through our boundaries."

"Boundaries?"

"Yes, you know, like running out of a club without talking to your Sub first."

He had though they were passed that. "I'm sorry about that."

"I know. Then there's that other boundary between us, like when we have a really great date and I go back to your place. We fool around a bit but this time I'm the one who runs off without talking first."

She looked away, embarrassed. She had said it as a joke, but he knew there was a lot more meaning behind her words. She was being vulnerable. He liked that.

"Can you talk about it now?"

She bit her lip and said nothing. He reached out and moved her face so that he was looking into her eyes again.

After a minute she took a deep breath. There was pain in her voice. "I trusted someone. I gave my entire self to them and they hurt me. They used my nature against me to get what they wanted. It's hard for me to submit now. That's why I keep slipping into high protocol to block the emotions." She paused. "This training is as much for you as it is for me."

He caressed her face. *Poor Mia. No, that's wrong.* Not poor Mia. Lucky Mia to have survived whatever had happened. Strong Mia for returning here to try and regain all that she had lost. Beautiful Mia, who needed him to be just as strong for her.

"Today's lesson is about body language. Read what your Sub needs."

Vincent nodded, lesson accepted. He could do this. Mia was so expressive it wouldn't be hard to read her body at all. The old Vincent would have probably given her a hug. This new Vincent knew that there was other ways to bring her comfort.

Okay, Dom, what does your Sub need? A reward for her honesty. Intimacy. Safety. Freedom to submit. He would give it all to her.

First, he wanted to turn her on. He wanted her to get just as aroused as she had been last night.

Vincent thought of the Mistress and her Sub out in the main room he had just seen and the way she watched her Sub's breathing and listened to the sounds he made. She used these clues to tell her when he was aroused and when he was close to coming. Vincent would try to read Mia the same way.

Focus. What would she like? He remembered how aroused Mia had become previously when she had undressed and he had admired her body. That seemed to have affected her. Yes, that would be a good place to start today and it would please him as well.

Slowly he took a step to his left and began to circle her. "I want to look at your body, Sub."

"As you wish, Sir." Mia stood straight and still. Even though she was partially shrouded by the candlelight, this close he could still see her body clearly.

With another step and he was behind her. His hand reached out to trace the lines of her spine. He trailed a line down her warm flesh. She shivered at the contact and then arched her back into his caress. His hand halted when it reached the succulent globes of her ass. "Very nice, Sub. High and firm."

"Thank you, Sir."

On a whim he touched the back of her knee. "Are you sensitive here?"

"Sometimes, Sir." He allowed his hand to linger in the spot then continue to trail down her right leg. "Nice legs, Sub."

"Thank you, Sir."

"The stockings you wore last night were sexy, but I much prefer your legs bare."

"I'll remember that, Sir."

He reached around her to cup her mound. Her tiny gasp made him grin. "I like this bare too. Remember that, no panties allowed."

She gulped and nodded. "Yes, Sir."

He smiled. She reacted to that well. He removed his hand and gave her a quick kiss on the neck.

He took another step, and as he came around her right side, he took his time to really give her the once over. His eyes passed over all parts of her, from the gentle slope of her neck to the graceful lines of her collar bone. Her eyes followed his movements closely.

She sucked in a breath when his hands found the swell of her breasts. "You have beautiful smooth skin, Sub."

"Thank you, Sir."

He returned to stand in front of her. His tour of her body had started to bring about the response he wanted. Although her breathing had quickened, he knew that he was far from done with the scene.

Now what was next? He would love the opportunity to take another taste of her flesh. Or, he could order her to her knees and watch her lips stretch to take his cock inside of her tight mouth like she had last night. Mmmm, that would be outstanding. No, this time he wanted something different. He thought back to James's scene and how Mia had reacted to it. He remembered this lesson was about pushing boundaries. Time to turn up the intensity.

He strode across the room with purpose. The candles on the cabinet were a beacon. He pulled open the first drawer. It was crammed full of dildos, every size, shape, material, length, and colour imaginable. Nope. Neither he nor Mia would need these tonight.

Focus. He opened another drawer. Anal plugs, hooks, metal shiny balls, and other stuff that might be fun for later. No, what he wanted wasn't in this drawer either. He tried to remember the tour Mia had given him and where everything was. He frantically pulled open drawer after drawer until he found one that was promising. Inside were the clamps they had used last time plus a variety of others. There were clamps with vibrating bullets attached, and even wooden clothes pins like the ones James had used on the Sub, Terry. Some of this looked like stuff he'd like to use, and he retrieved a few pieces. But still he hadn't found what he was really looking for. *Shit, where could they be?*

He rifled through another drawer—the electro drawer, maybe?—before he finally found the drawer he was searching for. Excellent.

He slowly walked back over to her. When he was almost beside her, he saw the barely veiled terror in her eyes.

"I know what drawer that was."

"Do you know what I picked out?"

She nodded sadly. "I think so. I bought everything in that drawer myself when the club first opened."

He was confused by her reaction. "So what am I holding?"

Her lip trembled, but she tried to rein it in, keep her fear in check. "H–h–handcuffs?" She shuddered.

"Why do they scare you?" he asked. She didn't answer. She didn't want to tell him. Time for a different question. "Can I put them on you?"

"No." Her head shook wildly.

He held out his empty hand to her. "Give me your wrist, Sub."

"No, Vincent," she cried.

He almost gave up, but instead the rising dominant in him pushed him to go further. "Trust me, Mia."

He thought she would scream at him again. Instead the fire was ignited in her eyes. She stared him down. She looked furious. Whatever the reason for her anger, it had nothing to do with him. They both knew it. This is what she needed to start to heal from whatever had happened to her.

She realized that truth about the same time Vincent did. This was therapy, nothing more. The fire in her died. She took two deep breaths and closed her eyes. Then slowly, like a timid kitten, she raised a hand and offered him her wrist.

He took this sweet gift in his hand. He turned it face-up and delicately kissed her palm. "Very brave, Sub." Then he snapped one end of the cuffs around her slim wrist.

When the cuff clicked close, her eyes fluttered open in surprise. Her mouth opened as she stared down at what he had retrieved. The jewelry that dangled from her wrists was a pair of fuzzy pink novelty cuffs. They were the kind that offered restraint in token only. One hard tug and they could be opened.

"You didn't pick the locking ones?" Her little voice portrayed her shock.

He shook his head. "No. I wanted to push you a little but I still want you to feel safe with me."

"I do," she said. He was flattered, but she had replied too quickly for his tastes. "Maybe you don't need any more lessons," she joked. She now freely offered her other wrist, and he clicked the cuff closed. "Thank you, Sir." She visibly relaxed.

"I also picked out something else."

"Oh?" Now that her fear was gone, she was able to concentrate on the scene. Her arousal swiftly returned with the promise of this new surprise. She stood a little straighter, and her plump nipples began to bead.

Perfect. Vincent softly touched his wet tongue to each and then pulled back to blow gently across each pink bud. They beaded impossibly more. Slowly, Vincent opened his hand to reveal the three leaf clover-shaped clamps he had hidden inside his palm. They were larger than the ones he had put on her before, and felt much heavier. He opened first one clamp and then the other and squeezed each one on each of her rosy tips, mindful of her pretty piercings.

Mia moaned. Her reaction to these clamps was more pronounced then her reaction to the previous clamps. Vincent had forgotten to test them first so he didn't know if they squeezed her tits harder or differently. Shit, something to remember for next time. Mia didn't seem to mind his forgetfulness. Her chest thrust out with the new adornment. Her tits looked amazing with them on. With no chain to link them, they just pointed straight out. Trapped inside his tight pants, his cock strained to do the same.

That's it. He had no further tricks up his sleeve or hidden in his hands.

He knew what he wanted to do next, but it would cross another line for him.

He took a deep breath and almost laughed at himself. Why would he hesitate now, when he had jumped over so many lines on the way to getting here? If he was afraid to leave his comfort zone he never would have stepped foot in this club the very first night. It's not like he hadn't already done this before when Catherine had begged him to.

Now it seemed different. Now he was in control.

He thought back to his discussion with James in the cafeteria. His friend had told him that the Sub wouldn't be here unless they wanted to. They submitted because they needed it. Did that mean that Vincent was a Dom because he needed that control?

Just do it, he told himself.

"Over here, Mia." She shuddered as he tugged on the cuffs and led her over to the spanking bench. Her eyes sparkled with excitement. She walked slowly in her bondage, trying not to move the clamps too much. They must be very tight.

He positioned her at the back of the bench and pushed her down over it. She groaned as her front hit the padded wood of the bench. That sound went straight to his cock. Even if she hadn't moaned it would have been impossible not be affected.

He ran his hand over the smooth skin of her back and she shivered. He remembered his first night here in her dungeon and how she had demonstrated this particular piece of equipment. He remembered vividly how good her ass had looked in her tight skirt and framed by those grey garters. Seeing her there now, naked, was even better.

Every part of her was on display. Here he had access not only to her clit or slit but to her fleshy cheeks and the sweet tiny rosette in between them. His mind swam with a million suggestions of things he wanted to try. God, he wanted to try everything with her.

First things first. Crossing that line.

His first spank was timid. He paused to gauge her reaction. Or maybe to gauge his own. He thought he would feel sick to his stomach hitting her, recreating some of the violence he had seen from James in the alcove. In reality, now after striking her, he didn't feel even the least bit terrible. Maybe that should have worried him more than it did. Instead it felt strangely right, and far more intimate than he would have imagined.

"You can hit me harder, Vincent," she whispered. She had turned her head to watch him. When their eyes met, she nodded encouragingly. No to handcuffs, but yes to hitting? Was violence a type of submission she was just comfortable with, or was she fighting through her fear? Was she just trusting him the way he needed to learn how to trust himself?

Taking her invitation, he spanked her again, harder, right on the fleshiest part of her ass. The contact made Mia move slightly with the impact. It was the red handprint it left on her that made his cock move. "Again, Sir," she quietly begged.

He spanked her twice more quickly. She reacted beautifully, gasping with each hit. His dick throbbed. Oh, he learned that he liked the way her body responded to his spanking. From this position she couldn't hide her arousal from him. It was made even clearer when her silky cream began to coat her thighs. Her pussy looked so pretty, pink as it swelled with desire.

He stopped spanking her to touch her. First her clit…and then he pressed two fingers into her. Mia squirmed as he penetrated her. She felt warm and tight, her pussy sucking on his fingers as he fucked them in and out of her. Her body language was clear. She was so hot, there was no way to mistake her fierce need as anything else.

"Please Vincent, please." She arched her back. Her breath was ragged and he knew what she wanted. His dick pressed hard against his zipper, begging to thrust home inside of Mia. If he waited too much longer he would come in his pants.

At the moment, the thought of Catherine invaded his brain. Catherine had never begged him to fuck her, ever. And what was Catherine doing now? She wasn't waiting for his call, that was for damned sure. Maybe she was busy, laying on a table, tied, legs open and begging for it from some stranger, some other Dom? He took a breath and pushed all thoughts of her of his brain. They weren't even together anymore. Catherine wasn't here, and Mia was. Wasn't Mia worth crossing this line for?

Mia wiggled as much as the bench allowed her to and made a small noise. Her soft mews told him how close she was. He hadn't known how to make her come then, but he did now. Although he wasn't quite ready to say the command that would give her release.

Mia looked over her shoulder at him, inpatient. "Please fuck me, Vincent." Her demand broke down any remaining barriers inside of him. And a latex barrier was the third and final thing he had taken with him from the drawers. He tore open the wrapper with one hand and unzipped his leathers with the other. Mia's eyes never left his face as he rolled the rubber down his length. He held that eye contact as his cock nudged Mia's entrance. He could feel her heat, even before he entered her body. He pushed inside of her. She was so wet that he met little resistance as he continued to push inside of her warmth all the way in to touch her cervix. Even as wet as she was, her tight pussy gripped his dick like a fist. He groaned. She left like heaven around him.

He began to move. He grabbed Mia's hips and she rocked back against him. Cuffed and in this position, she couldn't move much. Vincent enjoyed that. Her cries were the only things she could add to the mix.

He started to thrust faster. He liked being able to set the pace for once. In the moment he understood that this was his scene and she submitted her body to him to use as he wanted. It was amazing. This was how sex should be.

Although she couldn't move, the effect he was having on Mia was clear. Her skin flushed as if she was on fire on the inside. Her breath was ragged. She was enjoying this just as much as he was. That realization was freeing. It was like a shot of testosterone right to his dick. He could fuck her as hard as he wanted or as slow. He could turn her over and fuck her ass, he could do anything or nothing. He had the power. And he liked it.

So did Mia. "Can I come, sir?" Her voice was barely more than a pant.

"No," he barked and continued to pound into her. He was getting closer to coming but he selfishly didn't want her to orgasm quite yet. This power he had was amazing. Catherine had never let him control her this much before. She said she wanted him to dominate her, but she had never really let him, even when he tried. Although, he supposed, he never knew how to be a Dom until Mia taught him, until now when she had shown him with her body. It was one thing to take a spanking or to follow commands, but this was something else. Full sexual surrender was exactly what he needed. He fucked her harder. Mia hissed in a breath and he knew how close she was.

Being in control was an aphrodisiac, it made him want to fuck forever, but the tingling in his sack let him know that his body had other priorities. Mia's breath was now coming in short little bursts like sobs and he realized she had priorities too. Although he didn't want to, he knew that she had to come.

He reached in front of her and tugged on one of the clamps. Mia made a sound that was half hiss, half moan and all sex. She must have been dying to come. A good Dom knew what his Sub needed and he was going to give it to her.

"Please, can I come, Sir?" She sounded so desperate.

"Yes." Immediately he saw and felt her pussy clamp hard around him. Her body shook. Her head down, she trembled, as if experiencing the most delicious orgasm he had ever witnessed. It came in waves. Her orgasm was intense. She felt amazing coming on his cock, milking his hard length. The feel and the look was his undoing. He felt his heavy balls draw up and knew he was at the point of no return. Vincent thrust once more and held his dick inside her hard as he came.

His own orgasm was no less spectacular than hers had looked. It felt like it went on for minutes and stole all the strength from his body. When the final spurt left his cock, he felt like collapsing.

Instead, still inside her, and standing there on shaky legs with his leathers pooled around his ankles, he reached forward and snapped her cuffs open. She was freed.

Instead of moving or starting to stand, she instead let herself collapse onto the equipment, looking very much like she had no strength left. She looked sated, happy, relaxed. He realized that all she wanted was for him to take control. That is how she felt satisfied, and he had succeeded.

As his orgasm faded away, he slowly came down to Earth. His calf muscles were killing him, and he reluctantly had to move. He pulled out of her, and pulled the condom off. He tied one end and tossed it into a waste basket conveniently placed in the play area. Then he slipped his flaccid cock back into his leathers and zipped himself up tightly. He was barely able to remove the heavy clamps from Mia's nipples. If he had been in a bed, he would have been asleep by now, he was so spent.

When he turned back, Mia had regained her strength and was rising off of the bench. On shaky legs she stood there looking at him a second, almost as if she was deciding something. Then she changed her mind and she knelt, returning to the familiar slave position.

"What's next, Sir?"

He could hardly think. The blood was sure taking its time to return to his brain. Ah yes, aftercare. This time he didn't have the strength to pick her up or lift her. Instead he simply dropped to his knees beside her. She was startled as he wrapped his arms around her. After a minute she relaxed into his embrace. They didn't say anything. He rubbed her back and peppered small kisses into her hair.

"Thank you, Mia," he said, pulling back and looking into her beautiful eyes.

"You're welcome." She smiled. "You seem to be learning quickly."

He nodded. Without thinking, he said the first thing that came to mind. "I liked it."

His innocent honest words caused her to burst out laughing. "I hope so!"

"I don't mean *that*. The sex was awesome. I more than liked it, but there was something else..."

"You liked being in control."

He nodded. "Yeah, I did."

"You have to start to realize that you really are a dominant, James, and I can tell you all day, but if you don't believe it or if you deny it then there's nothing we can do. It will take a while but soon it will feel natural to you. One day you will wake up and it will be part of you, like breathing."

"Is that how it's like for you?" Her only reply was a quick nod. "Thank you, Mia, for letting me control you." Again another nod. She seemed as spent as he was.

Slowly, and inwardly groaning, he peeled his arms off of her and stood. Then he reached out for her hand. Connection. When she trusted him with her palm, he held it tightly and she allowed him to help her to her feet.

Her knees were red from kneeling on the bench. She had slight marks on her wrists and when he looked closely he could see an unnatural red hue to her nipples caused by the clamps he had used on them. Shit. Tenderly he caressed each mark, as if his touch had the power to take it away. He even sweetly kissed her nipples. He liked them, he didn't want them to hurt.

When he looked up at Mia again, she was smiling so sweetly. God she was so beautiful, even when being this tired and used. In fact, she looked even prettier for it. Man, he really liked having her as a teacher and as a Sub.

He cleared his throat, feeling again a little nervous and maybe a little shy. "So um, next week?"

She smiled sleepily. "I thought that was a given. A couple of successful scenes don't make you a fully trained Dom, you know," she teased.

"I know, so Saturday night I'll be here again. On time and…"

"And?"

"Would you like to have dinner again Friday?" The invitation popped into his head seconds before he said it.

"I guess that means I'm forgiven for running last night?"

"I'd say we're about even now."

"Absolutely." Gone was the professional. Here Mia was much more sweet and innocent. "Yes. Yes, Vincent, I would love to have dinner with you again. Just please promise me something."

"I promise," he said quickly before she had time to qualify the request. She laughed shyly.

"Good. You just promised to let me pick the restaurant this time."

"What, you didn't like the food last time?" he joked. "Okay, fine, lady's choice." He smiled and kissed her lips intending to give her a quick goodnight peck.

Instead, Mia took the opportunity to rise up on her tiptoes and wrap her arms around his neck. This kiss was not that of a Sub, or of a temptress hungry for more. This kiss was all Mia, and it seemed to have meaning. Her tongue licked at his lips and then snaked inside his mouth to massage his tongue. Their deep kiss was powerful and it had his spent cock coming to life again. He growled and pulled her hips to his so that she could feel the full effect her kiss had on him. If they didn't stop kissing, he would fuck her again.

Mia knew and reluctantly pulled back.

"What was that?" he asked.

"Lady's choice that got away from her?" Mia joked, but the effect of the kiss was visible on her as well. She turned to gather up the discarded cuffs and clamps and her hands shook a little. That made him smile. God she was amazing. He couldn't wait to see her again.

He was starting to think maybe Mia could be more to him than just his teacher.

Chapter Five

"Hi. Have you been waiting long?" Vincent asked as he took a seat at their table. He was careful not to muss the white tablecloth or knock over any of the many glasses on the table. Man, rich people must like to drink more than regular people.

Like last week, Mia had called him shortly after he had gotten off of work. He had stopped home briefly to ensure that Gus had food and water, and to take the chance to change clothes. He didn't have time to shave and hoped that the stubble would look fashionable instead of lazy. As soon as she said the name of the restaurant, he knew that his favourite T-shirt and jeans wouldn't cut it. Nor would leather pants, sadly.

Some guys would feel out of place dining at the most exclusive restaurant in town, but it didn't bother Vincent. He'd been walking on cloud nine all week. Neither the valet parking nor the line outside of the restaurant had broken his good mood. He was genuinely happy, for the first time in a long time. Some of that was because he was getting his old self back through training and learning how to be the assertive man he wanted to be. Most of it was because of Mia.

He was excited to see her again. Luckily he hadn't needed to stand in line to get in. The hostess had spotted him and waved him inside. Yes, Mia had told them that she was expecting someone that matched his description, and that had helped. The hostess had also recognized him. It took him a second to figure out where he knew her from. He got a clue when her eyes shifted down to the floor. "Your table's this way, Sir." As Vincent followed her across the restaurant he was both shocked and flattered. The hostess was obviously either a club member or a special club guest. She obviously remembered him from his time in the main room with James. What made him smile that she hadn't called him a Baby Dom, she had respected him as a Sir.

When she stopped at Mia's table, the two women shared a special nod. Vincent pulled out his chair and took his menu from her hand. It was only then that he fully recognized the Sub before him. She wore a lot more makeup than she had last time he had seen her and her hair was twisted into a beautiful blonde chiffon. Of course she was also clothed. Still, now that he realized it, there was no mistaking Terry. She gave him a nod as well and then was on her way back to the foyer.

He was still grinning when he took his seat at the table opposite Mia. Her smile was equally large and the happiness in her eyes was like pure sunshine.

"Great timing, I just got here myself."

She smiled. And he took time to appreciate that before diving headfirst into the menu. She wore a long-sleeved navy dress tonight. The bodice was pleated and played up her assets. Her dark hair was pulled back and restrained into a thick braid. Her makeup was closer to what she had worn the first night he had met her, smoky eyes and dark red lipstick. She looked very pretty.

"So am I going to have to take out a loan to afford this place?" he joked.

"Probably." Her dry wit matched his perfectly.

The waiter arrived and poured them each a glass of sparkling water.

"I've heard a lot about this place. Have you eaten here before?"

"I guess a few times since it opened. A former client of mine owns it and he always makes sure I get a table whenever I call." After the waiter left, she picked up her glass and had a sip of the cool water.

A former client? What did that mean? Mia wasn't giving anything away or offering up any more information. Did that mean another Dom that she had trained owned this place? He didn't know how comfortable he felt with that. He quickly looked around the room. No one was watching them and he didn't recognize anyone else from the club besides Terry. Maybe the guy Terry had been with last week was the owner. Maybe Mia had trained him for Terry.

A different waiter approached their table. Mia ordered a kale salad and raw zucchini pasta. He ordered a steak, felt guilty for a minute, then got over it. He could relax, no judgment, remember? If she wanted to eat rabbit food, that was fine with him. Although he did order a side salad to go with his meal.

When the waiter left, Mia leaned over the table and took his hand. She did it quickly, as if she had been waiting to do it since he sat down. It was very comforting. Then he wondered if holding hands was part of the training, if she had this connection with all her clients, including the client who apparently owned this restaurant.

"Looks like the gears in your head are smashing together. What are you thinking so hard about?" Her smile was kind. She was asking for honesty so he gave it.

"You said your former client owned this restaurant..."

"And you were wondering if I was a prostitute?" One finely shaped dark eyebrow raised, amused.

"No I didn't think it was that kind of client. Well, I guess sorta. I mean, not to say that I think you're a prostitute. I just thought it was someone you had trained at the club." His face flushed as he stammered through his words. Luckily her smirk was back, showing that she hadn't been offended and was probably just throwing around more of that dry wit.

"I'm a psychiatrist. He's a patient of mine. And that's all I can tell you."

Vincent was floored. She was a psychiatrist? "Of all the stuff I thought you were going to say, that one was not even on the list." He felt a little guilty for his poor thoughts.

"I don't speak about my work too much at places like the club because a lot of people look at me ten shades of fucked up when I tell them that. And then people get all nervous that I'm about to psychoanalyse them, or else they go the total opposite way and tell me that I'm the one who needs a shrink because of the kink I'm into."

"So you're actually Doctor Mia?"

She nodded. "That's right."

"Fuck, well you're paying for dinner then."

She threw back her head and had a good honest laugh. He chuckled right along with her and squeezed her hand. So she was pretty, smart, kind, and probably made more money per year than he could ever imagine. Great. He wasn't intimidated by her before but now maybe he should be.

Their food arrived then, startling him. It was impossibly fast and almost like they had known their order ahead of time or something. Mia didn't seem surprised so he let it go. Would the shrink have guessed ahead of time that he would have picked the biggest most obnoxious piece of meat on the menu? He sighed. Probably.

Mia squeezed his hand again, as if reading his mind. "Let it go, it's just a job. I just started working in a government-run free clinic and sometimes I still have a trouble paying my bills, just like everybody else."

Vincent nodded and unfolded his napkin. He felt bad for breaking the rule of no judgment. Mia had given him one piece of private confidential information about herself and he had immediately started making assumptions and seeing her differently.

Instead of reaching for his fork, Vincent held on tightly to her hand, forcing her to look up at him.

"I'm sorry."

"Don't worry about it. One day I'll get you to think twice about what's on your plate."

He shook his head. "No, I mean I'm sorry for making assumptions about you."

"It's okay."

He released her hand. Slowly, no hard feelings and no harm done, she eagerly speared her food with her fork and held it out toward him.

"Wanna bite?" she kidded.

"Ah, no thanks."

"You don't know what you're missing." Mia stuck out her tongue at him and took back her fork. Her first bite almost made her eyes roll back into her head. "Divine."

He laughed. "I never met anyone who enjoyed food as much as you do."

She winked. He remembered, it was one of the few things she controlled herself. "How was your week?"

"Boring, slow. Glad I had tonight to look forward to. You?" His knife cut through his steak like it was butter. His own eyes would have rolled back into his head if he was that type of guy. Thankfully he wasn't.

"The same." She sighed. "I spent a lot of time with my dad."

"Oh, that's good."

She shrugged. "My dad's throwing his big summer party tomorrow night, so I helped him with some of the details. Most of the stuff he hires someone for, but he still likes to try to make my brother and me a part of it. It's a charity event he throws at his house. He's expecting almost five hundred people this year."

Wow, Vincent didn't even know fifty people he'd invite to a party, let alone five hundred. "That's nice."

She shrugged. "It's a lot of work and my dad's pretty demanding. He wants everything to be perfect."

Vincent nodded to himself and stabbed into his salad. One mouthful told him that this restaurant was good at everything they prepared, even simple mixed lettuce leaves. He chewed slowly and thought about what she had said. "Are you going to the party?"

"He wants me to. I usually just make a quick appearance and get out of there."

"I don't mind if you'd prefer to go there tomorrow." He tried to keep the sadness out of his voice. Tomorrow was Saturday, which meant that if she went to the party they'd have to cancel their training session.

She shook her head. "No, Vincent, I'd prefer to see you. A quick appearance at his party is good enough." Relief washed over him. His heart did a little happy dance. "Besides, we have to start working on things to incorporate into your final exam."

"I wanted to ask you about that, you seemed surprised when James suggested it."

Mia twirled some zucchini noodles on her fork. "Yeah, I'm not sure why he's making us do an exam. Maybe it's a new thing with the trainers since I've been back. And he's never put a time limit on sessions before. Eight weeks is a lot of pressure. Thank God you're taking to the training well."

"How many weeks does the training usually last?"

"It depends." She bit her lip. "Usually I just train someone until they find themselves a Sub and are comfortable with them."

"Usually?"

"Yeah, usually." She looked away.

A waiter returned to refill their glasses. When the distraction was gone, he saw that Mia had put down her fork. Her eyes were far off, and he could tell that she was having an internal struggle.

"What is it?"

"Nothing."

"Please tell me."

She sighed. "Honesty and trust," she whispered to himself like a reminder. Then she took a sip of water. "The last Baby Dom that I trained was the reason why I took a break from the club. We were together for almost a year."

"You mean you trained him for that long?"

"No, we stopped our training together pretty early on and moved into a committed relationship."

Vincent didn't know what to say. He had to admit that he was a little jealous. But he had to put that aside for now. There was no mistaking the sadness in her voice. This hadn't been easy for her to admit. Was this the secret that she was holding?

"Was he—"

She cut him off with a wave of her hand. He could see tears shining in her eyes. "I'm sorry, Vincent. I can't talk anymore about it right now." She cleared her throat. "I'm sorry for ruining dinner."

Vincent looked down at his half-empty plate and back at her. "You're the one paying for it, so you can ruin it if you want to," he joked.

Mia's lips cracked a faint smile. "I guess you're right." She pushed away her plate. "Have you ever found someone that made you feel so special you would do anything for them?"

"No, not really."

"What about Catherine?"

"I don't even know if I find her special anymore."

"Don't say that." Mia's eyes swam with something he couldn't quite read. "How long were you together?"

"Three years before she left me."

Mia raised an eyebrow. "She stayed with you for three years even though you didn't satisfy her sexually?" Mia now sounded very judgmental. It was out of character for her, but cute. For some reason he needed Mia not to like Catherine and not to sympathize with her. He couldn't bear it if she agreed with Catherine's opinion of his sexual performance.

He shrugged, pretending to be casual. "She always came. I thought she enjoyed our sex."

"But it wasn't enough obviously. I wouldn't have stayed a week with a man who didn't satisfy me, let alone wasted years of my life."

"I don't think I wasted her life."

She smiled. "Well you are definitely not wasting mine, because you are satisfying me."

A mixture of machismo and pride surged within Vincent. This was the validation he had been searching for. He turned his head away so she wouldn't be off put by the enormity of his grin. He felt like celebrating. But he had to get them off of this topic. "I don't want to talk about her anymore."

"Okay." She sighed. "I don't think I'm very good at this date stuff. I killed the conversation again."

Vincent shrugged.

A thought flashed into her eyes which lit up her face. "I think I may know how to save the night."

She pushed herself away from the table and stood up. Vincent's good manners dictated that he stand as well. With a naughty smile she said, "I'll be right back." Mia walked away from the table toward the washrooms.

While she was gone, Vincent finished most of his steak and side dishes while thinking about what she said. Who was this other Dom? Clearly she had loved him. Did he still go to the club? Was it someone that James had introduced him to, someone that he never would have imagined would have crushed the spirit of his pretty little teacher? Questions, questions, millions of questions rolled through his mind.

Mia had sounded so sad. Was she still hurting? Vincent knew exactly the kind of bond you could form with a partner. He knew how attached you could get to someone and just expect them to always be there. Until one day they weren't. Was that why James had limited the training to only eight weeks? To save them from building that kind of bond together?

Mia returned to the table and pulled her chair closer to his. Instead of sitting across from him she moved to be almost at the side of the table. Vincent helped move her plate over, even though she didn't appear interested in her meal anymore. Instead of eating, she just smiled and met his eyes. She looked rather pleased with herself for some reason. The way she sat now, her chair was angled slightly toward him so he could see her head to toe. He looked her up and down, admiring the new view. Her pleased look grew and he could swear she looked a little mischievous too. What had gotten into her?

Mia took a long sip of her drink and moved her legs apart slightly. She seemed to be daring him to look. When he did he saw that her skirt had hiked up slightly and he could see her garters. And then he caught a glimpse of her bare pussy on display. Holy fuck. Anyone could see her. It was daring and so freaking hot!

Before he could say something, she quickly crossed her legs. Now, in this fancy restaurant, she wasn't wearing panties. Sure he had seen her fully naked, but there was something risqué about her little show that was just for him. She reached across the table for his hand. When he moved to take her palm, he found that she had a different idea instead of their usual line of connection. When his hand opened she dropped a navy blue G-string into his palm. He really hoped that his surprised gasp wasn't audible to the entire restaurant. Her surrendering her panties to him was even more shocking. He quickly closed his palm to hide the lingerie.

"I remembered what you said, that you prefer me to be bare there. Yet tonight I still wore panties. I'm sorry, Sir."

Quickly Vincent put the panties into his pants pocket. "Thank you, Mia."

She took a deep breath. "No, thank you. James says I need to talk about what I went through, but I can't yet. My submission is my reward to you for respecting that I can't tell you everything yet."

The meal was over for Vincent. Beyond the fact that he didn't have much of a meal left to eat, the only thing he could think about were her panties in his pocket, mere inches away from his cock. A cock which was now very, very hard. Shit, it was just an article of clothing! Why was her gift turning him on so much?

She quickly realized his focus. Or lack thereof. "Is there something wrong with your food?"

"Ah, no."

"Not hungry anymore?" She smiled, clearly amused.

"Something like that." From her vantage point she could clearly see the effect she had on his cock.

Mia nodded and signaled for the waiter. He brought over a card that she signed and handed back. "I think we should get out of here then."

They waited together at the valet stand. Mia had taken a taxi to the restaurant, so only Vincent's vehicle was in hock. The line wasn't overly long but any wait was too long. It felt uncomfortable to be so aroused in public. He took off his jacket and discreetly held it in front of his pants to hide his raging hard-on. His other hand was in Mia's as they stood side by side. Mia noticed what he was trying to do with his jacket, and laughed at his predicament. Her spirit was once again light and playful. Her eyes were lit up like the Fourth of July. She, too, was antsy for the valet to bring his car up. Good thing his house wasn't too far of a drive from where they were.

When the high-school kid working as a valet finally brought his car around, Mia held out her hand for the keys. "You seem distracted, Vincent. I think I should drive."

"Absolutely not." He shook his head. No one drove his baby. It had been hard enough letting the valet take his car. After his home renovations had been completed, refurbishing the 1970 Charger had become his hobby and obsession.

Mia mock-pouted. "But I wanna drive."

"Sorry, I don't let anyone drive my car."

"Please?" she asked softly. It was adorable. Shit. He couldn't say no.

"Fine." Hoping he didn't end up regretting the decision, he handed over his keys. Mia beamed.

Climbing into his own passenger seat was weird. He had worked hard on putting this car back together. It had come a long way from how it was when he had rescued it from the junkyard. No one else had ever driven it, but if he was going to continue the plan to give Mia some control during their personal time, he had to let go. He just hoped he wasn't gambling away his car in the process.

He was amused as Mia realigned the driver's seat and mirror for her height. "Careful, it's a fast car." He was not amused when she gunned the engine and took off from the parking lot, squealing the tires. She pulled out onto the road and weaved around the evening traffic a bit too fast. He didn't like the out-of-control feeling he was getting.

He held onto the dash as she took a left a little too close to the oncoming traffic. As he tried to choke down his anxiety he noticed that they were heading to the other side of town. "Where are we going?"

She smiled and took another quick left. "Vincent, do you trust me?"

"Yeah, sure."

"No, think about it. Do you really trust me?"

"I think so. I mean, I think I can." He didn't say that he didn't know if he still trusted her with his car.

"Trust is important. I trust you because I know you wouldn't do anything to hurt me."

"How do you know that?"

She shrugged. "Call it half intuition, half training. Trust me. I want to take you someplace special."

He agreed that he would never knowingly do anything to hurt her. That wasn't in his nature. Was that what Doms did? He didn't think so. Maybe that's what James had been trying to tell him. Doms give their Subs as much as they can take and nothing more. Safe, sane, and consensual for both of them, right?

She abruptly pulled off the road into an above-ground parking garage. It was connected to an office building. He vaguely knew the area. At this time of night, especially on a Friday, it was usually deserted. He couldn't imagine how this could be her someplace special.

She drove around and around the floors to get to the next floor up. The roar of the engine echoed against the concrete walls. There was no other traffic in the garage, so it didn't take long to drive out to the open-air top. She swung the vehicle into a spot and shut off the car. He was puzzled as she removed her seatbelt. "Come on, the view is beautiful from up here."

By the time he had unhooked his own seat belt, she was already out of the car. He had to move quickly just to catch up with her.

She was already half up on the hood and he helped her climb the rest of the way up and take a seat. He hoped it wasn't too warm for her. She looked so tiny up on the dark hood, her knees hanging off the top. She motioned for him to join her. He had pounded out this hood himself so he knew it could withstand her weight, but not his. So instead he took a seat on the front bumper. She scooted over so that he sat between her knees.

She was right. This was someplace special. The view was beautiful. Although it was far from being the tallest above-ground parking garage in the city, it was high enough to get an almost unobstructed view of the surrounding neighbourhood. The sun was setting and its orange and red rays lit up the sky, shining off of the glass of the buildings around them. It was awe-inspiring, and a sight he had never taken the time to admire. He was glad she had brought him here to see this.

Her hands brushed his neck and then started kneading. If the view hadn't been so spectacular, he would have been tempted to close his eyes and just enjoy the massage. The tension left his neck and shoulders and he relaxed. He never would have thought that he would feel so comfortable with someone so quickly.

"Once upon a time, my mom worked in this area. Around the time this garage was first built. She watched it being constructed and discovered this view the first time she explored it. She'd often come up here to take her lunch break. Later on after she married my dad and had my brother and me, she'd bring us here. She loved looking out over everything. She called it the 'heart of the city.' It's odd, my mom was not a sentimental person, except when she was here." She took a deep breath. "This was the first place I made James take me after I was uncollared."

"Uncollared?"

"Freed." The word took all her strength to say. "When I left my last Master."

He turned and kissed her knee in thanks for trusting him with more of her story. His brave girl. She was teaching him and showing him so much more than he had expected when James had first outlined the training. He was grateful to both of them. He was a little humbled to know that they both thought him capable of fitting into their world and taking on the role on of Master.

The fact that Mia was opening up to him was amazing.

Mia wrapped her hands around his neck and bent forward toward him as much as she could. He turned his head and she gave him a kiss on the lips. Soon the beautiful view he had thanked her for was forgotten as he turned to deepen the connection of their lips. He turned his head and gently put his tongue in her mouth. She sucked on it and then began to massage it with her own. She tasted sweet and light and free. As their kisses built, they became more forceful and more demanding.

She lay back on the hood, as Vincent stood and turned around. The sight before him now was far more beautiful than any skyline. He stood between her knees and she wrapped her legs around him, begging him with a little thrust of her hips. He grinded his hard length right back at her. Then he ran his hands up her legs, lifting her skirt to take a peek at her pussy.

"Do you like what you see, Vincent?"

"Absolutely. You have the prettiest pussy I've ever seen."

Mia's brown eyes softened a little at his words. Her hands left the hood of the car where she had been using them to brace her weight and to keep her from slipping down off the hood. With him standing there, she had no fear of falling. The movement gave Vincent an idea.

"Hold out your hands."

Mia's smile broadened. She slowly put her hands together and held them out in front of her. It was her turn to trust him now.

He dug the navy lace material of her panties out of his pocket. He held them up for a second before he wound the material around her wrists. He used the band to tie her hands tightly together. Now she was the beautiful sight—tied with her pussy on display, offering herself to him. She looked delicious and sweet and sinful all at once. He wanted nothing more than to bury himself inside of her. The only problem was that they were in public. The setting sun provided almost a spotlight on them. Although the garage was almost empty, it was far from deserted. Someone working late could look out of their building and see them there.

"Please, Vincent," she begged.

"We're in public."

"I know." The husky sound of her voice told him exactly how turned on she was at the thought of him taking her here and how real the risk was of being caught. The sexy rasp of her voice had strained his hard cock even further. If he didn't fuck her soon, he was going to come in his pants like a high-school boy.

Vincent took another look around them. Yup, they were still just as exposed as they were a minute ago, and no wishing on his part had changed that. Maybe they could go in the car, or drive down a level, or…

"Stop thinking and fuck me. Take a chance."

The dare in her words was all he needed for motivation. With a silent prayer that a security guard wouldn't happen by on patrol, Vincent opened his wallet and removed a condom he had stashed there. He quickly unzipped his pants and sheathed himself in latex. As soon as he was covered he raised her thighs and thrust home inside of her.

She was incredibly wet. Neither of them would last long. He slid his hands down her body and cupped her breasts through her dress. He squeezed them hard and she moaned as he rammed into her equally as hard. The feel of her silk as he thrust in and out of her was incredible. He could feel how it coated him and in this position he could clearly see how her cream coated his shaft.

When he could feel himself getting close, he released her tits and instead moved his hand to her clit. He rubbed rough circles that had her spewing dirty talk until he felt a tightening inside of her. "Mia, come!" he commanded. In seconds she was coming undone hard on his cock. Her gasp of pleasure caused him to instantly follow with his own groan of release. He collapsed on her as her muscles milked the orgasm from him.

When he had the strength, he rose up on his elbows and kissed her softly.

Mia still lay on the hood, her dress flipped up and her body exposed. He probably admired the beautiful sight a second too long before finally going to her aid, righting her dress and untying her hands. How amazing was it that she had brought him here and given him this experience? It was in his top five hottest. Fuck that, it pretty much was his hottest experience ever.

As she stood and straightened her dress, he took off the condom and tucked his dick back into his pants. He tied up the condom and put it in his pocket. He watched her adjust her dress and tuck her panties back into her purse. Vincent couldn't hide his huge grin. "Looks like we didn't get caught."

"Not yet." Mia grinned right back at him.

Reluctantly they both got back in the car. This time Vincent took the driver's seat without argument. He sat for a few minutes, trying to calm his breathing and get focused before turning on the car. He didn't want to leave this place just yet. Mia noticed all of this with a sexy smirk.

"So how was that?"

"Pretty amazing." He felt almost dumb saying that. Sex with Mia was awesome, fantastic, unbelievable and about a thousand other adjectives he couldn't remember right at the moment. He had to admit, he had hesitated, but when he was deep inside her it was pretty damned hot knowing that anyone could see them. A month ago he never would have considered doing anything like that. Being with Mia certainly brought out something daring in him.

"Could you take me home now?"

"Sure," he nodded, but inside he wanted to disagree, demand that she come back to his place. He wanted to spend more time with her, and see her more than the current few hours twice a week. He wanted to ask her questions and show her movies and…just be with her. It might just be the postcoital haze but he just wanted Mia in his life.

She patted his hand. "Sorry for the early evening. I had a long week."

"No problem." He guessed he couldn't fault her that. Even though his entire being was screaming at him not to, he started the car and drove down the garage and out onto the street. Mia gave him directions to her place and he took his time getting there. It gave her time to play with the radio, turning it to an urban radio station she loved.

Her neighbourhood was not a far drive from the parking garage. The closer he got, the more traffic thinned. For every pickup truck they had passed in the city, they now passed a Porsche.

He was noticeably intimidated when he pulled into her driveway. The house was on the small side for the neighbourhood but still was a luxurious place. It was cut into the side of a hill, and, like the parking garage, overlooked the city. Playing up that feature, the front side of the structure was entirely glass. The place had some age to it, and parts of the design looked pure art nouveau.

"The architecture is amazing."

"Fucking me was amazing and now my architecture is amazing?" She laughed as she slipped off her seat belt. When he started to turn off the car she stopped him. "I'm sorry but I'm not ready for sleepovers yet, okay?"

"Okay," he said, trying not to let his hurt feelings show. Again she was pushing him away.

"Don't be like that. I'll see you tomorrow." She crawled across the front seat and took his face in her hands. She gave him another sassy smile before she gave him a long kiss. This time she was gentle—her lips were probably just as bruised from their earlier kisses as his were. Then she pulled away and got out of his car.

He watched her start to walk up her front porch then change her mind. As she returned to the car, he rolled down his window. "One more kiss," she said and leaned in his window to capture his lips once again. Pulling reluctantly away she dropped something in his lap and then turned and jogged back up her pathway.

Vincent looked down to see what she had dropped in his lap. It was her panties.

When he looked back up, she had already disappeared into her home.

He put her panties into his pocket and then backed out of her driveway.

He grinned the entire drive home. Tomorrow. He would see her again tomorrow. He couldn't wait.

Chapter Six

"Did I wake you?"

It was before dawn, so of course she was waking him. He didn't mind, though. If he was still asleep he probably would be dreaming of her. Especially since last night after their date, he'd settled himself with a beer and a late-night double feature before jerking himself off. It seemed she was all he could think of these days.

His reply was a fake sleepy grunt. This made Mia laugh and he had to join in with her. She sounded alert and well rested. As if she had been up and about for hours instead of cherishing every minute in bed the way he and Gus were.

"Well since you're awake, I have a favour to ask." Her voice was hesitant. Vincent sat up in bed. Gus raised his head and gave him a puzzled look. Now they were both awake and intrigued. "You still there?"

He cleared his throat. "Yep, go ahead. What favour do you need?"

"You know how we were supposed to meet at the club tonight? Well remember my dad's throwing that party for charity? It looks like he really wants me to be there for the whole thing."

Vincent's heart sank. He had been looking forward to seeing her. "Oh."

"Don't sound so sad. This is where the favour comes in."

"Okay..."

"I want you to come to the party with me."

Inside he was cheering, but he decided to play it cool. "Done. Can I go back to bed now?"

"Is sleep all you think of?"

"No, ma'am, I also think about eating and sex," he joked in a fake southern drawl.

"You'll definitely get to do one of those things tonight."

"Damn, it's not *that* kind of party?"

"No it's not." She laughed.

This party sounded like a big deal. It was nice of her to invite him. Wait, was this the favour she needed? "Would I be going as your date?"

"Of course." She hesitated. "But you have to promise me to not mention anything about the club or BDSM."

"So no delighting your father and his friends with tales of his daughter's debauchery?" Vincent was joking but when she didn't answer he knew he had touched on a raw nerve. A joke was a joke, but Vincent did understand families. He himself wouldn't appreciate someone placing a long-distance call to his family in BC to spill the secrets of his training. Although his sister would probably understand more than his mom did. He shuddered to think of the questions dear old Mom would ask.

He turned back into their conversation when he realized that Mia was giving directions and reciting the address for the party. "I'll meet you there at six."

"What should I wear, my leathers?"

"Vincent!"

"Just joking."

"A suit and tie will be fine. Do you have a red one?"

"A red suit? Like Santa?" he joked.

"No, Vincent, a red tie." Mia didn't laugh.

He took a mental inventory of his wardrobe. Nice black suit, check. Any red ties? Nope. "I can get one."

"Don't bother, I'll bring one for you."

"Do you think I can use it later to tie your hands?" Vincent growled. His cock started to lengthen and harden at the thought.

"Maybe..." There was a slight hitch in her breath which showed that clearly he wasn't the only one imagining the things they could do together with a red tie.

"Are you wearing panties?"

She laughed. "Yes, Vincent. I don't always go around bare."

"That's too bad." Vincent reached a hand under his blanket and fisted his cock. He gave it a slow stroke. "Are you touching yourself?"

"No!" She laughed, surprised. "I can't."

"Sure you can. Touch yourself."

She hesitated. "I'm at work. I had to come into the office this morning to finish up some dictation from last week."

"Are you alone?"

"Yes but..."

"But what?"

"Anyone could come in and see me."

He laughed at her sudden modesty. "That didn't stop us last night. I want you to touch yourself, Mia."

"Okay." There was only a brief hesitation. She knew this wasn't a friendly request, but instead a Dom commanding her.

"I want you to pull your underwear aside and pleasure yourself while I jerk off."

"Yes, Sir."

By the sound of her breathing, and how her breath changed, he could tell the exact moment she touched herself. He listened close enough to even hear the tiny sigh that escaped her lips when her fingers first touched her clit. The sound inspired him to rub his hand over the crown of his now fully erect cock. His pre-cum coated his palm and he rubbed it down over his shaft.

"Are you wet?"

"Yes." She moaned softly.

"Are you imagining me there with you?"

"Uh huh." In his head, Vincent was dressed in his leathers and he stood beside her desk. She wouldn't be kneeling and naked as she should be. Although she was probably wearing a naughty little skirt. Maybe even a pair of those sexy garters. If he was there, there was one thing he'd be absolutely dying to do. Taste her.

"I want you to rub your clit like I was licking it. Get your fingers wet and use some pressure."

"Okay…Oh, that feels so good," she whispered.

"Mmmm yes." Vincent pictured himself between her spread legs, her cream filling his mouth.

"Take your time and rub your clit in tiny circles." If he was there eating her, he would want to take his time and savour every second that his face was pressed to her pink parts. In response, he slowed down his hand. He didn't want to come too fast.

"Has anyone ever gone down on you in your office?"

"No, never." She panted. "It's…"

"It's what?"

"It's always been a fantasy of mine," she confessed.

"Have you ever been fucked in your office, Sub?"

"No…"

He smiled. His talk was having quite an effect on his Sub. "Then imagine me there, stretching you over your desk and flipping up your skirt. I'd spank that ass first."

"Yeah?" She panted.

"Then I would shove my cock in your pussy. So hard I'd move the furniture."

"Oh yeah."

"Put your fingers inside of your pussy. Do you wish it was my cock there?"

"Yes Sir." He could imagine how good she felt inside. He squeezed his cock with his fist, mimicking the feeling of sliding into her flesh. He groaned. Her fantasy was quickly becoming his. He would come soon.

"I'm close."

"Good, me too." His hand moved faster over his cock. This fantasy was certainly getting him hot. He pulled down the blanket and let his dick spring free. "Rub your clit again. Faster. I want you to come quickly."

"Yes." She gasped.

"Mia, come now and come hard." As soon as he gave the command, he heard her sob. She tried to stifle the sound of her orgasm, but Vincent had been with her enough times to know exactly what it sounded like when she found he release. The last gasp had barely left her lips before his own orgasm overwhelmed him. He cupped his hands over his tip to catch every last drop of ejaculate.

"Thank you," she whispered. She sounded happy but spent. That seemed to be a habit for them, and he liked it.

"You're welcome. And thank you." Vincent rolled over and grabbed a handful of tissues from the box on his nightstand. He seemed to go through them like crazy these days.

"So um…see you at six." He laughed at her shy awkwardness.

"Absolutely." He smiled. "And Mia?"

"Yes?"

"Don't touch yourself again until you see me, okay?"

She laughed. "Deal."

* * * *

He checked the address he had punched into the GPS. Yeah, this was the place… Vincent pulled to a stop just inside the gate. A horn honked behind him. The car was easily worth his yearly salary or more. He swallowed the lump in his throat and stepped on the gas. *Holy fuck…*

As he drove down the long driveway, he realized he may just as well be driving into another world. The house he spotted was a huge gaudy monstrosity of a mansion. He had the feeling that you could easily fit the population of his hometown inside its doors. Roman columns, a grand porch, art nouveau roof line. What a hodgepodge of styles! What he recalled of his former architecture training made him look away from the train wreck of a home. It was old and had obviously been built onto several times over the years.

There was enough light that he could see other buildings on the property. One looked like a barn. Toward the east he could just spot fruit trees. The lawn was an impressive shade of golf-course green, and the gardens were well tended and in full bloom.

He was staring more at the house than where he was going, and he almost missed the valet stand. An older gentleman in full uniform stepped out in front of his car as Vincent slammed on the brakes.

When his heart stopped wanting to beat its way out of his chest, he turned off the engine and opened his door. As if he wasn't nervous enough to be there. Now he had to think of an excuse for nearly committing vehicular homicide.

A throat was cleared to his left. The older gentleman held out his hand for his keys. Vincent handed them over.

"The sun was in my eyes," Vincent offered in way of apology for almost running the man over.

The gentleman in uniform simply nodded and said nothing else.

Oh! He almost forgot! Before he let the gentleman take his car away, Vincent reached back into his car for his suit jacket and the special package he had brought for his date this evening. "Be careful, she's a classic." He shrugged on his jacket as the man took his car away to park in some far away area of the property.

"Nice suit."

She startled him. He hadn't spotted her when he pulled up, but now she came out of the shadows. While waiting for him, Mia had relaxed out here at the valet stand with the staff. She stood and straightened out her dress, then stepped up onto the driveway to join him.

She looked incredible. Her hair was clipped back, one side decorated with small finger waves. Her hot-red Asian-inspired dress left little breathing room as it showed off every curve she had.

"Nice dress."

"Thanks, I got it last time I was in China." As she walked close to him, he could see that although the dress covered most of her body, it did have a very revealing slit up one side. He would love to plunge his hands through that opening and feel her smooth skin. He restrained himself for now but promised that later his hands would separate that fabric and explore what was underneath the silk. "I brought you this."

In her hands was a red tie as promised. It matched the material of her dress perfectly. She wrapped it around her wrists, teasing him, and then gently trailed the ends over her hands. He was mesmerized by the flow of the fabric and the possibilities it presented.

Her hips swayed as she came closer. He bowed his head and she wrapped the silk tie around his neck. She smiled as her agile fingers quickly twisted it into a Windsor knot. She was obviously practiced at the skill. He was seconds away from asking if her former Dom had made her dress him, when she shook her head, anticipating his thoughts.

"I learned because when we were young, James could never figure out how to tie one. His dad always berated him for not knowing even the simplest of skills. So he'd come to me and I'd help him." She frowned, remembering a time long ago.

"He was lucky to have you."

She shook her head. "I'm the lucky one." She took advantage of Vincent's still bowed head to give him a quick kiss on the lips. "You look nice."

Vincent would have blushed, had that been his thing. "Thanks."

When she moved to take his hand, he was reminded of the parcel he had carefully picked out for her. "Is that for me?"

He nodded shyly and handed over the box. She looked delighted to receive this unexpected gift. He hoped she would remain delighted when she opened it. She opened the carton and peeled away the florist paper. Inside was a modest red rose wrist corsage that he had bought for her earlier today while his suit was at the one-hour cleaners. It was an impulsive purchase.

Mia was surprised. She stared down at the open box. Shit. He felt like a teenager who mistook this party for a silly prom.

"Forget about it." He tried to take the box back, but she held onto it tightly. "You don't have to wear it."

"No, I want to." She tore her eyes away from the box and looked up at him. Her cheeks were still flushed in surprise but her eyes sparkled brightly. "Help me with it?" Vincent took the delicate flowers from the box and used the attached ribbon to wrap it around her wrist.

"It's silly."

"No, it's perfect." She smiled broadly. "I love it, thank you."

The older gentleman returned from parking Vincent's car. He smiled at the two of them together. "Have a good time tonight, Miss Mia."

"Thanks, Stanley." She gave the man a kiss on the cheek, making him blush. He took the empty corsage box from her hands to dispose of.

Vincent held out his arm to her. She happily returned to his side, hooking her arm through his.

"Ready?"

He took a deep breath. "I think so."

"Don't worry."

It was hard to feel nervous with such a beautiful woman on his arm. As she walked with him up the rest of the driveway, Vincent did as she had requested and began to relax. "Did you grow up in this house?"

"Sure did. Maybe after the party I'll show you my old bedroom."

"Can we just go there instead?" Vincent wiggled his eyebrows suggestively.

Mia took his hand in hers and gave it a squeeze. "Believe me, if I could skip this party, I would."

Classic Motown tunes floated on the air. Instead of going inside the house, they followed the music down a lit pathway around to the back lawn.

The land in front of the house was nothing compared to the grand lawns around back. Vincent hesitated to estimate the acreage of the property. Land like this didn't come on the market very often. A developer would probably love to get their hands on this much real estate this close to the city.

A huge canopy strung with twinkle lights covered rows of tables. This was where dinner would be served later. Most of the guests were outside of that area, gathered together in small groups. Their attention seemed focused on several stations set up across the lawn.

Vincent looked around him. His eyes were greedy to take it all in. In reality this night wasn't much different than a night at the club. Suits and dresses were just a different kind of fetish wear—the clear fetish in this location was business and money. Which was more honest? The club members openly enjoying themselves and their bodies, or the people at this party acting openly conservative and doing who-knows-what in private? Mia looked fantastic all dressed up, but he knew this wasn't the true Mia. And the guy in the suit and borrowed red tie wasn't the real him either, and never would be.

A waiter approached with a tray of champagne and Mia waved him away. Her hands stayed wrapped tightly around Vincent's arm. "Wanna check out the stuff people are bidding on for the charity?"

"Sure."

Together they walked down a pathway and approached the first station. Here an easel held a small painting. The canvas was awash with vivid colours, brush stokes coming together to make up the flowers of a beautiful garden. It wasn't something he would hang in his house, but he could appreciate the artistry. "I like the lines on this one."

She nodded. "Me too. You sound like you know art."

"Just a little. My sister's the artist in the family." He stepped closer to the painting. This item had a small plaque on a table beside it that gave the name of the generous donator. This item had been donated kindly by the mayor of their city.

A few steps away, the next station was set up. Here a beautiful tapestry hung off another easel. The skillfully weaved brown and red strands came together to depict an ancient hunting scene between a warrior and a great animal. He was surprised to see who had donated it.

"This is my company."

Mia nodded. "Yes, the owners are always very generous to us."

"Wow, that's nice. I've never met them." And it was true. As far as he knew, his workplace was owned by a conglomerate that owned several different companies. Before now he hadn't questioned that there was no face behind the company name.

He tried not to let the new mystery bother him as they arrived at the next station.

Here was a large statue. It was created by an artist he had never heard of, and was crafted out of many different materials. The statue had the appearance of a featureless figure that looked to be reaching for the sky with oversized outstretched arms.

Mia raised an eyebrow. "Do you like it?" Vincent shrugged and Mia laughed. "Me neither."

On the table beside it, the plaque read, "Donated by Dr. Mia Stoyanovsky." Vincent looked up at her and she smiled. "Yeah, that's me. My father donated it and just put my name on it. I think he just likes the look of 'doctor' and his last name together. That's my dad in a nutshell."

Shortly before seven, an announcement was made for people to take their seats under the canopy. Although most partygoers hustled back up the pathway, Mia and Vincent took their time leisurely walking back up the lawn to the tent. By the time they found their assigned table, everyone else was seated.

The places reserved for Dr. Mia and guest were at a table toward the front of the room, near where a podium had been set up. Mia introduced him to the other people at the table. Each of their table mates were white males between the ages of fifty-five and sixty-five. Apparently all were business colleagues of her father's. The men resumed talking economics and stocks amongst themselves after making the minimum amount of small talk.

The sole exception was the man seated to Mia's left. He wore wire-rim glasses and a scowl. His place card read, "Lee Stoyanovsky."

"Vincent, this is my brother."

The two men eyed each other warily. Vincent stuck out his hand first and Lee reluctantly shook it. Shaking was a kind word. In truth, Lee clamped onto his hand with all his strength and gritted his teeth.

"Great to meet you, Vincent. Are you one of them?"

"If you mean an arrogant asshole like yourself, then no, he's not." Mia hissed.

Lee's frown deepened. The two men watched each other carefully as they sat. Vincent took a sip of his water. When he looked back, Lee narrowed his eyes. *Well this is uncomfortable.*

Mia unfolded her napkin and laid it on his lap. Her tone was purposefully light as she turned to her older brother. "How's your work?"

"Fine."

"Is Sage with a sitter?"

"Yeah, the usual girl is watching her upstairs, so you can peek in on her later." Lee took a sip of his Scotch and shot a cold look toward Vincent. "So how long have you been training?"

Mia sighed. "This isn't the place, Lee."

"I think I should be allowed to ask whatever I want from the person tying up my sister."

"I know you're protective of me, but you have to let me live my life."

"You said something similar before you moved in with that creep."

"Enough."

"Is this guy going to take you away from us too?"

"I said it's enough, Lee."

"It's not enough." His glass hit the table sloshing brown liquid onto the tablecloth and drawing the eyes of the other members of their table. Mia smiled in apology. When they turned back to their business conversation, Lee leaned in closer to his sister. "How is this guy any different from the last one?"

"He's James's friend."

Her words stopped Lee cold, as if a bucket of water had been thrown on him. Lee's features had lost all fight. He turned to Vincent and closely examined him. "Wow. I owe you an apology then."

"Don't worry about it." Vincent took another sip of his water. Never before had he known anyone whose reach seemed as far as James's. There seemed to be as many sides to his friend as there were connections. Work world, kink world, Mia's world.

Lee nodded. "Okay, if James vouches for you then you get a pass in my book too. But if you do anything to hurt my sister, I will not hesitate to ruin you. Understood?"

Vincent found himself smiling. Despite the thug act, he liked Lee. There was no harm in an overprotective family. "Understood."

As Mia and Lee made small talk, and gossiped about people there tonight that they knew, Vincent took a look around the tent. Not a seat was empty, and yet there was no sign of the eldest Stoyanovsky.

"Is your dad here?"

"Yeah. He's probably still in the house. My father likes to make an entrance."

As well-choreographed as a dance, about a dozen uniformed waiters entered the tent together carrying large trays laden with food. First each guest was treated to a pasta appetizer. Next came a roast vegetable dish and a chicken main course followed. Mia's vegan dishes were brought out separately but looked equally as delicious as the other meals.

She held out a forkful of food toward him. "Do you want to try this?"

"No, it's okay, I've had salad before," he joked. Whatever it was, it was definitely more sophisticated than simple mixed greens.

"One day you'll say yes." She gave him a mock pout and dug heartily into her meal. Whatever it was, she appeared to enjoy it.

As coffee and desert were served, the PA system clicked on. A man in a crisp suit stepped up to the podium and the room quickly silenced. "It's time to introduce our host for the evening. Please help me in welcoming the CEO of the Memory Foundation, Mr. Thomas Stoyanovsky."

With a hearty round of applause, the guests stood as their host walked up to the podium. Vincent was about to join them out of politeness when he felt Mia's hand holding him back. Neither she nor Lee made an effort to stand. Nor did either applaud.

Thomas Stoyanovsky was a man of medium height and medium build. He wore designer glasses and a designer suit. He had Mia's same dark hair, except his was grey at the temples. The fine lines at his eyes crinkled as he squinted into the light to look out over his guests. He gestured for them to be seated and he feigned embarrassment at the grand welcome from his guests.

"I want to thank everyone for coming. This has been a nice evening of good food and good friends and colleagues. I'm glad you were all able to join me and very glad that you were so generous. Individual auction results will be posted on the foundation's website in the morning. I'm pleased to announce that tonight we have been able to raise well over a million dollars." The man paused to allow a polite applause break. Vincent noticed that here Mia did allow her hands to clap softly. "On behalf of the many families who will benefit from the Memory project, I want to thank all of you for a successful evening." He raised his glass in a quick toast and then left the podium.

Lee quickly stood. "Excuse me, I need to check on my daughter."

"Tell Sage that her Auntie sends her lots of hugs."

"Will do." Lee smiled and gave Mia a kiss on the cheek. Then he extended his hand and Vincent was glad to receive a real honest handshake. "Sorry about before. It was nice to meet you."

"You too."

Thomas Stoyanovsky walked through the tables stopping to talk to his friends and colleagues, who were more than happy to shake his hand or pat him on the back. It was obvious that this man was well liked. Vincent tried not to be obvious as he watched the man who had made Mia. He was not what he had expected. Although Mia's clear animosity for the man probably had coloured his opinion. Her body was stiff. Her eyes watched her father closely.

"What's the Memory project?" Vincent asked her.

"It's the purpose of the foundation."

"Can you tell me a little more than that?"

Mia sighed, and tore her eyes away from her father. "It's a program that donates money to families to help young children deal with the death of a parent. It could be used for shelter, for therapy, for a trip or anything else that helps the child through their grief."

"What an amazing cause. It must be great for families to receive this money."

"Yeah, it's great. It's just one of my father's many endeavors." Mia drained her water glass. "Let's get out of here and go for a walk."

She stood and Vincent followed suit. Many of the people at their table simply nodded as they pushed their chairs in. Then he saw their eyes light up as if the Pope had joined their table. Mia had no such reaction. She audibly groaned as if caught trying to sneak out.

"Hi, Mia, thanks for coming." His voice was soft and kind. He looked older now that Vincent saw him close up.

The colleagues at the table all turned back to their conversations to give the family some privacy. They needn't have bothered. Father and daughter could have be strangers for all the warmth they showed each other.

Mia didn't even smile. Even though they hadn't been close either, if this had been Vincent's dad, he could have been guaranteed a big hug and some warm words. Looks like her family didn't operate that way. They held identical stiff postures as they regarded each other. "Congratulations on the fundraiser." Her tone was icy cold.

"Thanks." Their silence was awkward and lengthy.

"I'm Vincent Dupuis, Mia's friend." Vincent introduced himself. He stuck out his hand and the older man took it in both of his to shake.

"Nice to meet you, Vincent. What sort of name is Dupuis?"

"French, I think." Vincent fumbled over his words, but the man just nodded his head.

"You don't have to have a fake conversation and pretend to be interested," Mia commanded without raising her voice. Vincent didn't know if she meant him or her father.

"Did you bring James with you?"

"No, Dad, I brought Vincent."

"Oh." The man nodded absently and turned back to Vincent. "Do you know James?"

"Yes, he's a close friend."

Thomas's eyes lit up. "James helped us get Mia back. I owe him everything I have." Although Vincent believed what he said, he didn't seem like the type to be in debt to someone else, for gratitude or otherwise. "Last year when she brought that other man…"

"Enough!" Mia hissed. "Look, you know I'm only here because you *commanded* me to be here."

"I shouldn't have to order my own daughter to spend time with me." The man looked into Mia's eyes with some unspoken intent.

Mia shook her head in anger. "Well as usual, thank you for a great evening." Taking Vincent's hand, she led him leaving between groups of people back out of the tent and onto the estate grounds.

With the auction items removed, the lawn looked bare without the stations. Mia practically ran down one path with the singular purpose of putting as much distance between herself and her father as possible.

Once the sounds of the party were distant, Mia slowed their pace. Her posture remained cold, her lips knitted together in a harsh line of anger. "'Sorry about that."

"'Not your fault."

She nodded in agreement, but her mind was a thousand miles away. Or rather, probably a dozen yards back in the tent with her father.

"So you're probably wondering why I come here, and why I put myself through this. Don't you think I've asked myself the same things a million times? I reject the alpha males in my family and yet seek out the same type in my private life. I'm a psychiatrist, I should have my shit together. Instead I'm just as messed up as the rest of them. Abandonment issues, mother issues. Issues on top of issues. I'm thoroughly fucked up."

She stopped walking and wheeled around to face him, cold ice still floating in her eyes. "Say something."

"We all have issues, it doesn't necessarily make you fucked up."

Her shoulders sagged. Mia nodded, although it was clear that she didn't believe what he said.

They had stopped in a clearing with a little pond and a cement bench sitting beside it. It would be the perfect spot for reflection or relaxation on a sunny summer afternoon. Now it was the place Mia sat as she tried to calm her breath and of her temper. Both of which at the moment seemed to be a little out of control.

Vincent sat down beside her and held her hand. He waited while she got whatever this fight was out of her system. The summer heat had gone to bed with the sun and left the hard bench cool to the touch. The night air was cooling just as rapidly and he supposed that Mia in her light silk dress must be getting chilly too. He took off his suit jacket and draped it over her shoulders. She smiled at him in thanks.

"Why didn't you bring James tonight? It seemed like your family was expecting him to be here."

She shrugged. "I didn't have to bring him. He had his own invitation. He could have come if he wanted to."

Vincent looked down at his hands in his lap. "I bet he fits in with these people a little better than I do."

Mia nodded. "He does, but not for the reason you'd think. That's James's story to tell. He comes to these things only because it's good networking for him. I bet you'd be surprised at how many people here belong to different kink clubs."

"Really? I'm shocked."

"Don't be."

They sat in silence and enjoyed the night a little. He could hear the outdoor sounds of an early August evening all around him. This late in the season no mosquitoes buzzed around them, but that didn't mean there wasn't a buzzing in Vincent's head.

"James didn't come because he wanted you and I to have this time together," Vincent guessed.

Mia nodded. "This is a side of my life I don't share with many people."

"Thank you for inviting me."

She sighed. In the low light Vincent could see the perfect outline of her lips. She looked damn sexy sitting there in that pretty Chinese dress with his suit coat around her shoulders. The dress was tightly buttoned to the collar and he guessed it probably wasn't much fun putting on. She probably couldn't wait to take it off.

As if reading his thoughts, Mia trailed a hand over her hip to the top of the slit in her dress. Mia pulled it open further, revealing a long expanse of milky white thigh. Vincent's hands were drawn to her newly exposed skin like a moth to a flame. She felt silky and warm. He stoked her smooth skin, and felt the arousal uncurl in his belly. He shouldn't be touching her here, so close to where anyone could see them. He shouldn't keep touching her, pushing her further, but he couldn't help it. The thought of stripping that tight red silk dress off of her perfect body made him hard as a rock. He wanted her.

"Do you want me to make you feel better?" She didn't have a chance to respond before his mouth was on her, crushing her lips to his. They clutched each other as if desperate for a connection. His lips were not kind as he savagely claimed her mouth. She clawed at him, scrambling to get closer to him.

Usually with kisses this deep he would have held her head to his to hold on for dear life. Usually he would have held onto their foreplay as long as possible. His hands had another purpose now. They found her breasts and squeezed them roughly, crudely through the silk material of her dress. They were so soft, but he could feel her nipples beading in his hands. His thumbs pinched at them, making them strain against the bodice that held them captive. He traced her nipple jewelry through her dress.

Mia leaned into him, giving him free rein to her body. He wished her tits were free so that he could suck their hard little points. Frustrated, his hands moved lower to find purchase in another area, which they did courtesy of the split in her dress. Mia pulled away only to gulp a lung full of air before showing him exactly what her response was. She pulled open a row of ornamental buttons and opened her legs. Her own arousal glistened as the moonlight illumined her matching red panties.

He moaned as he cupped her pussy in his palm and then pushed his fingers around the side of the soaking garment. She opened her legs to him and his fingers barely skimmed her clit as they moved onto and into her heat. Her hips rocked toward him, sucking first one finger and then a second added digit into her. Her moan was loud, and for a second he thought for sure someone would have heard or had the curiosity to happen upon him finger-banging their host's daughter in the garden. The potential for discovery made it even hotter. He had no reservations this time.

"I need to have you," Vincent whispered against her lips. She nodded, just as hungry as he was for connection. They broke apart long enough for her to hike up her dress and swing a leg over the bench. She lay back onto the cold cement of the chair and he followed her, covering her body with his own.

Her panties were gone with a strong rip. The next sound was his zipper being yanked down and the tearing of a condom wrapper before his hard cock thrust into her. He liked how she was always wet and ready for him. This time was no different, and he relished slamming all of his inches home inside of her.

Her fingers grabbed at him, sliding off of his pressed dress shirt. He was sure that her nails would still leave marks on his chest and shoulders, in fact he looked forward to it. Until he had a better idea.

He kept up the pace of his thrusting as he grabbed her wrists. Using force he raised them above her head and pinned them to the bench. He was careful not to crush her corsage, but he didn't want her moving either.

He fucked her harder as he looked into her eyes. Yes, this was exactly what she had needed. Everything cold about her earlier was replaced with a heat that he had created. The sound of their breathing and the slapping of their skin together filled the night air. He shoved into her again and again, harder and faster with each thrust.

He knew her orgasm was close. She tried to fight it, to not move against him like an obedient Sub, but it was no use. "Come for me,

Mia," he commanded, and she did. It wasn't long before he followed her, his arousal shattering him into a thousand pieces.

When he recovered, he realized he was kissing her again. But it was much different this time. He peppered little soft kisses on her lips. He moved to kiss her chin, jaw, cheeks as well. He remembered the intensity of his kisses earlier and hoped that her face wouldn't be too beard-burned tomorrow.

Slowly, regretfully he sat up and, now flaccid, slipped out of her. She sat up too, but made little move to straighten her clothes or hair. He held her and just enjoyed the moment.

"It's so beautiful out here. It must have been a great place to grow up."

Mia nodded. "Yeah, it had its moments."

Vincent hugged her tightly and she rested her head on his shoulder. "Tell me one of your favourite memories of this place."

She thought for a moment and then smiled brightly. "When I was fourteen, I was obsessed with horses, just like every preteen girl. I asked my Dad for one and so he bought me five and had the stables built. He even brought up a horse trainer from Wyoming to teach me how to ride." She giggled, remembering. "The trainer used to ride bulls in the rodeo and he told me so many stories...probably stories he shouldn't have told a young girl."

"Do you still ride?"

She nodded eagerly. "I do, just not as much as I would like. We don't keep horses at the stables here anymore." She looked a little sad at the thought. "I still keep in touch with the horse trainer. He has a family now and a wife that he shares with his best friend. A couple years ago they welcomed twin daughters."

"I'd love to go riding with you sometime."

"You would?"

"Absolutely. I'd love to share something with you that you obviously enjoy so much."

Mia's entire face lit up in happiness. Her brown eyes swam with happy tears. "Vincent, I'm so glad that James suggested we train together."

"Me too." He kissed her softly, and felt a little choked up. He owned James a lot. She snuggled into him and lay her head on his shoulder.

"Mia!"

Just as quickly as their intimacy began, it was broken again. Voices raised in anger were so loud they reached their clearing and invaded their happiness. Mia recognized the voices and quickly righted her clothes before hurrying back toward the tent, where the shouts were becoming more heated.

As they approached, Mia visibly blanched. Lee had returned from the house. He and their father stood united against a third man. Guests, who previously had been the model of politeness, now openly gawked at this display of family drama.

"I'm calling the police," Lee shouted at the man Vincent didn't recognize.

The man looked like he was about to say something back to Lee, but when he spotted Mia, his entire demeanor changed. "Mia, baby." He turned toward her. "We need to talk."

The man moved toward her and Mia froze. Her terror was palatable. The man was dressed just as fine as the other people at the party, but there was something very wrong about him.

"I told you not to come here ever again," Mia cried.

"Calm down." He continued to walk toward her. Although meant to sound casual, Vincent recognized the request as what it was, a command from a Dom.

No way. Vincent stepped in front of Mia to shield her. He had never seen her so afraid. He put out a hand to stop him as the man approached.

He continued as if he didn't see Vincent. "Mia, you need to hear what I have to say."

"No, I don't think so, buddy." Every possessive bone in Vincent's body was screaming out but he tried hard to keep his tone flat and emotionless.

The man's head snapped toward Vincent. "Who the fuck are you?"

Vincent took a step toward him. "I'm the man that's with Mia."

He didn't know who this guy was, but the effect he had on Mia was clear. His beautiful brave girl had every ounce of strength scared out of her by this man. Vincent's instincts as a protector clicked in and his hands curled into fists. He hoped his size and his stony features were enough to prove to the man that he wasn't someone to fool with. If not, Vincent was prepared to do whatever he had to in order to protect his Sub.

The man stopped in his tracks. He eyed Vincent warily. Then, slowly, a smile lit up his face. He laughed. The sound made Vincent sick to his stomach, but he held his position.

The man turned to retreat back up the path. "This isn't over, Mia, not by a long shot." He pushed past Lee, Mia's father and other guests. Their eyes followed him as he retreated to the car he had abandoned without waiting for the valet. He slammed the car into reverse and disappeared back up the driveway.

Good riddance. Vincent calmed his breathing. His fingers hurt as he released his fists. He had been holding his fingers down so tightly they had bit into his palm leaving long red marks.

He barely noticed.

Mia was still shaking. She was pale, and tears freely splashed down her cheeks.

"Are you okay?"

Her lips were held tightly closed to keep the sound of her sorrow inside. Instead she just shook her head sadly.

Without hesitation, Vincent wrapped his arms around her and picked her up in his arms. He turned toward the house, and her father nodded. "Take her inside. Her room is upstairs, the first door to the left."

The crowd respectfully parted as Vincent carried Mia away. A waiter opened the door and pointed out the way to the stairs. Vincent held onto his girl tightly as he quickly took every step. Mia clung to him soundlessly.

First door to the left. Thankfully it was easy to push open. He used his hip to bump it closed. Mia needed safety and privacy.

Chapter Seven

Vincent sat gingerly on the bed, Mia cradled securely in his arms. She curled into his chest and he could feel the dampness of her tears through his dress shirt. He tenderly stroked her hair and cheeks, letting her cry her fill.

The twilight and party lights shone in through the window, partially illuminating the space. He looked around the room. The walls and the bedding were a light yellow colour. A dresser and a long mirror were against one wall. Beside the bed was a small study area with a desk and a corkboard covered with pictures and postcards. It appeared to be the only personalization of the room. The cards were from places a little less exotic than he had expected, small towns in Florida, Colorado, and Wyoming. The photos were old, and a young Mia was smiling in many of them.

As her tears slowed she opened her eyes and looked up at him. There were a thousand different emotions bubbling on the surface. Vincent just kept silent and strong for her. He would gladly hold her as long as she needed, but his stubborn girl sat up and moved out of his arms. She looked everywhere but at him, as she straightened her dress and brushed her hair back out of her face.

"Thank you." Her voice was quiet and a little sheepish. She was embarrassed at her outpouring of emotion.

"Of course." He smiled, hoping to ease some of her awkwardness.

"You should go. I'll be okay now." Sure she said it, but Vincent wasn't buying it.

"It's okay. I'd like to stay with you for a bit."

"I'm fine now." She stood and paced away from the bed. Ah, he knew now that she didn't like this vulnerability, this closeness. *Silly Mia, didn't you always say that trust was the most important part of their relationship?* And yet she didn't trust him with this side of her. "You should go."

"Fine. Come with me. We'll go back to my house. You could see Gus."

Her lips curled up almost into a smile. "And watch a kung fu movie?"

"Sure."

She kept pacing and, he hoped, actually thought about the offer before declining. "No, you go. I have to stay and talk to my father after the guests leave."

"Don't do that. Come with me and call him tomorrow or something."

"No, I have to. It's our ritual." She chewed at the side of her lip, debating clearly whether to share more with him. Finally she sighed and stopped the internal struggle she was having. "Tonight is the anniversary of my mom's death. That's why he has the fundraiser every year on this date."

"I'm sorry to hear that." She was opening up a little, so Vincent chanced a question. "Were you one of the children…."

"The first child," she interjected.

"…to benefit from the Memory project?"

She nodded then sat back down on the bed beside him. "Yeah, when my mom died. Lee was older than I was, so I needed more help understanding. But really, I'm fine. You go home and I'll talk to you tomorrow. I promise I'll call and wake you up again."

Vincent smiled. He liked the promise and the thought of talking to her again tomorrow, but he wasn't going to let her push him away. If she honestly wanted him to leave he would, but he felt that maybe she was pushing him away again to protect her secret. It was time for her to finally tell him everything. He needed to know who that guy was and why he scared her so badly.

Although his tone was soft, Vincent's voice sounded far too loud for the silence of the room. "Was he your ex?"

Some emotion played at Mia's lips. For a minute he didn't think she was going to answer. Then she sighed, deciding to let him in. "His name is Robert and I was his twenty-four-seven slave."

"What does that mean?"

She looked up at him, meeting her eyes. He knew this must be incredibly hard to talk about. "In the BDSM world there are many types of relationships. Some are like ours. We play in sexual circumstances and you are in charge in the bedroom only. Outside of those doors, in our lives, we are each in charge of ourselves, no one owns us. Even if you collared me, I would still be in control of myself." She paused, trying to find the right words.

"I had worked as a Dom trainer since the club opened. I can't even remember how many men discovered their true nature while inside the walls of my dungeon. Each of those men was carefully vetted and had purchased full membership to the club before they began training with me. Robert was different. I met him online in a BDSM chat room. He knew the lifestyle, he knew what he was doing, and I found that refreshing after years of men that I had to teach everything to. I agreed to meet him. James didn't want me to, but I went behind his back and set up a date. Robert was charming. He had a goofy sense of humour that put me at ease. He was a little awkward, a little immature outside the club…but in a scene, he was a hard and merciless Dom. To me, at that time, there was something very attractive about that. I thought I needed someone to take full control of me.

"I brought him to the club and we trained together. Behind my locked door, no one knew the amount of punishment he doled out or the depraved acts he liked that became almost second nature to me. I wanted to please him. Our first public scene together made James's one with Terry look absolutely tame by comparison. I was manipulated into thinking it as no big deal. Yet it was horrific enough that James stepped in, breaking the club rules of never interrupting a scene. He dragged Robert off stage and threw him out of the club. I chose to go with him."

Mia took a deep breath. The secrets were spilling from her lips so quickly she barely had time to breathe. The dam had burst and she couldn't stop. Vincent tried to calm his fiercely beating heart. He couldn't imagine that things that Mia had just described, and he feared what she would say next. Whatever it was, he knew it would be bad. He reached out and took her hand. She smiled faintly.

"Soon after that, within four months of knowing him, Robert asked me to be his slave full-time. I had never been anyone's slave before, but I was just so…I don't know, flattered that someone wanted me to be theirs. I was in love with him and couldn't say no. At this point my relationship with James was very strained. He begged me not to agree to a slave relationship, but my mind was made up. The next day I walked in and quit my very successful practice. I packed up my home and moved in with Robert. He had bought a small remote cottage for us to live in together. He said that he had been in the area one day and fell in love with it. That it would be the perfect place for us to start our life together. From the minute I arrived, he had full dominance over me and every aspect of my life. I owned nothing. I wanted nothing. His will was the only thing that mattered." Her tone had gradually taken on a removed quality, as if she was talking about someone other than herself.

"I can't imagine that people do that."

"Some twenty-four-seven relations work well and prosper into loving relationships that last years, decades even."

"But not yours?"

"No." She fidgeted, and refused to look him in the eye.

As much as he hated that, Vincent was also a little glad that she couldn't see the anger in his own eyes. He was still trying to wrap his mind around the concept. "I don't think I would want to be in control of someone all the time."

Mia sighed. "No, I don't think it would work for you either Vincent. You're not the type of man who needs that. Plus it's a tremendous amount of responsibility. And it won't work if there are differences in the idea of what the Sub's care or punishment should be…"

"You and Robert disagreed?"

"Not at first. I knew the rules, having taught them to new Doms for so many years. I tried to protect myself a little. Like every BDSM relationship, terms were negotiated and agreed to before the arrangement began. You should only continue with a scene if you trust the person to stick to those terms." Her voice trailed off. She was getting closer to the horror and she was beginning to resist. He couldn't blame her for not wanting to relive the experience, but he needed to know the rest.

"Was he mean?" he whispered, already guessing the answer.

"Yes."

Vincent closed his eyes, feeling like the air was knocked out of him. "Did he hurt you badly?"

"Yes." Mia paused. Her voice shook and he thought that she was going to cry again. He squeezed her hand. The connection between them had never been so strong or as important as it was now. He stayed silent with her, allowing her all the time she needed to find the words.

"At first our arrangement was amazing. He would go to work and I would have free time. I even cooked. When he came home I would sit with him and serve him. I felt cherished." Her voice broke on the last word.

"That changed?"

She nodded sadly. "It wasn't enough control for him. Gradually the stakes were raised and then we got to a point that anything I did was an excuse for him to punish me. "She took a deep breath. "I started to crave his anger because it was the only attention I got from him. The goofy charming guy he once was disappeared completely. Maybe he hadn't existed at all. Robert was a cruel sadist. Right before it ended, I hadn't been allowed outside for over six months."

"What? That's inhumane."

"Robert has been accused of many things, being humane was never one of them." She paused. "I was chained for the last month I was with him."

"Chained?"

"To the bed, naked. Unable to do anything for myself. I couldn't even go to the bathroom alone. For an entire month I was held captive. He even stopped going to work so that he could stay home and control absolutely every aspect of my existence." She was angry, she was hurt. She fell into silence as Vincent processed the last bit of horror she had admitted. How could anyone want to do that to a person?

"How were you able to get out of there and away from him?"

"James. He's always been there for me. Like I said, he never liked Robert. At first I thought he was jealous of our relationship. I was blind. I thought I knew better. James made me promise to keep in contact with him, and I agreed. But when things changed and I was totally under Robert's spell, not only couldn't I call James, I didn't want to. The last time we talked, James knew that something was wrong. He started looking around, and used all of his connections to get info on Robert. The cottage had been purchased privately, so it took a while for James to find out about it. He had to camp out and wait almost a week before he could get inside. He said the wait almost killed him and I believe him. It almost killed me.

"The opportunity finally came when Robert left me alone for some reason. He was clearly upset but he didn't tell me why. He just rushed out and left me. James made his move as soon as he was gone. He didn't know if Robert had booby-trapped the cottage or if there was someone else in there guarding me so he couldn't just waltz in the front door. He took off a screen and pushed out a window then crawled through the small rooms until he found me. I was practically comatose. He said he didn't recognize me when he found me." She shuddered. "He didn't have chain cutters so he practically had to rip the bed apart to get me free. But he did it. He freed me, carried me out of there and burned rubber getting me back into town and to the hospital."

Vincent exhaled a breath he didn't know he had been holding. "Thank god."

"No, thank James. Now you know why my family loves him so much. If he had stopped looking, I would be dead now. I believe that."

"I'm sorry that all of this happened to you." He kissed her forehead and held her closer. He wished that he hadn't asked. No, actually he was glad he had asked. This fucked-up stuff affected who she was and made a few things clearer. He now wished he had known all of this earlier. Then he would have justification for beating the shit out of that creep for doing this to Mia. "Was he arrested?"

"No. James made me take out a restraining order but that's all I would agree to."

"What?" Vincent was incredulous. Assholes like that should have been in jail, not out in public dressed in expensive designer suits crashing benefit parties. "That's ridiculous. He should be behind bars."

"That would never have happened. As it was, I was probably lucky to get a restraining order. There's little the police can do when you willingly agree to be someone's slave. Besides, I never would have testified against him, had he been charged with anything."

"Why not? The man tortured you."

"You can call it Stockholm syndrome if you want. I called it love." She looked up now and Vincent could see tears shining in her sad brown eyes. "Do you think any less of me now?"

"Why would I?"

"A better question would be, why wouldn't you? There were many people in my life that rejected me when they found out that I had willingly agreed to be someone's slave. My brother, for one. I don't think he'll ever fully forgive me for missing out on an important part of his daughter's life, or for not being there for him when his marriage ended. I'm lucky we have any relationship at all now." She sighed. "I'm not a dumb woman, Vincent. I am educated and strong and I still let that happen to me. I'm a psychiatrist. Logically I should have seen the signs of a sadist."

"Come on, Mia, it wasn't your fault. You didn't know he would hurt you or treat you the way he did."

"No, I just thought he loved me. But he never did."

Vincent didn't mean to say the words, hadn't even thought them before, but it was true. He said them and he meant them. He loved her with everything he had and he would protect her from this creep or any other horror of the world. He wanted to be her Dom and take her as his Sub forever. The old Vincent he used to be would have thought it was impossible to fall in love with someone so quickly, but it was impossible to ignore the evidence. She had trusted him with her truth and now he had to trust her with his. "I love you."

"Don't say that."

"It's true."

Mia pushed away from him and sat up. She didn't say anything for a long time. He hoped that she was just thinking about what he had said, and was trying to find the courage to say the same.

He was wrong.

"I don't think I can ever love someone again. He broke that part of me. I can't trust those types of feelings. I didn't even think I could go back to BDSM for a long time. James talked me back in. That's one of the reasons why I agreed to train you, Vincent. We have the perfect arrangement. Remember, you're *so* in love with Catherine that we'll have no worries of ever having romantic feelings between us. Remember?" That last word was said almost desperately. Her eyes found his and implored him to agree with her, to take back what he had said, to kill any idea of love between them.

He couldn't. "Maybe that was our arrangement originally, but it's not now. You changed something inside of me."

Her bittersweet smile almost broke his heart. "I wish something could change inside of me."

"It can if you let it. Let me love you."

She didn't answer.

He needed to hold her. He stretched over her and wrapped his arms around her. She closed her eyes as he held her. They sat in silence. He matched his breath to hers and he could hear her heart beat. He had never felt closer to her.

He kissed her softly, tenderly. He felt her arms still shaking a little as she wrapped them around his neck and pulled him closer. Maybe she wasn't ready to accept love, but she would accept this attention from him now. Vincent kept the kiss light, and used his hands to brush the new tears off of her face. If he could use them to brush away all of her hurt, he would.

Instead his hands traveled down over her shoulders and back. She mewed as he caressed her. She opened her eyes and he saw a need there. He understood what she needed without saying a word. Sex was the only way she could show him affection. It was enough for now. He would take care of her and take care of her needs. He pushed her down on the mattress.

She was still as he unbuttoned her dress and removed it from her body. Her creamy skin shone in the low light. She looked so small and so fragile. Her dark hair spread out against the pale yellow comforter. She was so beautiful and yet so hurt at this moment. He pulled back from her only for a second, to remove his own clothes. He needed to take the hurt away from her, erase the tears and worry and fear from her features. To show her that he loved her, not just tell her.

Vincent pressed his lips to her skin, trying to impart strength and comfort to all of her limbs. He kissed her neck, her shoulder blades and the red *X* wrist tattoos. His lips ran over her body and touched every inch of skin he could see.

When his mouth found her breasts, she responded. Her back arched toward him, and his own body answered, drawn like a magnet. He pressed his hips against hers as he took a nipple into his mouth. He sucked on it gently, pulling another mew from her.

He caressed down her legs and over her thighs. Her legs parted to give him better access and his caress continued across her mound and down to her labia. His fingers parted her folds and he kept his touch very light. He read her reactions. This wasn't about speed or force. This was about kindness and affection.

Mia's body arched when he touched her clit. He knew she was likely still sensitive from their play in the garden, so he was gentle in his intimate caress. Even with her recent orgasm, she was already wet and ready for him again.

His eyes found Mia's. There was a quiet desperation there, waiting for him to comfort. He did his best by kissing her lips as he continued to touch her. He was touched by how vulnerable she was allowing herself to be. She was always open and honest with her body, but this was different, as if she was finally sharing her whole self with him. This was a new Mia.

He removed his fingers from her as his emotion swelled. He needed to be inside of her. Without letting her go he angled himself between her thighs. His cock slid against her, and she moved her hips to give him full access. He didn't want to break their embrace to get a condom. As he pulled away to go searching for one, Mia held tighter to him. She met his eyes and shook her head. It was clear she didn't want a barrier between them.

Accepting her gift, Vincent kissed her. Then he lined up the hard length of his cock with her opening. She was slick and ready. As he began to press into her, his cock coated with her silky wetness. He slowly thrust inside, feeling every inch of her wrap around him. It felt amazing to be inside of her. He would never tire of her unique heat.

Once he was in to the hilt, he paused. He met her eyes and she gave him a soft smile. Her face held as much emotion as he was feeling. It took everything he had to choke back the tears that came to his eyes. He had never felt this way before, but wanted to feel it again for the rest of his life. Had he been in love with her from the moment that he had walked into her dungeon? Had she won his heart when such a sweet, generous girl had offered to teach him to be a better man? He closed his eyes and kissed her again.

Mia moved beneath him, wanting more. So he gave it to her. His cock slid out of her and then back with a little more force. Mia responded wonderfully, her hips flexing toward him, pulling him back each time for more. He tried his best to keep his composure and be gentle, but it was impossible with her body moving off the bed to meet his with every thrust.

Vincent sat back just a little and moved her legs wider and placed her ankles on his shoulders. She was fully open to him now, and ready for everything he could give her. It was a beautiful sight.

Vincent wanted to last, but she felt so good. Every thrust was harder and faster. He couldn't even register the surprise when he felt Mia's body tighten with her orgasm. Her body pulsed against him as she came apart without being commanded to come. He followed her, himself coming hard and fast.

They lay there together and tried to catch their breath. After a few moments he gently moved to let her legs down. Rolling to the side, he pulled her into his arms again. Her head resting on his chest, he hugged her tighter to him and kissed her forehead.

Mia no longer shook. The coldness was gone from her skin. She snuggled into him and it felt wonderful to hold her and have everything out in the open.

"I'm glad I told you."

"Me too."

A banging on the door caused Vincent to bolt upright. Was the creep back? Was Mia in danger?

"Just a minute, sweetie." Instead of being scared, Mia smiled, recognizing easily the source of the childish thumps on the closed door. "Don't worry, she won't open the door without permission. But you should get dressed."

Vincent quickly pulled his shirt and pants back on and helped Mia with her dress. When they were both fully closed again, Mia opened the door. Instantly her arms were full of an energetic five-year-old in pink pajamas. "Hi, Auntie Mia."

"Hi, Sage. Isn't it past your bed time?"

The little girl didn't answer. She had realized that her aunt wasn't alone in the room. She looked at Vincent and ducked her head shyly.

"Hi there," he said softly.

Again the little girl didn't answer.

"Sage, this is Vincent."

She took a deep breath and found her words. "Hello, Vincent, nice to meet you." The girl was adorable. She had her aunt's dark hair and freckles. She also had two deep dimples in her cheeks. She smiled at him briefly before turning back to Mia. When she spied her aunt's wrist corsage she tried to grab onto it. "Pretty flowers!"

"Thank you, Sage, but be gentle with them."

The girl nodded and continued to hold onto the flowers and feel their petals with her fingertips. "I was wondering…"

"Yes?"

"If you would read me a story."

"What do you say?"

"Please?"

"Okay."

The little girl danced in happiness. It was impossible to resist her youthful charm.

"Go back to your room and I'll be there in a minute, okay?"

"Okay!" With a squeal of laughter, Sage was gone, running back down the hallway toward her room. Mia shook her head and closed the door again.

"So that was my niece. I'm not sure where her sitter is. Either gone home early or somewhere fucking my brother would be my two best guesses."

"No worries. She's great."

"Yeah she is." Mia walked over to him and wrapped her arms around him. "It was an adjustment getting to know her again after missing a big chunk of her life. And now I can't resist her. So I'm sorry, but I'm on story duty now."

"Okay." He bent his head and collected a kiss from Mia. Their interruption hadn't dampened her hunger for him. "So will I see you again before Saturday?"

"Maybe." She smiled coyly. "Remember this Saturday is the halfway mark of your training. We'll have to start thinking about what you want to incorporate into your final exam."

Possibilities ran through his head. "I think I have some ideas…"

"I bet you do." She kissed him again. "Are you okay to see yourself out and find Stanley to get your car back?"

"I think so." Another kiss. He didn't want to let her go or the evening to end.

"She's waiting for me."

Reluctantly, and after stealing just one more kiss, Vincent pulled away. He continued to hold her hand as she opened the door again. He followed her out into the hall.

Now she was the one who didn't want to let him ago. She threw her arms around his neck again. "Thanks for coming tonight, Vincent. I'm so glad you were here."

"No problem."

"Night, Vincent."

"Night."

She waved and walked down the hall away from him. He watched her disappear into Sage's room before he turned to leave. If his footsteps hadn't echoed as he walked down the stairs, he would have thought he was walking on air.

He loved her. Mia didn't know it yet, but she was still capable of love and trust. He was going to teach her how.

Chapter Eight

The next Friday night, Vincent spent the time he would have preferred to spend with Mia at the police station.

Everything had changed during the week and yet nothing had changed. As he sat with Eve to his left and Allison to the right, he reflected over the past five days.

He hadn't heard from Mia at all. He hadn't really expected her to keep her promise of calling him the next day. He hadn't expected, but he had hoped. He had even set his alarm so he would be up and cognizant when she called. He waited. He put off taking Gus for a walk as long as he could. He watched the clock. He just really needed to hear her voice. And yet no call came.

He could have called her, but maybe she was curled up with Sage, having fallen asleep at her side after dazzling her young head with classic child-approved fairytales. Maybe she was having the yearly talk with her dad, cooling their fiery tempers down to ashes as they shared their grief over a woman they had both lost a long time ago. Or maybe she was spending some long-overdue time with her big brother, listening and finally getting forgiveness for her absence from his life.

Maybe. Maybe she was doing any of those important things. Or, maybe she was avoiding him. And maybe she was avoiding him because he had said the L word. He definitely didn't want to think about that last maybe at all.

During the week he kept his cell phone close by and checked it frequently, just in case she needed him. Or wanted to talk. Or whatever. They had never spoken during the week before, so why did he think it would be a possibility now? He just really hoped that his fun girl Mia would call. Either for some naughty talk or else to invite him out someplace to eat salad and have fun.

He just really wanted her to call him.

But she didn't. And the week dragged on. He felt like a teenager mooning over some girl that didn't feel the same way about him. He was supposed to be a Dom. Funny, he didn't feel in charge of anything right now. Mia had all the power to make him or break him. What a wimp! It felt like his relationship with Catherine all over again.

Catherine was the reason why they were at the police department. Neither Allison nor Eve had been able to contact her. Cell phone, text, e-mail. All had gone through, but no one had received any response. This was odd because Catherine always kept her pink jewel-cased cell phone with her at all times. Sure, she'd always been a little flighty, and truthfully this wasn't the first time she had "disappeared." Usually she told at least one person what her plans were before she took off. Allison and Eve were her closest friends. You would think if she was going somewhere, they would be first on her list to tell.

On his way home last night, walking through the parking lot, they had cornered him. Allison demanded to know what he knew that he wasn't telling them. Eve, in a much nicer way, admitted that he did look like a man with a secret. And why wasn't he more upset that his very recent ex was missing? That last question had come from Allison. It sounded like she watched too much true crime drama on TV. She had a glint in her eye that told him that in her view, he was seconds away from being named suspect number one in Catherine's disappearance.

Although he had to admit, he was starting worry too. Sure, the girl had been pretty cold when she had ended their relationship, but he hoped she wasn't really cold now, as in dead. Mia's story was so fresh in his mind. She was lucky to have survived being some guy's voluntary slave. Catherine was interested in the lifestyle. Had she gone to a club looking for a Dom? She wouldn't have had someone like James to guide her, or someone like Mia to train her. Would she have been naive enough to allow herself to get pulled into a relationship where she couldn't contact her friends and family? Could she have gotten involved with someone who had taken a scene too far?

He certainly didn't have James's reach to search for her. Filing a missing person's report was the best thing they could do. Allison had mentioned it first and eve had begged him to come with them.

He had never been inside their local precinct before, and was a little shocked when he walked through the doors for the first time. The place was cheerful enough and lit brightly. The desk clerk was a little too cheerful and happy in her job. But she did make sure to say all the right things when she heard they were there due to a missing friend. The station also had comfortable chairs as they sat and waited to speak with an officer.

One thing they didn't allow was cell phone. He wondered if his would have rung if it was turned on. He folded his arms across his chest. Six days without a phone call was too long. He was going to tell Mia that, too. Maybe a good spanking would get it into her head.

That is, if he got another chance to get his hands on her. What had happened to make her avoid him? Was it because he had said "I love you" to her? Certainly she didn't feel the same way. He could accept that. Ugh. He ran what he could remember of their intimate conversation through his head. He felt so stupid saying corny things like she had changed him. God, what was he, some loser guy from a silly romance novel?

No he was a dummy, who thought a few weeks of training had made him into a Dom. Sure, he felt like a powerful stud that could make any lady swoon. Instead he was just some guy who walked into a sex club and had made the mistake of falling in love with his teacher. Hadn't he just gotten out of a bad relationship? Why was he struggling to get back into another one? Mia had no interest in that, she had said so herself, she had agreed to train with him because he was so over-the-moon for Catherine.

He was an idiot! Right after sex, and right after Mia pouring her heart out, he had told her that he loved her. Sure, it seemed right at the time. Talk about moving too fast. Was it real or was it just his emotions rebounding? He had to get his head on straight so that when it came time for their next training session his head was back in the game.

No, that would be pathetic. He couldn't continue training with a woman he had embarrassed himself with. So yeah, he would go Saturday night. He would walk right in there and tell her that he didn't need her anymore. He didn't love her. He didn't need membership at the club. Forget all that other stuff, it wasn't for him, not anymore.

And yet, he found himself excusing himself from Allison and Eve as they still sat waiting to talk to an officer. He crossed the room to an ancient-looking pay phone and dropped two quarters into it. Fishing his cell out of his pocket, he discreetly turned it on. He shielded it with his body as he scrolled down to the number he had saved. Ten digits punched into the pay phone and the line began to ring.

No answer. He hung up the phone with enough force to garner a few looks. He was getting tired of this bullshit. Why was no one answering his calls? First Catherine, now Mia.

As much as he tried to tell himself that he didn't want Mia, it wasn't true. He scrubbed a hand across his face. No anger or machismo would change that fact. It wasn't rebound emotion, it was real. He did love her. That girl was it for him.

A uniformed man called Allison's name. Only one person would file a report at a time, and she had decided that she would be the one to do it. Classic Allison. Luckily they were allowed to be informants on the report. Allison and Eve hurried to follow the officer into his office. Vincent hurried as well, but for a different reason. He was anxious to get home to Gus and start his old Friday ritual. He'd feel better after he ordered a pizza and popped the top on a beer. And hopefully shut up the confused, pathetic yammering in his brain.

"Have a seat." The officer's name tag read "Rodriguez." His posture read Dom, and his face read familiar. Shit. He was the Latino Vincent had seen with Terry at the club, but he was cleaned up and dressed in a uniform. Were Doms and Subs everywhere?

"Thank you." Allison and Eve each took a seat while Vincent elected to stand. Rodriguez perched on the corner of his desk, close to the ladies. He held a clipboard and tried to look casual, but control rolled off of him in waves.

"So who is our missing person?" His voice was friendly, almost casual even to those outside the lifestyle.

"Our friend, Catherine Mentier."

Rodriguez nodded and wrote the name down on his clipboard. "And when did you last see her?"

"Friday the twenty-second. We went out for drinks," Eve offered.

"Where?"

"O'Malley's. We had never been there before, Catherine suggested it."

Rodriguez's expression revealed nothing as he wrote down the information. "Did she meet anyone there?"

"No."

"How many drinks did she have?"

"I think she had four Bellinis." Eve frowned as she tried to recall the detail.

"And how many did both of you have?"

"I don't see why that's relevant." Allison stuck her chin out sullenly.

"It's just a routine question." Rodriguez smiled at them, a perfect charming smile filled with honey, but with an edge. "How many drinks?"

"I had two, I'm a lightweight. But Allison had five beers," Eve piped up.

Rodriguez's smile broadened. "Thank you. Did you all leave at the same time?"

Eve nodded. "Yes, we shared a cab."

"What time approximately did you drop her off?"

"One fifteen. I have the receipt from the cab."

"Great, thank you, that will be very helpful." He wrote a few more details on his clipboard. "Have any of you heard from or seen Ms. Mentier since?" Rodriguez looked at all three of them, but his gaze landed on Vincent for only a second.

"No, unfortunately."

"Next, I have a form here I'd like you to fill out. With next of kin, address, her cell phone number if she has one, and a brief rundown of what occurred that last time you saw her."

"Okay." Eve took the clipboard from him eagerly.

Rodriguez stood. "Mr. Dupuis, can I see you outside for a moment?" The two girls shared a look. And an "oh shit maybe he really had something to do with his ex-girlfriend's disappearance" look flashed across their faces. Rodriguez's expression revealed nothing as Vincent followed him out to the hall.

Rodriguez wordlessly gestured for him to keep following him to an empty office across the hall. Once they were both inside, he closed the door. "Mark." Rodriguez held out his hand for an introductory shake.

"Vincent." Vincent gladly shook his hand.

Rodriguez nodded. "Yeah, I remember from when James introduced us at the club. You looked like a deer caught in headlights that night."

"I think I *was* a deer caught in headlights." The men laughed. Vincent liked Rodriguez.

"So what do you think happened to this girl?"

"I have no idea. She's done this before though."

Rodriguez nodded. "She's your ex?"

"Yeah. She's the one that motivated me to go to the club and train."

"And you're with Mia now." It wasn't a question. It was statement. But that didn't mean it wasn't ambiguous. Did he mean that he saw Vincent as Mia's trainee—true—Mia's Dom—maybe true—or Mia's boyfriend—close to being true if he hadn't fucked it up with the L-word?

"You're with Terry?"

Rodriguez shook his head sadly. "I wish. It takes a strong man to handle someone that broken." Vincent nodded, thinking the same thing about Mia. "Maybe if it doesn't pan out I'll try one of those Subs in there."

"I never thought of Allison or Eve as Subs. Certainly not Allison."

"Subs come in all different packages, Baby Dom. You'll learn that soon."

"Yeah…" Vincent let his voice trail off, thinking of one Sub in particular.

"Stick with it. Mia's a great person. She needs something good to happen to her."

"How can you be so sure that I'm her something good? My ex-girlfriend is missing and I'm probably the prime suspect."

"No way. You have an alibi. The last time she was seen, we were both at Club Perfect."

"Would you testify that in court?"

Rodriguez winked. "Not a chance, but I know eight or nine Doms that all met you that night and would testify you were at a *card game* during that time."

"Gee, thanks."

"Don't thank me, thank James. The members respect him, and by extension, respect you."

"I owe that guy a lot."

"Everyone does." Rodriguez opened the door again. "And if that Robert guy shows up again to bother Mia, call me." He slipped a card into Vincent's hand a second before he regained his cool cop expression.

When they returned to the office, Allison looked surprised that Vincent wasn't in handcuffs.

"I think we're done here, ladies. If you think of anything else or if you hear from your friend, please give me a call." Rodriguez fished out two more cards that he offered them, along with a smile so warm it would melt butter in the Arctic. The two women noticeably flushed as they took their cards from his hand. Hmmm, maybe Mark was right and they both were Subs after all.

Now he just had to figure out how to deal with his own Sub. He loved Mia. He had said it and he couldn't take it back. He took a deep breath. He remembered what Rodriguez had said about Terry. It takes a strong man to handle someone that broken.

Rodriguez had also said not to give up, but what if Mia had already decided that they were done and that's why she wasn't calling him? So many "what ifs."

No more self-doubt, Baby Dom. That stuff had to end, now. Going forward he had to be strong. If he had ruined things with Mia by telling her the truth, by saying what he honestly felt in his heart, then so be it.

He had to know.

Chapter Nine

He procrastinated. He sat on the couch with Gus far too long. He watched some classic sitcom episode that he had seen a thousand times and hadn't found funny even the first time he had watched it. He cleaned up a bit, he made a grocery list. He put off getting ready as long as possible.

Not knowing what Mia was thinking made him nervous.

He didn't dress in his club clothes. He left them stashed in the back of his closet and instead dressed in clothes that made him feel comfortable, well-worn jeans, boots, a white T-shirt, and his favourite well-worn hooded sweater. If he was stepping through those doors tonight, he was going in as himself. He didn't care what anyone thought about that.

It was dark when he got to the area the club was in. He parked his car in the usual anonymous lot nearby and took his time walking to the club. He passed the café where James had tricked him into meeting Mia.

He thought about stopping in for a coffee, but there were too many memories of Mia there. The way she had smiled and taken his hand. She had won him over that night and asked him to continue training with her. It was that night that everything had started to change for him. It was when he had decided to train to be a Dom.

What if tonight she told him that the training was over?

He was walking past the café when he remembered the small pub that was between the club and the café. He had never been inside before. Now was as good a time as any.

He walked into the dark smoky place and headed straight to the bartender. The guy looked him up and down and then set an unsolicited shot in front of Vincent. "Liquid courage," the man laughed. Seeing the confusion, he explained. "Before I met my girl I used to go next door for a bit of slap and tickle too. We Doms know our own kind." Vincent was shocked as the man walked away.

Vincent quickly downed the shot. The whiskey burned going down, but the instant calm he felt in his gut was worth the discomfort. Catherine had told him that he couldn't satisfy her in bed and her words had made him angry. He had come to the Club with more passion than he'd had in a long time. Mia had basically told him that he could never satisfy her heart enough to make her love again. Both women's words had been a call to arms. This time he wouldn't let his girl walk away without a fight.

One more shot for the road couldn't hurt. The bartender seemed hesitant as he slid the glass across the bar. When it was in his hand, before he even tipped it to his lips, Vincent knew he'd had enough. He placed the shot glass down on the coaster. None of this was helping, it was just putting off the inevitable. Whatever happened next was already decided. Either Mia was there waiting to welcome him into her body with open arms, or she simply wouldn't be there. End of story.

He took a deep breath and stared down at his glass. He couldn't drink his sorrows away. He had tried that after Catherine had left him and it hadn't worked. He took another second to summon his strength, and then he slid the glass back across the bar back to the kind bartender. It made a long wet mark. Vincent used the coaster to wipe it up.

Wait. The coaster said O'Malley's. This was the bar that Catherine, Eve, and Allison had come to that Friday? Shit. Why this bar? It wasn't the type of place Catherine usually went. This whole neighbourhood was a little low rent for her tastes. So why had she picked this isolated bar to go to? He was surprised the bartender even knew what a Bellini was let alone how to make one.

He waved the bartender over. He had just finished dumping Vincent's shot so he was curious about being waved over again.

"Want to try a different drink?"

"No thanks. I actually wanted to ask you about some women that were here a few weeks ago."

The bartended took a step back. "Are you police too? Officer Rodriguez was in earlier asking about that redhead."

"No, I'm not police. Just interested."

The bartender gave him a long look, trying to decide if what Vincent said was true or not. Finally he relented. "Look, pal, all I know is that she came in looking a little sad, after that the other two joined her, then they had some fancy drinks and left sometime before last call. That's it."

"Thanks." Vincent slapped some bills down on the bar along with a nice tip and got his ass out the door. He had to talk to Mark about this. He had to figure out why Catherine had been sad. That bar was so close to the club. Is it possible that she saw him there the night she had disappeared? That's why she had been sad and called in Allison and Eve for reinforcements? He felt a little sick at that thought.

First though, he had a date with Mia.

The bouncer went through the usual security checks. You'd think after being here so many times he would be fast tracked or be on a list or something.

The place was just as busy and as loud as usual. Why did it have to be so damned loud? Didn't people like to have a decent conversation along with their kink? The scenes happening right out in the open held no interest for him.

His head was spinning when James joined him by the front door.

"Mark told me that you had been by the station. We increased security in case someone in the area is targeting women."

Vincent shuddered. "Do you think she was taken?"

"We don't know. Despite my personal feelings for her, I put out feelers. I don't like the thought of anyone being held against their will."

"Thanks."

James was silent for a moment. "You're wondering if she was there that night because of you or because of the club. It's possible that she knew about Club Perfect. I've owned this place a long time."

Vincent couldn't hold in his surprise. "You own the club?"

His friend nodded. "Yes. Although I do have a few shareholders, Mia being the largest. But at the end of the day it's my name on the line if this club prospers or fails. It's a lot of responsibility making sure it's a space that remains safe, sane, and consensual. It's a lot different from just coming here a few days a week, but I love it."

Vincent didn't find it hard to believe that every word the man said was true. The more time he spent here with James, the more he realized that before he only knew one small side of him. This was the true James. "It's your life."

James sighed. "Absolutely."

"I think the old me would have found it strange, but now…"

"It's not so out there?" James laughed.

"Nope." Vincent grinned.

James slapped Vincent on the back. "I feel like a proud papa. Pass your final and you can consider yourself a full member for free." His voice was a little choked up.

"That's very generous, thank you."

"No problem. Maybe one day you'll consider buying into the business as a partner too."

"Let's take it one step at a time, okay?"

"Fine, I'll wait until you're ready." James laughed.

"Were you and Mia betting on how long it would take for me to ask to become a member?"

James's look said it all. "Maybe…"

"Great." Vincent shook his head.

"Don't worry about Catherine, if there's something to find, my team will find it." He paused. "And don't worry about Mia either. Just have patience with her."

Vincent didn't have time to ask what he meant before his friend disappeared back into the crowd that filled the club he loved. He just hoped James's advice was right, about both women.

He checked his watch and then started toward Mia's dungeon with a newfound swagger. Suddenly his stomach dropped out and he remembered why he was here and what was at stake behind that door. Ugh. Mia. Either she was here or she wasn't.

He took a deep breath and swiped his key card. The door opened but the room was empty.

Almost an hour later she hurried in, flustered. She quickly hung up her jacket and stripped off her street clothes before she turned to him.

"So are you early or am I late?"

"A bit of both." Vincent sat on an arm of the leather couch and watched each of her nervous little movements. Something was definitely up. He had never had to wait for her before. In fact, he had almost left, convinced that his L-word confession really had chased her off for good. It had been hard to sit in that room all alone, not knowing if she would show. James had said to be patient, so he had waited.

"Hi." She smiled sheepishly. His voice was calm, as he carefully cloaked any annoyance that had built as he waited. "Where were you?"

"Nowhere. I'm just running late I guess." She shrugged. A clear lie.

"Come on, Mia, tell me where you were."

"I had to do something okay? Let it go." She kicked off her boots, her strained mood still very evident. "Are you ready?"

"I thought you didn't top from the bottom?" Vincent was careful to keep his own tone in check. She cast him a bratty look.

"Well, someone has to top if you're not going to do it."

"Excuse me?" Vincent stood as Mia threw herself to her knees violently and took the classic submission pose. Her attitude and the hard line of her shoulders didn't read submissive at all. Her comment stung.

He took a deep breath and slowly walked over to her. Each step echoed in the room.

Mia shoulders slumped. She took a deep breath. "I need to be punished, Vincent. You're right. I'm being a brat to get what I what. I wasn't being honest with you."

Vincent was at a loss for words. The anger he felt dissipated. Instead he felt a little happy. Not that he had a Sub to punish, but that she respected him enough to be honest. "Why do you need to be punished?"

Mia's eyes wouldn't meet his. "I was late, Sir."

Vincent raised an eyebrow. This was her tactic to get past telling him the truth. He saw right through it. "Mia, you know our schedule isn't firm and no one minds if we stay later…"

"No. This is the next lesson." Her words warbled. Her words were quick and chipped. She was trying to hold onto her tactic of distraction. "I didn't mean it to be, but we might as well cover this since we're here."

He walked around her in a slow circle but said nothing. The sound of his boots on the hard stone floor was as firm as his need to not let the truth slip away.

"Vincent, Subs need to be punished when they're late." Mia pressed on. "You're punishing me because I was disrespectful and late. I didn't tell you where I was and you could have been worried that something happened to me."

He stopped, standing behind her, lips inches away from her neck. "I was worried. You didn't call me all week or return my call yesterday. Then you left me standing here, waiting to see if you'd show up eventually."

Mia shivered at their close contact. He was getting to her. "I'm sorry, Vincent. I need to be punished and a Dom needs to be firm with their Sub."

If she wanted him to be firm, she would get it. He walked around her again, stopping in front of her. "Sub, I demand you tell me why you were late."

Mia paused. She cleared her throat. "I'm sorry, Sir, but I can't tell you why I was late."

"Are you late because of work and cannot tell your Dom because of some hypocritical oath?"

Mia gave him a look that was pure brat. "Hippocratic," she corrected.

He lifted her chin so that her eyes met his. "Sub, I demand to know why you were late. You have to trust me and tell me the truth." She was silent. "Do you want to stop our lessons?"

Surprised, her eyes jumped up to meet his. "No, of course not."

"Then tell me."

Mia tried to evade his look again and cast her eyes down. Because he still held her chin, she wasn't able to hide the truth. "I was late because of my phone."

"Really? Who is more important than our time together, pet?"

"I only answered once, the rest of the time I ignored the calls."

"Who's calling you, Mia?"

She didn't answer. At first he thought he was too soft on her by calling her pet. James had used the title on Terry, and it seemed to fit now with Mia. Although it didn't seem to help grease her tongue. He was starting to think up a plan B, another way to get the information from her, when she said the one name that he knew she would say, but dreaded to hear. "Robert."

Vincent would not show weakness. He needed to let her know how putting this creep before him had made him feel. "Do you want him to be your Master again?"

Mia's eyes snapped up. "Of course not. But, he's been calling and sending me text messages…"

"And you ignored them, just like you ignored my call." Vincent shook his head. "Don't you trust me at all?"

"I'm trying to," she whispered. "Vincent, he sent flowers to my house and other things." Her posture was defeated. She didn't like admitting these things to him. She didn't know how to let a Dom help her. Vincent's palm left her chin and caressed her cheek. He needed to both soothe and reward her for telling him.

"Pet, you should have told me this was happening. I could have talked to him for you."

She nodded. "If you were my Master you would have."

Vincent started to react to her words. Then he realized it may be part of her bratty play to get punishment and distract him from the truth. His hand dropped from her face. "Sub, you have earned five swats for being late. Five more for being disrespectful. Five for not being honest with me. And five for thinking I'm not your Master."

Mia's eyes blazed fire. "But you're not…"

"Pet, until my exam, or until you find another Dom, I expect you to respect me like your Master. I need you to tell me if he contacts you again. Do you understand me?" Mia didn't answer, but her anger showed that she understood. If he was going to be her Dom, he needed to keep up the rules and receive her full consent. "Pet, how does a submissive answer her Master?"

"Yes, Sir."

"Try again."

"Yes, Master." The words were said between clinched teeth, but it was progress.

"I like the sound of those words on your lips."

"I'm glad to have pleased you. Now I need my punishment."

Vincent walked to the wall of torture. There was a soft flogger he liked the look of. He wondered how it would feel on Mia's soft skin. "Brat, you try my patience. Remember this punishment isn't a reward." He carefully unhooked the flogger and felt the suede lashes. He tried it out on his palm and found he liked the weight of it and the tiny sting when it made contact.

"The cane, Sir." Mia's voice was small. Vincent's eyes located the cane on the wall. It looked old and hard and very unforgiving. It also looked like it hadn't been used often. It would feel terrible.

"Mia, are you sure?"

She nodded reluctantly. "Robert can be very charismatic. I need something harsh so that I remember what he did to me."

Every part of Vincent's body didn't want to do this. His old natural response was kicking in. He was sweating. He was anxious. He didn't want to be here, but this wasn't about him. It was about Mia. He had to trust that this is what she needed and that he would do everything in his power as her accepted Master to punish her but not hurt her. He had been taught to never hit women. Did her consent change that rule? She was practically begging for it. If he said no, didn't it prove that he wasn't ready for this?

Vincent replaced the flogger on the wall and took down the cane. From the floor he could see Mia's body visibly relax, even though his anxiety ramped up another notch. He didn't like the feel of the hard unyielding stick in his hands. He tested it against his palm. The soft buttery feeling of the flogger was gone. He winced at even the lightest tap. Fuck. This was going to hurt.

"Get up, go to the bench, and lie across it," he ordered.

Mia nodded, got up and stalked across the room. Her constantly changing attitude was starting to affect him. The brat was gone and his sweet Sub was left. With almost a joyful gallop, she reached the bench and climbed up on it. Her manner was so confusing. You would have thought she was getting a nice treat, and not a beating. With perfect contentment, Mia stretched across the bench, ass up in the air, in perfect position. She was ready for him.

He still didn't know if he could do this. He grabbed the flogger back down along with several other instruments of both punishment and pleasure. Maybe because he felt they were more of what she needed. Maybe because they were what he needed. He still brought the cane with him over to the bench but he placed it away from them on a nearby table.

"I'm ready for my punishment, Master."

"I can see that, Sub. You have pleased me, but that doesn't get you out of some pain." He rubbed a hand over the pale creamy skin of her ass. There were scars there, probably from her time with Robert, and he tried to not let them worry him. He knew he wouldn't be adding to them today. He touched a hand between her legs and was surprised to find that she wasn't turned on at all. Maybe she was as freaked out as he was.

Her skin felt smooth against his palm as he let his hands roam her body. They made a slow sweet journey up her back to her shoulders before his fingers wandered into her hair. She sighed as he gently combed through the strands.

"This isn't punishment, Vincent."

"I need a moment first, Mia. I've never punished anyone before."

She nodded and silently allowed him to continue caressing her. He stalled as long as he could. Finally he took a deep breath. It was time to get her Dom. "Are you ready, Sub?"

"Yes, Master."

He picked up a paddle and weighed it in his hands. It was flat and heavy, designed to cause the least amount of pain but high intimidation. He took a deep breath. He drew back his arm and quickly smacked her across both ass cheeks. It made a hollow sound as it connected with her flesh. Although it reddened the skin, his Sub didn't flinch. The same for the next four times he hit her. Nothing.

"That's five. One more for being late?" Her voice was sweet. "Maybe use the cane now?"

"Pet, you will take what I give you and thank me."

She nodded, disappointed. "Yes, Master." He placed the paddle back on the table and picked up the flogger. He liked the sound it made as it hit her skin. "Five. For being late." It felt good in his hands. Yes, the flogger would be his instrument of choice going forward. It worked for him, but sadly seemed to have little effect on Mia. He tried it again, striking her skin quicker.

"One, Two, Three." She counted off the strikes again. She could have been rattling off a grocery list. "Four. Five. For being disrespectful."

The flogger was discarded on the table. Next he grabbed a riding crop. It was small and light and could be used for pleasure or pain. The thinness of the strap worried him. It stung when he snapped it on his palm. He could just imagine how it would feel against Mia's reddening bottom. He tried not to think too much about it whistled in the air as he swung it down over one cheek and then the other.

"One, Two." Mia counted off the strikes, her voice taking on a different tone. Each time she was hit now she did react, albeit only slightly, her spine a hard curve. He put a hand to her pussy again and she was still bone-dry. Strikes three, four and five didn't seem to make a difference either. When they were finished, Mia noted, "That's five for not being honest."

"Do you remember what these last five are for, Mia?"

She nodded. "For not thinking you were my Master."

"These last five are for me and will be given how I see fit."

Mia closed her eyes and squirmed a little. If she thought now was the time for the cane, she would be mistaken. Instead he touched her reddened backside with only his bare hand. He was a little surprised and a little awed by the heat of her skin. He caressed her bottom as he had touched her face earlier. He took his time. His touch extended up onto her back. The bench required her to hold her body in a slightly contorted position, and the muscles in her back looked tense. He kneaded the cords with his hands. Mia sighed. She may think that she wanted pain, but he knew better. He wondered when the last time someone had taken the time to see to her comfort. It was a priority for him.

Lightly and quickly he tapped her ass five times. She would remember his mercy and his caress. That's what would make him her Master. "That's it, pet. Punishment received."

Mia's eyes snapped open and she snapped her head feverishly. "No, that can't be it. I told you, I need to remember."

"Will you forget that I'm your Master?"

She shook her head. "No, that's not it. I need to remember how…Robert…" Shame blushed her features. She looked vulnerable. This was the real truth she was hiding from him.

He knelt beside her head and pushed back the hair that had fallen into her eyes. He needed to touch her, to have the connection. "What about Robert do you need to remember?"

A tear slipped down her cheek. "I need to remember that he hurt me."

Vincent stood. He wished that Robert was here now so that he could be the one to feel the cane. But he wasn't. It was just Vincent and his Sub. A Sub who was still very much broken by what that creep had done to her. "Did he use a cane on you?"

Mia nodded. "And other things." Vincent closed his eyes briefly. He didn't want to picture and he didn't want to know what these "other things" were. Hell, he wished he hadn't asked about the cane. Now he knew why Mia had asked. She didn't want emotional pain, just the physical pain to remind her that Robert was not what he appeared to be. She trusted him to give it to her. It was both humbling and very, very sad.

Vincent's hand gripped on the cane, an instrument of pure hell. It felt destructive in his hands. He lifted the cane above his head. His breath sped up, with one final moment of incisiveness. It vanished when she met his eyes, her mouth set hard. She nodded. This was what she needed. He swung.

He stopped himself before he made contact with skin. Mia's body still reacted as if struck.

She jumped slightly when the cane fell from his hand. He couldn't do this. He could never bring her true pain.

Mia was still bent over the spanking bench, but now she was sobbing. He was paralyzed only for an instant staring at the car crash scene he had created. He gathered Mia up in his arms and moved her from the bench to the leather couch. She weighed nothing, felt like nothing in his arms. Ashamed at the anger he had felt, he sat and held her against him while she cried. She had no fight in her now, only tears.

Minutes passed and her sobs slowed and then stopped. Then there was a long silence where he kept holding her. Finally she raised her head up and he could see her eyes. They were no longer blazing with anger, the tears had extinguished all her flames. "Thank you," she whispered. "That was exactly what I needed."

Her words broke Vincent's heart. He felt the full weight of what he had done, and how he had beat her. He loosened his grip on her when all he really wanted to do was hold her tighter, but he was desperate to know.

"How could you ever want to be with someone who hurt you like that?"

"He's not the only one who hurt me, Vincent."

"What?" Her words spun in his head. Who else had hurt her?

She nodded. "I've been realizing these past weeks, with your help, that it wasn't just Robert. I've allowed myself to be the training ground for dozens of sadists."

"Sadists?"

"Remember I'm the girl with no safe word. You're not the first man I've trained, Vincent. I've been here a long time."

He didn't know what to say, so he asked the question that had been on his mind for a while now. "How long? How old were you when you first became a Sub?"

"I was nineteen when the club opened." She looked away. Classic giveaway. She was avoiding the question.

"Is that the truth?"

She thought for a moment. "Yes."

"And how old were you when you first tried the lifestyle?"

"Nineteen." Didn't she know that he knew her well enough by now to tell when she was lying?

Vincent sighed. "Is that the truth?"

Busted, her tone turned angry. "Vincent, that's none of your business."

"How old were you, Mia?"

"Nineteen!" Lie. Lie. Lie.

"No."

"Sixteen. I was sixteen when my mother died. That same year I met James's father. He was the married man who taught me how to submit." Here was the truth. Mia's eyes focused on her hands in her lap. Vincent tried not to show all the shock that he felt. How could she have been so young?

"You were a child."

"No. I was old enough to know what I wanted. I was born a Sub. Don't hate me because you weren't."

He took a step back. "Mia, I don't hate you. I love you."

"I know you do. But I don't know if that's the right answer." She sighed. "I don't know what the right answer is."

"Me neither."

"I've always pretended to be this strong woman. I didn't even really let myself mourn when my mother died. I threw myself into my rebellion and thought I was such a progressive adventurous chick for trying BDSM. Don't get me wrong, the lifestyle is who I am now and I wouldn't change that for anything. But for a long time I tied sex to my self-worth. And then I began confusing sex with love."

"I'm not confused. I enjoy the sex, of course, but I do love you, Mia."

She shook her head sadly. "I have to be sure." He didn't know what to say. He didn't know if he was a strong enough man to love her, but he decided he wasn't giving up without a fight.

"Are you going back to Robert?"

"No." Was that a lie? Hard to tell. Maybe she didn't even know what the truth was. "Sometimes it's hard to remember that all those things happened to me. Sometimes it seems like it happened to another person and I'm just watching myself, removed from the scene."

"But it did happen."

She nodded. "Yes."

He couldn't say anything to make her pain go away, so he said nothing. The silence between them grew so that it filled the room. All he could hear was their breathing, the beating of their hearts, and something that sounded suspiciously like her phone vibrating in her purse. They both heard it at the same time.

Mia groaned. "He keeps calling and calling. I don't know what to do. He keeps asking me to meet up with him. He says he just wants to talk and try to explain."

Vincent growled. "Explain what?"

"I don't know."

Vincent saw in her eyes the truth. She didn't know. He saw a girl who was a little lost. One who had been running since she was sixteen and didn't know any better. One who believed that she couldn't trust love because love is what that creep—no, what that monster—had given her. Pain was love?

Needing the connection, Vincent returned to her side and took her hand in his. Her palm was so cold against his skin. Vincent would do anything in his power to protect the woman that he loved. He would talk to Rodriguez about Robert in the morning, but he had to do something immediately to keep her safe.

"Come home with me."

"I'm not really in the mood, Vincent."

"No, move in with me. You took care of me when I needed you, so let me take care of you."

"I don't know if that's a good idea. The last time I moved in with a man it didn't work out so well."

Vincent's voice was firm. "Mia, I'm not him."

"I know." She smiled. It was the truth and she believed it.

"He doesn't know my house, and I have a security system in case he tries something. I think it's the best solution for right now." He paused. "And besides all that, I want you with me."

She didn't say anything for a long time. He was afraid that she would say no. Instead, tears began to stream down her face. "Do you really love me?"

"Yes."

"Okay." Her voice was small. She was scared, but trying very hard to be brave.

"Okay what?"

"Okay, I'll go home with you."

"Thank you." He wrapped his arms around her and held her close. She hadn't said that she loved him back, but this was close enough for now.

"Do you want to do a scene with me tonight?"

"I don't know if I can." A scene now wouldn't just be a scene, it would be him acting out everything he felt with his heart.

She placed a quick kiss on his lips. "You helped me feel better, now let me make you feel better." She ran her hands down his body. Over his T-shirt and down his leathers. His leathers? Wait, he could have sworn that he had worn his favourite jeans. That had been his plan. Had he unknowingly reached for his comfort clothes but put on his leathers? Shit, the pants had probably been what had given him away earlier to the bartender at O'Malley's. Normal people didn't wear kink clothes in regular establishments. Had he really been so out of it that he had dressed in his Dom attire?

He must have, because now Mia unzipped those leathers and let them fall to the floor. He hadn't realized exactly how aroused he was until his cock, unfettered, bounced up toward his abdomen. She looked into his eyes for a split second before she bent at the waist and swallowed him to the root.

It felt so good to be inside her skilled mouth again. Hot and wet, with just the right amount of pressure. She swallowed him down to his balls and held him there inside her throat for an impossibly long time. Then she slowly slid back up his cock and down again. Her hand followed the path her mouth had made. Expertly, she knew exactly how to suck him. It was hot watching her lips devour him, and the position she was in let him see her ass move as her mouth bobbed up and down on his cock.

He wouldn't help himself. He reached out and spanked her. Not a timid little hit, but a full-force slap that probably stung her bottom as much as it stung his hand. Mia gasped but didn't move away and didn't stop sucking his cock. So he slapped her again, as hard as he could, because he wanted to and he knew she wanted it. Her sore ass grew pink and then red as he spanked her. The more aroused she became, the more that fine ass wiggled, taunting him for more punishment.

Suddenly he felt the familiar tingle in his balls that let him know he was close to orgasm. He pushed her down on her knees so he had better access to her mouth. Ruthlessly he thrust his cock into her willing face until he knew it was time. He pulled out of her mouth and stroked himself until he came with jagged breaths and hot spurts that covered her chest. He was spent but became impossibly aroused again as she watched the best part of him drip down across her tits. He couldn't take his eyes away as her hands found those drops. They rubbed his cum into her skin and then were brought up to her mouth for a taste. "Mmm, thank you," she commented as her bold tongue licked him off of her long fingers.

He smiled. She was so sexy. She was a successful doctor, she could have anyone she wanted and do anything she wanted. But instead she chose to be here, with him, giving him pleasure.

"No, thank you."

"You're welcome." Her voice was barely above a whisper. "Just like it's a Dom's job to know what his Sub wants and needs, it's a Sub's job to know what she can do to please her Dom."

"Well then, you're very good at your job."

"Thanks." She stood and took a towel from the cabinet. They both used it to clean off. Vincent had trouble standing. "Is it time to go home now?"

She smiled and he did too. She was so sweet. God, he was a goner for this girl.

"Absolutely."

From this vantage point he was up close and personal with her ass and the red marks he had left on her skin. "I'm sorry, Mia."

"It's okay," she said, meaning it. "It was just part of the lesson."

"I promise I'll never hurt you again."

She smiled. "I believe you."

He helped her dress. When he helped her slip on her sexy heels, he saw how red her ass and legs were. "I'm sorry, Mia."

"It's okay," she said, meaning it. "It's just part of the lesson."

Vincent nodded, agreeing, but still he felt ashamed of what he had done. Tonight was a night of many lessons, perhaps the most important ones that Mia had ever taught him. Anger had no place in their relationship. It wasn't who Vincent was, and even though it got her talking, it wasn't what Mia needed. He would find a way to make it up to her, he swore. As soon as they got home he would see to some much needed aftercare for her. "I promise I'll never hurt you again." Mia was his submissive. He would do everything in his power to ensure that Robert would never be her Master again.

Chapter Ten

He tried not to watch the clock or the door, nor the driveway through his front window. He did anyway, but he tried not to.

He smiled to himself. This felt right. Last night when they got home, he should have been kind and soothing with her. Instead they had gone straight to his bedroom and made love twice before she curled up in his arms, exhausted. They spent Sunday much the same way. When the alarm had gone off this morning they had made love again before they each left for work. He had felt so lucky and so happy that she was there in his arms when he woke up.

It was hard to remember why she was staying in his home. It wasn't just because he loved her, and it wasn't entirely because she wanted to be there. Mia was in danger. Catherine could be in danger too, but she wasn't his to protect any longer. Hopefully, by keeping her close to him, he could keep Mia safe.

He finished work a few hours before she did. He didn't feel like going for a run and getting all sweaty, so instead he sat on the couch and tried to watch the game. Usually he lost himself in the plays, but right now his brain was only focused on her arrival. He turned the TV off and picked up a book. When he realized that he had read the same page four times, he put it back down again. Nothing was going to distract him this close to Mia coming home to him for the first time.

Even Gus seemed anxious. He sat at Vincent's feet and demanded attention. They both contented themselves with mindless scratching and staring off into space.

Vincent had never lived with a woman in his adult life. Catherine had hinted at it for a while but in the end they had both decided they preferred the independence of living separate. Besides, Catherine wasn't the type of person that would make a good roommate.

He shook his head now, considering it. If Catherine hadn't left him, where would their relationship have gone? Probably nowhere. It was doomed to fail. He realized now that his heart had never really been in the relationship. In retrospect it was a miracle their relationship had held out as long as it did. He had fooled himself into thinking that he was happy. If she hadn't ended it, would he have just continued on, blind to their problems? He hoped not.

He tried to remember a time when he had been as excited to see Catherine as he was now to see Mia. Never. Although he would love to run into her now, to make sure she was okay, and then show her how he had changed in the past weeks. It would be nice to thank her, in a backhanded way, for being the catalyst that got him out of his old life. If she hadn't spoken up, he would never have met Mia.

He smiled. She would fucking hate Mia. Mia wasn't fake. She came from money but didn't need a thousand-dollar handbag to let everyone know. She wasn't pretending at BDSM. Mia was a real, flesh-and-blood submissive who lived and breathed the lifestyle in every aspect of her being. Mia had challenged him and opened his eyes. Mia was who he loved.

Damn, Vin, you got it bad.

A car door closed outside. Vincent and Gus both jumped to their feet. Vincent tried to calm himself, tried to look a little less like he was just sitting around waiting for her. It was impossible. Instead he decided to not be ashamed to let his true feelings show.

He opened the door with a huge grin. "Hi there."

"Hi." She smiled just as brightly. Her arms were loaded with paper bags. She did her best to balance them as she stumbled up his front path in her high heeled shoes.

"Do you need help?" He took the bags from her and placed them on the counter just inside the door. She looked relieved…and maybe a little nervous?

"Sure, if you wouldn't mind. There's a few more in the car." She went inside his home while he jogged down the driveway to her car. The trunk of her car was open, and packed with identical paper bags. He loaded up his arms and then noticed the small satchel with her clothes. He swung it on his back and successfully fumbled with the trunk to get it closed with his full hands.

Back in his kitchen he found her rummaging through cupboards trying to figure out where to put things away. She looked up and blushed when he placed his huge load of bags on the counter.

"I guess I bought a little too much."

"I do have some food here," he joked as he took a bag of quinoa from her.

"Yeah, but I just wanted to make sure there was enough." One entire grocery bag was just canned beans. "Looks like you got enough in case the entire membership of Club Perfect drops in for dinner." Vincent took the cans from her hands and lined them up in his cupboard. How could one person eat so many beans?

When she turned to hand him the next cans, he surprised her. Instead of emptying her hands, he swooped in and claimed her mouth with a kiss. It was tender and sweet. He could have lost himself in it if she hadn't pulled back.

"Vincent, just because I'm here, you don't have to…"

"I know."

Mia looked into his eyes, seeing the truth there. She relaxed a little and sighed. "I'm new to this."

"Me too."

She smiled. "I like that."

Mia went back to unloading more paper bags. "I noticed you brought more food than clothes."

"I'm not really a clothes girl."

"I noticed." She looked up and smiled at his double entendre. "Although my sister Jennifer would say there's no such thing."

"I think I'd like to meet your sister one day." She smiled. She looked so pretty and normal and just right in his kitchen. She wasn't Mia the Sub here. She was…just Mia.

"I think I'd like that too."

She paused before she opened the last bag. "I brought some other things with me, I hope you don't mind."

"Why would I mind?" She held open the bag and gave him a preview of the contents. "Geeze, Mia, what did you do, raid the dungeon?"

"Absolutely. I brought some things that are my favourites, and some that you seem to like." She took out the flogger that he had used last time they were at the club.

"So what do you want to do tonight?"

She brushed back a lock of dark hair that had fallen into her face. "Maybe we could make some popcorn and finally watch that kung fu movie you promised me? Or maybe we could take Gus for a walk?" She cocked her head to the side as she tried to think of other activities to suggest.

Maybe it was the truth, or maybe it was the added response of seeing her in his space, but he couldn't help the emotion he felt for her. With her hair pinned up and in her conservative work clothes, she looked like the most beautiful woman ever. He knew he should wait, give her some space to adjust and relax, but he couldn't help himself. If he was going to have her staying in his home then she deserved a proper welcome. Her last bag had inspired him in a big way. She could stand there and suggest options all night, but she had put an idea in his head that sounded the best to him right now.

In two long strides he crossed the kitchen to her. He led with his mouth and his lips touched her first. Mia, to her credit, this time didn't hesitate a single second. She saw him coming and stepped into his kiss as if expecting it. As if there was no better activity she could suggest than wrapping her arms around him and pulling him close to deepen the kiss.

His hands ran down her body, wanting to touch everywhere at once. He couldn't get enough. His fingers fumbled with buttons and zippers and her jacket fell to the floor, soon followed by her blouse. She panted against his lips as his palms cupped her breasts over her bra and rubbed against her nipples. She reached back and unclasped her bra while he licked her neck, her chest. Her skirt soon joined the puddle of clothes abandoned on the tile floor. When she bent down to take off her shoes, he stopped her. "Leave them on, pet."

"Yes, Master." She smiled. She liked this.

She stood there naked except for her heels. He admired the view for a short moment, but he was too hot to wait. "Take out my cock."

Her hands flew to his zipper and pulled it down. He groaned when her fingers located his dick and dragged it outside of his jeans. He groaned again when her long fingers slid down his thick shaft, and she rubbed the deep purple head against her palm. The sensation was incredible, but he wanted more. "Lick it."

His wish was her command as she dropped to her knees. Her tongue played over his length, leaving a sexy trail of saliva across him. She looked up at him as she parted her beautiful red lips to take the tip of his dick into her mouth. It was hot and wet inside her mouth. He stretched her lips as her tongue continued its flicker around his shaft. She slid down to deep throat him, and then surfaced again, using her hands to add to the sensation. He held back her hair and she increased the pace and the suction. He was so turned on watching her that he almost blew right then. She was so incredibly sexy on her knees. He made a mental note to thank her later for her service. "To bed, now, Sub."

Mia jumped to her knees and took off for the stairs. Vincent took the time to shuck his pants and shirt before joining her, running naked through his home.

She made it to the bedroom before him. "On your back," he ordered, and she gladly lay back against the white sheets and spread her legs, her feet dangling in the air as she held them up over her head. He dove onto the bed, his face meeting her pussy. She gasped as he took a long lick of her cream, and moaned when he did it again. Her face was so expressive. He reached up and grabbed one tit as he continued to lick. He could tell from her expression that she loved the sensation of his tongue on her sex. He indulged her for a few more swipes, but he couldn't hold off being inside her any longer.

He grabbed a condom from the bedside table and rolled it down himself. She was watching, so he made a little show of it. Continuing the performing, he rubbed his cock against her pussy, teasing the opening until her legs began to shake. "Do you want me inside you, pet?"

"Yes, Master, please," she begged.

As the words of her sweet submission left her lips, he plunged inside. He knew she could take it, so he wasn't slow or easy with her. He pushed inside until he was balls deep. And then stopped. Her hips gyrated against him, begging for more movement, more stimulation. He barely held off. He wanted to savour the feeling of her tight walls holding him. When he finally relented and began pulling out, her body tugged against his hard shaft, drawing him back in and making it irresistible not to push back in.

He captured her mouth with his, and swallowed up her sighs as he quickened the pace of his thrusts. The sounds of skin hitting against skin echoed in his room, and just heightened the experience. Breaking away he now captured her hard nipples with his teeth. She arched off the bed, enjoying the delicious mix of pleasure and pain.

He sat back and pulled out of her. She groaned in protest. "On your knees," he ordered, and she happily complied, bouncing easily onto all fours. Ready and in position, she wiggled her ass at him. He took the opportunity to give her a good smack. "Ready for more, pet?" He thrust hard inside her and any answer she may have been ready to give was lost from her lips. She started bucking on his cock and he held still, allowing her to set the pace. He admired the view of her ass thrusting back against him. He pulled a fistful of her hair so that her neck was pulled taut, and she faced the ceiling. She was so incredibly hot.

He smacked her cheeks again to let her know that he was the one in charge and not her. Immediately her hips stopped moving. In punishment for her trying to set the pace, he slowed down his strokes to a crawl.

"Please, please, please," she begged again and again.

Feeling generous, he picked up the pace. Soon he was pounding into her as hard and as fast as he could. He could feel his control slipping. He could also see the changes in her body. Her skin flushed, and she shivered as a thin line of sweat made its way down her back. She needed to come, bad.

He kept thrusting as he reached around and pinched her clit. "Oh Master," she yelled.

"Come now, Mia," he barked, although he hadn't needed to. As the words left his mouth, he could feel the squeeze of her muscles as she clamped down on him. She didn't need his command to come anymore. He tried to watch his beautiful Sub as she climaxed, but it was impossible as she milked his own release out of him. A few final thrusts and he was there, coming inside of her.

He panted as he climaxed, and held himself seated deep inside of her. For her credit, Mia remained still and let him enjoy the moment. Then, as his legs began to shake, he pulled out and collapsed on the bed.

She joined him, lying on her back and trying to catch her breath. The smile she wore was unmistakable, it was the smile belonging to a very satisfied woman.

"Welcome to my house."

"Thanks. I think I'll like it here." She giggled and he pulled her into a hug.

She snuggled closer and put her hand on his chest. It felt like a possessive move, but he couldn't be sure. But her small hand felt good there, red X tattoo on the wrist and all. He thought about all of her tattoos and how they seemed to be so much a part of her and yet, also a little out of place. She was a complete contradiction in terms.

His hand ran over her thigh, feeling the ink there. "When did you get this?"

"Right after my mom died. I paid the best artist I could find a lot of money to copy a photo of her." there was a melancholy sigh in her voice.

"That's your mom?" She turned her thigh to give him a better look at the artwork. The thigh tattoo was large, the style was classic 1970s, a cheeky pose you might see in the stag magazines of the era, but pretty tame compared to today's standards. The young blonde in the tattoo looked happy and healthy as if she had just come back from a night at the disco.

"Yeah. Mrs. Amber Braden Stoyanovsky."

"You don't look like her."

Mia nodded. "That's true. I always wished I did. Maybe that's why I got the tattoo. I found the photo among her private papers when we were dealing with the estate. I found a lot of things..." Her voice trailed off.

"Like what?"

"Like, she was headstrong and successful but liked giving up control." She stretched out her leg, admiring the tattoo now as well. "My mom belonged to a club too, when she was younger, way before she had me or my brother. Except it wasn't an organized club like ours is. It was more a collection of likeminded people, like James's father, that opened their homes to the lifestyle." She paused. "That's where she met my dad. He was her last Dom."

"Really? This was all in her papers?"

Mia shook her head. "Enough of it was. I pieced it together and confronted my father about it. Back then I couldn't imagine any of this being consensual, sort of like how you felt after you watched James's scene. My relationship with my Dad has always been a strained one, my fault really. I was difficult growing up. I acted out for attention. After my Mom passed, I was uncontrollable. I had no discipline, no drive. It took me months to go through her personal things that she had left me. Then I found her letters and her diary. I stayed up all night reading them. When I was finished I confronted my father with what I had learned of their lifestyle. Of course he told me that I didn't understand…and it's true, I didn't. I used the fight as an excuse to leave, get out on my own."

"And to try the lifestyle?"

"I guess. It didn't start out that way, but I had to know what it was like. Maybe it was even my way of getting close to her again. To walk a mile in her footsteps or whatever they say. Turns out I was a natural at it. I met some really great people, and some not-so-great people. Like everything there was both good and bad. Unfortunately there still weren't many safe places to go to practice BDSM. James had the idea to open a club of our own. Lee and I inherited quite a bit of insurance money when my mom passed. I saved half of my share for my schooling and the other half I gave to James so that he could make his dream of Club Perfect a reality." She paused. "Would you believe me if I told you that no one else knows that story? Usually I just make something up, or lie because it's easier than reliving the truth."

Vincent nodded. "I have my own kind of past with that type of thing. Secrets can be really harmful. We found out some stuff after my dad died too."

"Like what?"

"Like, that I have a younger brother."

Mia sat up in bed. "Really?"

"Yeah. I still don't know the whole story. We just found out that my dad had been sending money to a woman for years on the side to cover child support. We have a copy of my brother's birth certificate and an old address, but that's it. Jennifer was hurt the most by it. She lived her life thinking she was the baby and the apple of my dad's eye. Since we found out, she's been searching for our brother, mostly online, but hasn't found anything yet. I don't know how much I really want to find him though. Putting a face to the name will mean that it's really true and that my dad really wasn't the great guy we thought he was." He shrugged. "It feels almost like a soap opera, like something that would happen to other people. My mom was heartbroken, but I think in some ways maybe it was a blessing in disguise. Her anger allowed her to move on after my dad's heart attack and find someone else. It just didn't fit with the type of man I knew. He was so loving with us, but didn't even care to know this other child. I just can't imagine ever doing any of this to my family."

"I know what you mean. I wish you and your sister luck. I'm still trying to process everything I learned about my mom and it's been years." She scratched absentmindedly at the red X tattoo on her wrist. It was not as artfully done as her other tattoo. In fact, the X almost looked vulgar, crude, and almost painful. A contradiction on her beautiful smooth skin.

"When did you get the others?"

She looked down at the tattoo now, made redder by her scratching. "Last year. Shortly after I was freed. James has the same one." Mia held out her wrists for Vincent to see. Each X covered a scar. The kind that were made after being chained to a bed for months.

Vincent took her hands in his as he had done many times before, but for once perhaps understood her drive and need for connection. She didn't have to say anything else, he knew she had been incredibly candid with him. Perhaps he was one of the few to ever see her this vulnerable. He placed his lips against her wrist, and gently placed a kiss on her tattoo.

"Thanks for bringing me here into your home."

"Thanks for trusting me enough to come."

She nodded. "It's been a while since I let myself trust anyone this much. It's a little scary."

"I know." He grabbed her around the waist and pulled her to him, spooning in his bed in the middle of the afternoon. He kissed her softly on the cheek and closed his eyes.

She was right. Trusting someone this much was hard. It was scary allowing yourself to be this vulnerable and risking everything was not something he had ever done before. Sure, Catherine had given him a massive kick to the balls of his ego, but she had never really had his heart. And Mia clearly owned his heart now, and had his full attention.

He knew he should probably be out putting up posters or canvassing the neighbourhood for any sign of Catherine. He should, but he couldn't. It almost felt wrong to be thinking of her at all. She was the other woman in their new relationship. The woman who had motivated him to talk to James, go to the club and train, who was beginning to feel like less of a priority and more like a stepping stone to this moment and to the future.

She may be lost, but Mia was here with him and safe. He would do everything in his power to keep her safe and by his side always.

Much later on, they sat at his table eating a delicious salad that Mia had worked her magic on. They also had some fresh bread she had brought and some weird kind of non-cheese that tasted pretty good. And they each had a tall glass of sparkling water. His usual meal came in a cardboard box, or a takeout bag. This was a nice change.

Gus whined at his feet for a little attention. Mia patted his head and snuck him a few bites of bread. "Keep that up and you'll be his favourite in no time."

"Is that so? The way to his heart is through his stomach?"

"Something like that." Vincent finished his salad and pushed the plate away. What was the way to her heart? Would she ever share it with him? "Can I ask you something?"

"Sure."

"Was it hard to train me?"

Mia smiled. "A little. You can be a little dense at times," she joked.

"Thanks. No, I meant was it hard to get back into training?"

She took a forkful of salad and chewed it as she thought about his question. "Yes and no, I guess. I did this for a lot of years so it's what I know. I'm more comfortable naked in my dungeon than in front of a boardroom of directors at my clinic. The hardest part was always trust."

"Why did you trust me?"

"Because James trusts you, and that was enough."

"I've known James for years and yet I don't think I really knew him until a few weeks ago."

Mia nodded. "That sounds like James. He has many secrets so he doesn't let anyone get close to him. An odd trait for a narcissist. Why did you go to him for help about your problem?"

"Because he knew Catherine, although he never liked her. And because subconsciously I guess I sorta knew he was into the lifestyle. Not overtly, of course. Just from certain things. I would never have imagined that his club *was* the scene. He's just always so put together, so in charge of himself."

Mia nodded. "Value his friendship. He doesn't give it out lightly. But it's been my experience that he could be the best friend you ever had if you let him. I owe him everything. I owe him my life."

"Do you sometimes wish that James hadn't found you and helped you get away from Robert?"

"I did for a while. I think that's just the Stockholm syndrome speaking. Living with him wasn't always horrific, though. Sometimes I miss the early days of our relationship when he treated me like I was the only one in the world. He was my first official Master."

"And who is your Master now?"

She rolled her eyes. "You. But it's different now. He was my first."

"A girl never forgets her first?" Vincent teased gently.

"Something like that."

"I can't say that I understand how you felt, but I do understand that sometimes it's hard to let go and move on. Even when you know you have to."

"Thus the training?"

"Yeah." Vincent pushed his plate away and sat back in his chair. "Pretty dumb, huh?"

Mia shrugged. "We all react differently when we're hurt. I'm just glad your pain eventually brought you to me."

Vincent smiled. "Me too."

Mia pushed away her plate too. "You know, I was thinking, I have some vacation time owing to me. Why don't I take the rest of the week off? Then we can just relax and hang out."

Vincent frowned. "I don't know if I can get the time off right now."

"That's okay, I don't kind. I'll have Gus here to keep me company." Mia leaned toward him. "And I'll have all day to think up things to train you on."

"Deal!"

Mia laughed. "I'll just let my assistant know so she can rebook my patients." She left the table to retrieve her purse, her cell phone inside. She quickly dialed the number for the clinic she worked at and left a brief message. When she was done, she scrolled through her missed calls. "Did you say that you called me last week?"

"Yup." Vincent picked up their plates and placed them in the sink. "I called from the police station."

"Why?"

Vincent nodded. "I was there with friends of Catherine's. They're worried about her and wanted to file a missing person's report." Vincent shrugged. "I want to believe that she just fell off the radar for a while and everything is fine, but…"

"No, you did the right thing. If you think there's even a chance that something could have happened to her then you should report it.

And you should talk to James about it. He's got connections that can look into it as well."

"He knows, but I'll check in with him again and see if he's found anything out."

"Good." Mia yawned.

"Ready for bed?" Vincent smiled. It was obvious that sleeping wasn't on his mind. Mia still felt a little uneasy, but being close to Vincent would help.

Mia let her smile match his. "Absolutely."

Both of their smiles vanished as the cell phone in Mia's hand began to vibrate, indicating that she was receiving a call. She dropped it on the table as if it was too hot to touch. Together they watched the vibration make it dance across the wood.

"Shouldn't you get that?"

"No, it's fine." A lie.

Vincent's eyes landed on her cell phone. Who was the asshole who was interrupting their nice evening together? The screen lit up as the caller tried to ring through again. With the first ring, the name saved in her contact list lit up the screen. "Master."

Vincent grabbed the phone in fury.

"No, Vincent, just leave it!"

Vincent punched the button to connect the call and put it on speaker phone. "Mia?" Robert asked from the other end of the line.

"Wrong." Vincent smirked. "Leave her alone."

"Never." Robert's one word answer was chilling.

Vincent wasn't scared of the creep. "Listen now and listen well, because you won't have a chance to call this cell phone again before she changes her number. Your time with Mia is over. You are no longer her Master. Leave her alone, or I will find you and I'll…"

"You'll what? Call Mark the cop? Call rich kid James? Yeah, I know them all. I was once the Baby Dom like you, welcomed to the family with open arms. Before you I was the one who trained on

Mia's body, and she molded me into her perfect Dominant. She made me this way, buddy, she'll do the same to you."

The line clicked as Robert hung up.

Vincent's hands shook as he turned off the phone and placed it on the table. Adrenaline made his heart pound, and his head spun with all of the things he wished he had been able to say to the creep.

"Thank you," Mia said quietly as she stepped toward him and wrapped her arms around him.

"I'll pick up a new cell phone for you in the morning and we'll have this one disconnected."

"We'll do this?"

Vincent nodded. "Absolutely. No hiding anything anymore, for either of us. I should have told you earlier that I was concerned about Catherine, and you should have let me talk to Robert when his calls first started. If we're going to be together you have to trust me to protect you and to not leave you just because some guy from your past thinks he still owns you."

Mia nodded. "Okay. But he's not *just* some guy from the past."

"He is to me." He gently kissed her.

"Let's go to bed."

His arms were slow to release her, but he accepted her invitation gladly. She was still shaking. It worried him how much the creep's call had affected her.

For now they would try to go to bed and try to block out the toxic words Robert had spewed. Did the creep love Mia as much as Vincent did? Was it love that eventually drove him to such extreme lengths in order to try to keep her? Would Vincent one day do the same?

The troubling thoughts clouded every step he took. Mia seemed to understand, at least a little, and gave him some space. On separate sides of his bedroom, they both quickly undressed. They slipped under the covers wordlessly, as if this was something they had done millions of times before. Once settled, he lay on his back. A naked

Mia curled into his arms and laid her head on his chest. She closed her eyes, but like him, knew that sleep was a long way off.

"He was wrong," she whispered in the darkness.

"I know," Vincent answered, and hugged her a little closer to him.

"No, not about him being my Master. Of course he's not." Mia took a deep breath. "I mean, he said that I molded him into my perfect Dom, but I didn't really mold him at all. He came to me with experience. I think it's the other way around and he molded me into his perfect Sub."

Vincent kissed the top of her head. He hated to think about what tactics Robert had used to mold her. "Don't worry about anything he said, I'm not. He can't scare me with a few phone calls."

"I think I'm falling in love with you," she whispered, so low he barely heard her.

"I think so too," he whispered back. There were no further whispers and Vincent tried to fool himself into thinking it was because she had finally been able to fall asleep.

Chapter Eleven

James looked up from his laptop. Vincent flopped into one of the two white leather chairs opposite his friend's long wooden desk and yawned. Although James was concentrating on something on his laptop, he didn't appear overly busy. He closed the browser window before Vincent could see what had held his interest. Knowing what he knew now about James, he could have been looking at just about anything.

Everything in this office was utilitarian and had been in position longer than James had been. Anyone else would have photos, framed awards, knickknacks, maybe a plant. Not James. There was not a single personal effect in this office. He knew James enough now to know that it wasn't an oversight. There was nothing of James here, because this wasn't the real James. Why did James do double duty, working at both the warehouse and at the club? Was this just a front to legitimize him somehow? Make him feel normal?

Vincent had rarely been in his friend's office before. He'd rather be at home right now instead of asking his friend's advice. It had been a long week and he hadn't slept well. One reason was because…well, it was very nice having his hot sexy teacher stay in his home. The other reason was because, even days later, that creep's words kept repeating in his head. He needed to get James's take on it and try to figure out a way to keep that creep away from Mia. Once she had changed her cell number the calls had stopped. Although that didn't necessarily mean that Robert had stopped trying to contact her.

The emerging Dom in him wanted to take Mia away somewhere isolated and keep her hidden and safe always. Unfortunately that wasn't practical. At this point he didn't even know if that was an exaggeration. Was there a real danger out there? Just because Catherine had gone missing didn't mean that she was kidnapped. If he was honest with himself, what scared the shit out of Vincent was that Mia had gone to Robert willingly last time. What if she chose to go back to him again? What if he charmed her just enough that she decided to walk out of Vincent's house and his life forever? Would she choose Robert's experience and their history together over what Vincent was building with her?

That's why he was here. James knew Mia better than anyone. He also had experience with this creep. "I need your help." He had said the same things to his friend weeks ago. The request then was motivated by a different girl and for a different problem. Funny how fast things had changed.

"Does my secretary just let everyone in here these days?" James's lips curled up in a mock sneer, clearly joking.

"Your secretary is practically ninety years old. My grandmother could get by her," Vincent joked back. His brain was overworked with serious thoughts, and it felt good to just kid around a bit.

"She's retiring in a few weeks." James grimaced. Arlene had been his assistant since the great Catherine exodus a few years back.

"Good for her."

James nodded. "But it does create a problem for me. I need a secretary that I can trust." He leaned back in his leather chair. "What's up, Vin? You look like shit. Did Mia keep you up too late last night?"

"Something like that." Vincent took a deep breath. Time to lay it on the line. "I'm worried about that prick Robert."

James frowned. "Mia told me about how he crashed her Dad's party. I can't believe the balls on that asshole."

Vincent nodded. "I agree, but there's more. He's been calling and texting her."

"Shit." James's hand kneaded his now-furrowed brow. "He is the most manipulative person I've ever met. If he's contacting her than he wants something."

"Yeah, her."

James leaned back in his chair and considered that. "I don't think so. He could have had her back if he wanted her. She was so messed up that she would have gone back to him if her friends and family hadn't stepped up to keep her safe."

"That's what I'm afraid of. Would she go back to him now?"

"No, absolutely not. She's done a lot of work on this. She's not the same person she used to be." His voice was sad, but his wild eyes were a contradiction. Probably coloured by memories he wished he didn't recall. Vincent understood now. It was one thing to call James a hero and vaguely speak about how he had saved her. The reality was probably far too terrible to imagine.

"It must have been hell finding her that way."

James closed his eyes for a minute before speaking. "It was bad. Mia had always been this wild child, free spirit. She and I had been in all kinds of crazy situations before, but nothing like that. Finding her that way was a nightmare. It was sick and depraved and…" His voice trailed off as he tried to keep his anger in check.

"I had waited days to get into that cabin. I didn't even know she was there, but I had a hunch. Like you guys with Catherine, I filled a missing person's report. That's how I met Mark. He was more connected than I was at that time. The police couldn't investigate because there were no signs that Mia was being held against her will. The police couldn't do anything because she had voluntarily gone with Robert. They couldn't even search the cabin because they didn't know if they were even there. But I had a hunch. I knew in my gut that she was in trouble and that this is where he had her. Mark put his job on the line by giving me the address of a place Robert had bought. I went and I waited for the opportunity to go in. It killed me to wait as long as I did, but I couldn't afford to risk spooking him. Who knew what he would do to her if he knew I was there.

"When he left the cabin, I went in. I had enough time to plan it out, but once inside I knew my plan was for shit. I should have taken the time to get some proper tools to free her with, but I didn't know…" His voice broke as he relived what was probably one of the worst moments of his life. Vincent had never seen his friend any less than calm and controlled. This was James stripped to the real, raw emotion. Vincent could hardly believe he had once accused his friend of being a monster. Clearly James had seen the work of a true monster firsthand.

"Her family told me that I was a hero, but I don't feel like I was very heroic. When I found her—when I realized it was her, Mia, chained to that bed—I froze. I know that I was in shock, but to me it feels like weakness. It I had eaten anything that day I would have thrown it up. That's how bad she was. I didn't even know if she was alive at first. Her eyes were open but she wasn't there. I don't know if she was in subspace or some different headspace that allowed her to keep sane while she was tortured. She was so thin I could see her ribs. And I saw her breathing. I had wasted so much time trying to get in safely and then wasted even more time frozen in shock. I needed to get her out of there. When I was trying to loosen the chains she snapped out of it. And she fought me with what little energy she had left." He shook his head. "But I did it. I got her out. She refused to let me take her to the hospital, so I took her home and helped her get better. It was a long process. She didn't have any contact with him after that at all. At first she waited for him to come, to want her back, but he never came."

"Until now."

"That's right. It would have been easier to lure her back to being his Sub then. Now she's in recovery and has moved on."

Vincent nodded and thought about that for a moment. "So why does he want her now? What's changed?"

"Who knows. I think the best thing to do is to wait and see if he plays his card. Until then we have to watch her and protect her. If he did those things to her when she was his Sub, who knows what he would do to her now that she's not."

The realm of possibilities that streamed through Vincent's mind were all incredibly bleak. If he was contacting Mia now there was a reason for it. Every possibility was equally terrifying. "She's at my place now. She's taking some time off of work and is just lying low."

James smiled. "That's a good idea." The less-than-calm James of a moment ago who had relived his private hell as he told James the story was gone. Regular Dom James was back in control of himself. He sat back in his chair, looking very relieved but also a little like the cat that had eaten the canary. "I knew you two would work out well together."

Vincent laughed. "So now you're trying to get me to believe that you we're playing matchmaker all along? I don't buy it, buddy. I was the one who came to you with my problem, not the other way around, remember?"

"You just gave me the opportunity to put my plan in motion." James shrugged.

"Whatever. I still don't believe it."

"It's true. I knew both of you and I knew that you would be perfect for each other. You just needed the opportunity to meet and fall in love."

Vincent didn't know what surprised him more, the vulnerability that James had shown before or this James who talked about love. Neither were a fit for the guy he knew. He just tried to chalk it up to being one more thing he was learning about his friend.

"I never would have suspected that you believed in love."

James shrugged. "At the end of the day that's what everyone wants, isn't it?"

"So what about you, where's your Sub to settle down with?"

James shook his head. "Vin, love for me is found in the time between when a scene starts with a promise, and when that scene ends with an orgasm and true submission. That's my high. I can't imagine anything better than that. That's it for me."

Vincent nodded, unconvinced. "Do you always lie to yourself like this?"

James shrugged. "It's worked so far." He opened a drawer in his desk and removed a folder. "Since you're here, I have some information for you, on your other little problem." James took several pages out of the folder and placed them on the desk. Vincent sat up closer to take a look. It wasn't much. A few grainy photos, surveillance of Catherine's apartment, a copy of the missing person report they had filed. None of it held any real information on Catherine or where she could be. Looking at each was a little frustrating. "Looks like Catherine bought a plane ticket to London the same day she disappeared." James handed him the last piece of paper. It was a boarding pass with her name on it. The document was for a direct flight from Pearson to Heathrow, and was purchased two days after her night of drinking out with the girls. This must be why she hadn't been seen, she had gone back home to England.

Vincent breathed a sigh of relief. "That's great. So I guess she just went home to visit her parents. Have you told Allison and Eve yet?"

"No I haven't, because she didn't get on this flight."

"What?"

"Security cameras caught her entering the airport and then later leaving with a man."

A terrible thought popped into Vincent's head. "Was it Robert?"

"No. Here's the photo we pulled off of the cameras." James slapped it down on the desk and it was clear. The guy in the photo looked nothing like creepy Robert. "See, it's a big guy, sort of about your size. If I didn't know you were here mooning over Mia I would have some tough questions for you." He paused. "It's a good thing Mark knows you just as well and was able to divert suspicion."

"Thank God. So if it's not me she left the airport with, who was it?"

James shrugged. "I can't give you a name yet but I know that the plane ticket was the last purchase she made."

"That's a little surprising."

James nodded. He knew about Catherine's shopping obsession as much as he did. It was one of the many reasons she was fired from her job here. James had spotted her returning late from her break, arms full of shopping bags. To her, lunch break meant a perfect opportunity to warm up her credit cards. Who needs to eat anyways?

"What about her apartment?"

"Messy, but looks pretty much untouched. She packed a lot of things for her trip and took them with her. Nothing of value was missing."

Everything was so odd. Catherine liked to party but she always said that no matter what she would end up at her apartment as a home base. Those four walls were the only things that had been constant in her life. She loved that apartment more than anything, probably even shopping, and definitely more than she had ever loved him.

"I've given a copy of this to Mark and he'll put it in her file."

"Why am I not surprised that you have better sources than the police?"

James grinned. "Sometimes it pays to have someone owe you a favour."

"I bet it does." Vincent didn't want to think too deeply on James's comment, considering he now owed James not one, but two favours. "What does your gut say?"

"She's not in danger. She probably just doesn't want to be found. Personally, I'd drop it if I were you. She'll come up for air soon."

"Okay." Vincent stood. Their need to talk was over and so was his break. "So do you have someone in mind to be your new secretary?"

James opened up his laptop again and tapped a few keys to wake it up. "Why, do you want the job?"

"No way, and especially not when a certain brunette named Eve is better suited for the job."

James's face flushed red. "Get out of here, Vin," he bellowed.

Vincent smiled. Two could play at this matchmaking game.

"Hey, thanks for helping me with Catherine."

"No problem. Thanks for helping me with Mia, her happiness means a lot to me. And Vin? In all seriousness, if I see that asshole again, he better be ready, because if he makes one move toward Mia, this time I won't just walk away."

Vincent nodded. "You and me both, buddy."

"Good man."

Chapter Twelve

The minute his keys slipped into the lock, the barking started. Vincent groaned. Gus sure was loud. He hoped that in the past week Mia had gotten used to that part of living with a dog. Gus had sure gotten used to having her around. He now preferred to sit beside her on the couch at night, and was content to silently follow her throughout the house as she went about her day-to-day life. Maybe other dog owners would be jealous of their pet taking so well to a new roommate. Instead of it making him jealous, it made Vincent happy. He liked how well she fit into both his and Gus's life. Besides if Gus was always by her side, then she had one level of added protection in case Robert tried something.

Vincent pushed open his front door with a smile and a lighthearted feeling that was new to him. He had always loved Fridays, but now Fridays meant that he would have two full days to spend with Mia.

Stepping into his kitchen, he saw that not only was his favourite four-legged friend Gus the barker waiting for him, his favourite two-legged friend was waiting there too.

"Welcome home."

"Hi there." Vincent wrapped his arms around her and accepted a welcome-home kiss. He could sure get used to having someone around besides his dog that was glad to see him home after a long day at the warehouse.

"How was work?"

"Fine." He gave her another kiss. When he tried to deepen it, Mia pulled away laughing. Vincent pouted, he had nothing better to do with his evening than kiss his beautiful girl.

She gave him a sexy smile. Tonight Mia wore her hair down and had on a comfortable pair of yellow shorts. It seemed out of character for her to be so casual, but he liked it. She was letting her guard down a little, and making herself at home. Which was exactly what he wanted her to do. His home was her home.

Wait, was she wearing his shirt? Yup, looked like she had taken this sharing thing to heart and helped herself to his clothes. The top was big on her but it still looked great.

"Nice shirt."

"I thought so."

"I think it looks better on you than me."

"Is that so?" She leaned back on the counter. Her shorts were very short and showed her long legs off well. His hands were drawn to the exposed skin and before he realized it, his palms were rubbing up her thighs.

"You look hungry, Master." There was no mistaking the innuendo of what it was she was offering to him to devour.

"I am very hungry, pet."

Vincent kissed her lips and tasted her mouth again. This time she didn't pull back when he deepened their kiss.

Something had changed since her late-night confession. She didn't seem to be just learning how to love him, she was actually doing it. Although she didn't say it again, it was there. She was beginning to trust that feeling more and more each day and show him how she felt. It was in the little things. It was in the shy looks she gave him, the way she cuddled into him on the couch at night, and it was in her touch. Their connection was stronger now than ever. The electricity hadn't faded. In fact, it had just grown more intense. He wasn't sure where the lessons began or where they stopped, but he kept in mind the fundamentals—trust, response, pleasure.

"I want you."

"Where?" The question was barely a breath upon her lips.

Vincent looked around the kitchen. Luckily she hadn't set them a place for dinner yet. "The table."

Without hesitation she walked the few steps to the kitchen table and bend over onto the strong oak tabletop. She looked so beautiful and so submissive, perched there, waiting for him. She kept her head down, and did not look for him. She simply trusted that he would be there soon to pleasure her.

The sunlight streaming through the window made her look impossibly more beautiful. Although she was for all purposes, still fully clothed, she was the sexiest he had ever seen her. Perhaps because now she was here in his home, and now she was his.

He moved behind her and ran a hand over her ass. The shorts she wore were taut against her sex. As he moved his hand lower he could feel her wetness through the fabric. "Use me, Master," she pleaded. He nodded. He already loved her but he needed to get inside her. He peeled the shorts down and pushed them to her thighs. The framed her perfectly, from the bud of her ass to her pretty little clit. He knew by how wet she was that if he put his finger there, touched that small little button and said the right command, that she would come undone.

Instead he just admired her. She let him look his fill and didn't turn to look at him or rush him. She was the perfect little Sub. After minutes, he didn't know how many, his hands found his zipper and then his jeans found the floor. His cock was high and hard and seeking her heat. He barely had to guide it into her, by now it knew exactly where to find her centre.

The first push into her folds was nothing like before. When he was fully seated inside of her against her cervix, he stopped moving. He could barely hear her heated breathing over his own harsh breaths. Again she did not move, she let him take control and set the pace of their lovemaking. When he couldn't stand it anymore, he began to rock his cock hard inside of her. He started with long, slow strokes so that she could feel the length of him and know his total dominance of her body. He fucked her so slow that he could feel every inch of her as well. He took his time and memorized every feeling. Then when he couldn't stand it anymore, he sped up his strokes. She held onto the far edge of the table to steady herself so that she could take everything he gave her. As he approached climax, he realized that this was exactly where he belonged, inside her, and that he wouldn't be able to continue to live without having her this way every single day for the rest of his life. At this revelation, he felt his balls draw up. Now his hand reached for her little button and roughly stroked it. She was getting close. He stroked her clit one last time and she came undone.

"Vincent!" she screamed as she came without being told. The act was so primal and so sexy. His chest heaved as he found his own release.

They stayed joined this way, he leaning over her, her leaning over the table, until they both caught their breath.

Then he gathered Mia up in his arms, not bothering to stop and pull up her shorts. He walked to his oversized chair and sat down with her in his lap. She felt like nothing and yet everything in his arms. He closed his eyes and breathed in the scent of her, knowing that finally she had surrendered to him and given him everything she had. Being a Dom didn't mean big scenes or fancy punishments. It was this, a beautiful Sub offering up her body and herself to please him, no questions asked.

Minutes passed and they said nothing. Finally she raised her head up and he could see her eyes. They were vulnerable and beautiful and truly Mia.

"I love you," he said to her for the second time and her smile grew.

It was true that you never really knew someone until you lived with them. Having Mia with him every single day changed something between them. They had an ease together, a comfort that he hadn't expected. He was surprised how sentimental she was and how that played out in little things. He loved the little candid moments between them. Even after she had decided to take time off work, she didn't sleep in. She got up when he did so that they could shower together. Then they ate breakfast together. Then she would insist that he continue getting ready while she made his lunch. Every day was something different, healthy and delightful. He'd eat it later at work and think about how much she cared about him.

Last night James had invited them over to his place, but they had decided to stay home instead. They ended up finally watching the kung fu movie he had promised her. They snuggled on the couch and ate popcorn, and then they argued over the ending of the movie. They seemed like a perfectly normal couple. Although later, he had spanked her for being a brat and she loved it. Maybe that part wasn't perfectly normal, but it was normal for them.

Now he held her in his lap. The excitement and adrenaline dissipated after their lovemaking. Her eyes were closed and her breathing regular. She looked like she was close to sleep. He would have loved to continue to hold her and let her rest. Unfortunately he wanted to show her something that she would miss if he let her sleep through the evening.

"Mia?"

His girl slowly opened one eye and squinted at him. "What?"

He laughed softly. "Do you want to go to the night market?"

"The what?" Mia sat up and rubbed her eyes.

"The night market. There's a little neighbourhood a few blocks from here that has a farmer's market Friday nights during the summer."

"Wait, do you think it's safe for us to go out?"

"Why wouldn't it be?" He took her hands in his own. "Look, you can't live your life locked inside the house. That's what he wanted, remember, and you fought your way out and to have a life."

She chewed on the corner of her lip. "Does the market have a good produce section?"

"The best. It's at the end of the street all by itself. You'll love it."

"Okay." She smiled, her excitement returned.

They walked the streets, holding hands. They both wore grins that said they didn't have a care in the world. Mia stopped every ten feet or so to look at something, a booth, a tree, a building.

She had changed into a sun dress. The light material flowed as she walked and was coloured in shades of light pastels. He had on his favourite pair of jeans and the shirt she had worn earlier. If she wasn't going to wear it, he would make good use of it. Besides it smelled like her now. When he had slipped it over his head it was still warm from her body.

It was an hour or so away from sunset. Cars passed blasting the songs of summer. If she recognized the song, Mia would sing along and laugh. Her happiness was infectious and he was sure that he had never been so happy in his entire life.

This sweet outgoing Mia made friends with many people they happened upon. A man selling street art was happy to talk about his work with her. A woman selling jewelry showered her with compliments as she tried on bracelet after bracelet, finally finding one with little roses stamped into the metal.

Next Mia pulled him into an adult shop that was slightly off the strip. Although she had spent many hours in places filled with every device known to man, she seemed titillated to be there with him. He supposed it was different stocking a dungeon than it was picking out select instruments of pleasure with the person you intended to use them with. They left with a small black bag filled with toys and promises.

Their walk through the market took them all over the neighbourhood. When they reached the produce area of the market, Mia grabbed his hand, excited.

"I bet they have a ton of local organic produce there, let's go and I can get something for us for dinner."

Mia was enamored with each booth. She stopped at each one and chatted with the seller. She got especially excited if the seller just happened to be the farmer too. Then she'd pepper him with all sorts of questions, from questions about the seeds and GMOs, to harvesting. It was nice to see her so happy and so passionate.

Vincent was more than happy to step back and just let Mia go. It was remarkable to him that this creature had only been in his life a few short weeks. Instead of looking at his coming final exam as a deadline, he saw it as a transition to the next step of their relationship. Mia said that she stayed with her trainees until they found a Sub, and clearly this trainee had found his Sub in his teacher. He thanked James. The man had given him friendship, a job, a door into the lifestyle, and the best gift yet, a beautiful girl to love.

Mia didn't know it yet, but he fully intended to turn their temporarily living arrangement into a permanent one. He loved his little house that he had renovated with his bare hands, but he would gladly give it up if she preferred to live at her house. It didn't seem so bad. It had a good architecture, for sure. Curb appeal was always a plus. As long as it had Mia, a good TV and a yard for Gus to run around in he'd be happy.

His sister would love her. Well first she'd probably do that whole "stake my claim, protect my territory" thing but when the dust cleared he knew that they would be good friends. He groaned internally. Oh man, he bet that when those two teamed up, there was going to be trouble.

His mom would probably be a little harder to convince. She was protective of her firstborn and only son. It had been a battle to be allowed to move out here in the first place. His mom would come to love Mia too, in time, and accept that Mia was now the main woman in his life.

He would have to suggest a trip out west soon to see them. He had about a dozen places in mind that he'd like to show Mia, from his parents' house to his grandparents' old place to his high school. Maybe he could even convince her into a little hanky-panky under the football field bleachers.

Vincent laughed to himself. He was making so many plans for the future. He didn't think he had ever felt so good and so right about life. That was Mia's doing. He was right before, she had changed him for the better. She had not only made him into a dominant, she had made him into the man he wanted to be.

Mia smiled at him as she moved onto the next vendor. This vendor was selling something called kale and it looked to Vincent that there were about a thousand different varieties. Mia and the salesman *oohed* and *aahed* over each bundle as if it were gold.

Vincent distracted himself by looking at the many different street performers set up along the side of the market.

"Do you mind if I just go over to the performers for a bit?" he asked.

"Sure, I'll be a little while here." She gave him a quick kiss and then waved him away before going back to her kale study.

Hands in his pockets, he strolled on toward the main grouping of buskers. The performers gathered to entertain and earn some change from the audience. It was a tradition at the market that culminated in a grand festival at the end of the summer. Vincent made a mental note to take Mia to that as well.

As Mia was still fully engaged with the produce vendor, he moved onto watch the next performer. As he moved closer, he spotted a small café just off a side street. At first he couldn't understand why the café's small patio had caught his attention. Then his brain registered the glimpse of red hair he had seen.

It wasn't just any redhead on that patio, it was Catherine!

Chapter Thirteen

"You know, a lot of people are worried about you."

Catherine looked up from the menu. "Vincent?" she asked, apparently just as surprised to see him as he was to see her.

"Where the fuck have you been?"

The force of his words disturbed her. She frowned and put down her menu. "Vincent, is that how you hello now?"

"Can you give Eve and Allison a call please?" Catherine's frown deepened. "They're worried about you."

"Really?" Her hazel eyes grew wide as saucers with her surprise. "I knew I fell off radar for a while but I never expected…" She shook her head, seemly understanding the amount of worry she caused her best friends. "I'm sorry," she whispered, her soft English accent becoming more pronounced by the shame in her voice.

"Don't apologize to me, apologize to them."

"I will, but I do think I owe you an apology too." Catherine motioned for him to sit down at the table. "Can we talk for a minute?"

"No, I can't, I'm here with someone and I should get back…"

"Vin, please. It's me. Just please sit down with me for a minute." Her eyes pleaded with him.

He couldn't see her, but he was sure Mia was still busy sorting through produce so a minute spent with Catherine should be okay. He pulled out the chair at the table opposite his ex-girlfriend and sat down.

"How have you been, Vincent?" She smiled now for him and he could remember the girl he had thought he loved…wait, how many days ago had it been since she had dumped him? Before he met Mia he counted every bit of time that had passed since she had ended it. Days, minutes, hours. He had held onto all of them in his misery. Now he didn't have a clue how long it had been. It felt like a long time had passed, instead of five or six weeks.

"Fine." Vincent frowned. He wanted to get back to Mia and not sit here and make chitchat.

"Come on, Vin. I appreciate this new tough guy act, but you can at least be civil to me."

"You asked how I was, I said I was fine. Now can you tell me where you were this whole time?"

Catherine took a sip of her water. "Right to the point, eh? This Dom training must be working."

Vincent was stunned. "How do you know about that?"

"I know a lot, Vincent. Probably more than you want me to know. I saw you that night when I was at O'Malley's. I had gone there in hopes of scoring an invite into the secret ultra-exclusive BDSM club next door. Imagine my surprise when I saw you and jerky James go walking in dressed like a couple of leather twins."

Vincent's mouth went dry. He had gone into the club with James hoping to become a Dom and surprise Catherine, but now the tables were turned and she was surprising him.

"You saw us?"

"Yeah. Is James training to be a Dom too?"

Vincent would have laughed if he wasn't in so much shock. "Nope, he doesn't need any training." He almost added that James was the owner of the secret ultra-exclusive club she mentioned, but didn't think his friend would appreciate him revealing that tidbit of information. Plus Catherine didn't need to know. It wasn't like she would be offered membership any time soon.

"I tried to follow you, I tried to get in, but the big guy in the lobby threw me out. So I went back next door, called up my girls and drowned my sorrows." Silently Vincent gave thanks to the meathead at the front door. He wasn't big on customer service, but thank God he did his job well. Vincent couldn't imagine that James's secret life would have remained secret very long if Catherine had witnessed his scene with Terry. He could imagine her placing two phone calls before the first welt had appeared on Terry's skin. Once she blabbed to Allison and Eve, James's reputation at work, and possibly even Vincent's own, would be in the gutter. Although Mia had assured him that the BDSM lifestyle was enjoyed by people in all walks of life, he didn't think the faceless, nameless owners of his company would like the fact the two of their managers were heavily involved in an alternative lifestyle.

"Yeah, so what if I went to a BDSM club. You were the one who told me that I wasn't dominant enough and needed to change."

Catherine cringed. "I'm sorry, I did say that, didn't I?"

Vincent nodded. "Yes. You were a bitch to me."

"Vincent!"

"It's true."

"I don't think I like what this training has done to you."

Vincent crossed his arms over his broad chest. "Tough. Deal with it."

Catherine laughed. "Well I must say that woman is very good at her job."

Vincent's stomach dropped out and any tough-guy composure disappeared. What else would Catherine surprise him with? How did she know about Mia? She said that she had been thrown out of the club. Had she gone back another night and been granted access to the main club room? Suddenly he felt a lot less like hugging the meathead and more like kicking him in the stones.

"How do you know about the training?"

"I have a friend who belongs to the club…" Her voice trailed off. "That's who I've spent the last month with. Before we met I planned to go back home. I even bought a plane ticket and went to the airport but he talked me out of it."

"I know, I saw your boarding pass."

It was Catherine's turn to be surprised. "How did you see that?"

"You're not the only one with friends, Catherine." Vincent was smug. He was done. Catherine was found and he could get out of here, go retrieve Mia and get on with his life. He never had to think about this particular ex-girlfriend again. Well, except to thank her a thousand times for giving him the push he needed to become a Dom.

Unfortunately, Vincent's ego wasn't as easily satisfied as his head. He needed to rub this in. "That woman you mentioned happens to be the best Dom trainer ever." Vincent's smile grew, time to drop the big bomb on her. "And she's living with me now."

"That's great!" Catherine's smile grew as his bombshell announcement backfired on him. She looked genuinely happy for him. *Shit. So much for revenge!*

"I'm pretty sure she's the love of my life."

"That's awesome, I'm so happy for you." Catherine reached across the table and patted his hand. Funny, when she touched him there was no electricity or anything else between them. She was just Catherine. There was no connection between them anymore. It was actually comforting to realize that.

"I didn't think you'd be so happy about me being in love with another woman."

"The old Catherine probably wouldn't be. But now I understand that we were never meant to be. Vin, I didn't just need a Dom, I needed someone else. We had a good relationship for the most part. We tried, and at times it did work. Unfortunately it just wasn't enough." She checked the time of her cell phone. "Neither of us would have been happy in our relationship for long term."

"I used to think I could be happy with you."

Catherine nodded. "Used to, right? Everything's different now for both of us."

Vincent couldn't help but agree. He had been with Catherine three years and had never once thought about how she would work into his life long-term. He had only been with Mia a handful of weeks and already he knew that he was trying to figure out how soon he could convince Mia to let him put a ring on her finger.

"So how did you come to this understanding?"

Catherine leaned in toward him, excited. "Well remember that friend I mentioned from the club? He took me home, he treated me like a human being. Like a normal person instead of the airhead shopaholic expat that everyone assumes I am."

"Catherine, you are that person. You got fired from jobs for taking extended lunches so you could go shopping, remember?"

She nodded. "Yes, that's how I used to be. Even I got tired of it after a while. I think that's why I had decided to go back to London, to try to start over. My old friend Jill was set to meet me at the airport. We were going to spend a couple of days down on the Isle of Wight having fun before going home to Southampton. After that I planned to figure out who I could be if no one knew my reputation. Maybe I could get a job and hold onto it for more than a few weeks. Maybe I could even do something I loved. Or I could go back to school and change my fate. Maybe meet some bloke and settle down, have a couple of kids and forget all about the mess I made out of my life back here.

"But it seems like my bloke was right here after all. He's not like anyone I ever expected to meet. He's big like you, maybe even a little bigger. But he's different. I don't even know how to describe it beyond the fact that he is someone I can't wait to go to bed with just so I can wake up next to him." She laughed. "Totally corny, I know, but it's true."

Vincent felt himself smiling and starting to feel happy for her. "I understand completely. I have to confess. I started training so that I could win you back. I had the stupid thought that I'd show up as big bad Dom and you would either immediately take me back or else realize exactly what you had given up. But that's changed."

Catherine nodded. "I figured as much. You're a good guy, Vin, a very good guy. But just not the guy for me."

"I agree." Vincent smiled. He couldn't help thinking about the woman whom he was the guy for.

"After that day at the airport I moved into my new friend's apartment. I didn't mean to make it permanent, but that's what it's turned out to be. He's my complete opposite. He's serious, studious and a hard worker. I used to think I was so sophisticated and above everyone else, but it was just fake. I don't even know if Eve and Allison will even want to be my friends now that I'm a new Catherine, stripped bare. Hopefully. If not, I hope one day they meet someone who helps them find their real authentic self. I sound a bit like a chat show, but I don't even know what to say. It's amazing, Vincent."

"You sound like a woman in love."

"I am."

Vincent tried to gauge how he felt about this new Catherine and about the revelation that she had met someone from the club and had apparently fallen head over heels in love. Sure he had imagined how seeing Catherine again would go. He would be the heavy Dom, and she would be the repentant ex, who begged forgiveness. Now that he himself had moved on, how did he feel about Catherine doing the same? Deep down, even when he was angry and looking for revenge and maybe vengeance, he still had feelings for Catherine. Perhaps not feelings as deep as those he now had for Mia, but feelings nonetheless. He had spent a decent amount of time in a relationship with her. Enough time that he still cared about the person across the table from him. She seemed so happy, but he wanted her to be careful and not fall too far too quickly.

"Just look out for yourself. Don't get in too deep or do anything you don't want to do or can't handle."

"Nope, I know. Safe, sane, consensual. Don't worry. You're not the only one who's been training. I'm okay, Vin. Better than okay."

"Good. I'm glad to hear that."

Catherine's smile brightened again. "So, when do I get to meet the new woman in your life?"

Vincent thought about that for a minute. Was he ready for his two worlds to collide? He decided that yes, he was. He wasn't ashamed of Mia or the life they were building together. There was no reason for her not to meet Catherine. He was sure she wouldn't mind, perhaps would even appreciate the introduction. He'd just quickly give her a rundown of this conversation with Catherine before he brought her over. Perhaps Mia would know the club member that Catherine had made friends with.

And if Mia didn't want to meet her, fine. Now that this chapter of his life had closed, and Catherine was happy, he knew he could easily live with never seeing her again. All he cared about was a sweet brunette who had tattoos and a thing for kink.

Whatever she wanted to do would be good enough for him.

"You're in luck. She's here at the market looking at the produce."

"Really?" Catherine patted down her hair, a nervous habit. The fact that she was nervous made him happier than it should have. He was glad that Catherine realized that Mia was an important person in his life. She should be nervous. Mia was everything that Catherine could never be.

Vincent stood up from the table. "Just give me a minute, I'll go find her."

Chapter Fourteen

Great, where is she? First he tried to find her at the kale vendor's stall. The farmer behind the booth told him that yes she had bought some of his leafy greens, but that she had moved on a while ago.

Vincent circled the area he had just come from. The street performers were still there, and Catherine still waited at the café. It didn't look like Mia had followed him, so where had she gone?

Maybe she had gone to the right, back the way they had come through the market. She must have wanted to see it again or thought that he'd catch up with her on the way back to his house. Vincent walked from stall to stall, backtracking through the market. She didn't seem to be there either.

How long had he been talking to Catherine? It had felt like only a few minutes, but the sun was almost finished setting. It would be dark soon. He never should have sat down. What a dumb move. Maybe Mia was angry for leaving her alone for so long. As soon as he found her he would apologize. Catherine was definitely not worth them fighting.

Oh, he should just call her cell phone. Great idea. Instead of running around the market, he should just call her and find out where she was. He took out his phone and tried her cell. *Come on, pick up.* No answer.

He tried to think of where else she could be. Could she have gone back to the adult shop to pick up a special surprise for him? A wide grin split his face as he opened the door to the shop. Now what section could she be in? It didn't matter, Vincent checked them all. She wasn't inside this shop either.

His was starting to feel desperate. It really was getting dark. He found the jewelry cart they had stopped at earlier. The owner was packing up for the night. He asked her if she had seen Mia again. The woman just shook her head and continued loading up her vehicle.

Where was she? She must be angry at him. Would she have been angry enough to go home without him? He didn't want to leave the market in case she was still there. He called her cell phone again. Again, no answer. He decided to chance it and head home.

He walked the few blocks back to his house hoping to catch up with her on the way. He had a feeling in the pit of his stomach that he didn't like. He couldn't lose Mia over this. Catherine was his past, case closed. He was so stupid. He could just imagine what it had looked like, seeing him having an intimate conversation with his ex.

He had let his pride get the better of him again. He didn't have to be such a macho asshole, marching up and demanding to know where Catherine had been. It was none of his business. He should have just confirmed that it was her and went back to the market and his Sub.

He unlocked the door. "Mia? I'm sorry," he called out, trying to be heard over Gus's barks. "You'll never believe who I ran into."

His words were too loud. They echoed in the darkened space. He held his breath as he flipped on all of the lights. She wasn't in the kitchen. Maybe she was in the living room? He walked into the room, Gus following behind him. He stared at the empty couch where the night before they had sat and watched the movie. They had eaten popcorn and read the movie's subtitles out loud.

Where was she? He was beginning to panic.

He took the stairs up to his, no their, bedroom two at a time. He flung open the door so hard that it hit the wall behind it with a loud thud. No Mia waiting for him there with their new secret bag of toys, ready to have some fun.

She wasn't anywhere.

He desperately tried to call her cell again. He tried both her old number and her new number just in case. Neither number was answered.

Vincent ran back through the house to the kitchen and grabbed his keys. He was in big trouble. Bigger than big. So big that he was now afraid that their relationship could possibly never recover from it. Could Mia have been so angry that she had gone back to her own home?

He made good use of his car's speed as he flew through town to her neighbourhood. Her car wasn't in the driveway. Shit, he should have checked if it was back in his garage where it had been safely parked all week. In his panic he hadn't thought to look. Did she take a cab here? He rang the doorbell. When she didn't come to door after the first or second or even the third rings, he tried the door. It was locked tight. He was so frantic he banged on the door with all of his strength. His knuckles were bloody before he gave up.

He tried her phone again and again.

If Mia was this upset, where would she go? Where would she feel safe? The parking garage, maybe? She had said that this place was one of solace for her. He rushed over there, but when he reached the top floor it was empty. He pounded his steering wheel in frustration.

There was one last place he could look. He prayed that she was there, because after that, he was out of ideas. Vincent's rough hands gripped his steering wheel tightly as he drove and he said a silent prayer under his breath as he headed down the freeway to the industrial part of town.

He didn't waste time trying to find a parking spot. He abandoned his car at the curb and ran inside the doors of Club Perfect. Immediately, he noticed something odd. The meathead bouncer was missing. In his place was another man, almost as big but equally as menacing. Because he was new, it took a longer than it should have to verify Vincent's ID and allow him access to the club.

The main floor was packed. Vincent remained focused on his quest and did not stop or allow himself to be stopped as he stalked across the room. Adrenaline made his feet move and he had to consciously stop himself from running. He walked straight to Mia's dungeon. The door was locked. *Fuck*! The key card James had given him was at home. Vincent banged on the door, but knew that even if Mia was inside she wouldn't have heard him through the room's sound proofing.

James! He owned the place, he would have a spare key card.

Vincent now took time to look around the floor. No Mia. No James, and oddly enough, no Terry or Mark either. He made a beeline over to the bartender. In his panicked state he couldn't remember the woman's name, but hoped she remembered him.

"What can I get you, Vincent?"

Great, he was in luck. "Some information actually. Have you seen Mia tonight?"

"Nope, sorry."

"What about James?"

The woman's smile broadened and he wondered if she had once been one of James's scene partners. "Yes, he's up in his office." Vincent was off running before he had even finished speaking. After he found Mia he would give the bartender a big tip, but he had no time for that now.

Vincent's feet pounded up the stairs to James's private office. The sound matched the pounding of his heart. The hair at the back of his neck was standing up and he didn't like the feeling. Vincent was becoming afraid.

James wasn't alone inside his office, but that didn't matter to Vincent. Nothing he was currently engaged with was more important to Vincent than finding Mia.

"Is Mia here?"

"No, why would she be? She hasn't been back since she moved in with you."

Vincent's heart sank to his feet. "I lost her."

"What do you mean?"

"We were at the market. Mia wanted to get some vegetables for dinner. I saw someone and I left Mia alone for just a few minutes." The words came out quick, Vincent didn't know if he was rambling, but he desperately tried to make them understand the seriousness of the situation.

"Who? Who was so important?" Lee asked, incredulous. Vincent realized that Mia's brother had been the one talking to James with the door closed. Whatever secret meeting they were having was now cancelled. Everything needed to take a backseat to finding Mia.

"I found Catherine. And I had to talk to her, to find out where she had been while we were all so worried about her." Vincent hung his head sheepishly. He hoped to hell that Catherine hadn't cost him the best thing that had ever happened to him.

"Shit, Vincent, I told you to leave her be. How could you let Mia out of your sight when you know that Robert is stalking her?"

"I don't know. I wasn't thinking. I just wanted to talk to Catherine and rub her face in how much I've changed." While he wallowed in his guilt James immediately dialed Mia's cell phone number on his office phone. When the call wasn't picked up, he disconnected and called again. Same result. Lee tried from his cell phone as well. Again no answer.

James shook his head. "Shit. That's bad. Even if she was mad at you, she'd still take my call."

"Gee thanks."

"It's true. I've always been able to reach her, except when…" He didn't have to finish the sentence. They all knew the time he was referring to and what that might possibly mean now. He quickly typed out a text message and sent it to Mia's phone.

"What do we do now?" Both Vincent and Lee looked to James for answers. He was silent. The man who was so calm and cool always, was neither of those things now.

A terrible idea came to mind. Bile rose in Vincent's throat and he had to choke it back in order to get the question out. "Should we call the police?"

"Vincent, we don't know for sure that anything has happened to her."

No one said anything for a good minute. Vincent had learned honesty and trust while inside the walls of this club, but he had also learned something about intuition. And his friend James had an intuition second to none.

"What does your gut say?"

"I think he's taken her."

Vincent's heart broke. His own intuition had told him the same, that's why he had come to James. But hearing James confirm his feelings was an entirely different experience. The pain of those words was so intense he almost fell to the floor. But he couldn't lose control of himself now. His grief would be increased a hundred times more if he didn't do everything he could to save her.

"Would he take her back to the cottage again?"

James considered this. "It would be pretty foolish of him, considering that I know exactly where it is. But if he's desperate, and if he didn't expect to be able to take her today, he might not have had time to get another place ready."

"I think it's the best lead we have right now."

"The only problem is that the cottage is over an hour away."

Shit. If Robert had taken Mia from the market, he would have had enough of a head start to have reached the cottage already. Vincent cursed. He had wasted so much time running around town. He should have just come straight to James. They needed to get on the road pronto. Vincent couldn't stand to waste any more time. "Let's go."

"I'm coming with you," Lee announced.

James sighed. "Lee, I don't think that's a good idea. Both of you should stay here in case she turns up."

"She's my sister," he said firmly.

Vincent growled, he didn't like being left behind any more than Lee did. "And she's my Sub."

Lee groaned. "God, I didn't need to hear that."

"Welcome to the lifestyle, Lee." The welcome was grim, but relayed everything Vincent needed to know about why he had found Mia's brother here at James's office at the club. He must have been applying for membership, having realized that like his sister, his sexual appetite ran a darker flavour than the norm.

"James, I love her. Don't ask me to stay. If Lee wants to come, let him. Let's just get on the highway and go."

"Fine, it's your choice." James stood and unlocked the wall safe behind him. "Unfortunately I only have two of these. I never thought I'd need more than my two hands could carry." He pulled out two Sig Sauer pistols from the safe. He stuffed one in his belt and handed the other to Vincent. "I got these from my friend Clay in Detroit, he's ex-army and wanted me to be prepared in case I ever saw trouble again. He always says there's no better security than having cold steel in your hand."

"What about me?" Lee's eyes never left the guns.

"You don't get one, Baby Dom." It felt good for Vincent to pass on the title to the Club's newest member.

"Don't call me that." Vincent and James shared a look. At any other time they would have shared a laugh as well. It wasn't long ago that Vincent had shown just as much angst when saddled with the title of club newbie.

"I do have one other thing to bring." Before he closed the drawer, James pulled out a large pair of industrial-strength chain cutters. Lee hesitated before he took them out of James's hands. What those chain cutters symbolized scared each of them. "I promised myself that I would never be without them again when I needed them."

"I'll take them." Lee solemnly reached out and claimed the tool.

The three men jogged side by side across the club floor and out the main doors. With each step, Vincent could hear his heart pounding. They had to get on the road soon and they had to find her. "We'll take my car," he offered, pointing out the vehicle he had left at the curb.

James nodded, looking at the fast car. "Okay but I'll drive."

"No way."

"Think about it, Vin. I know where we're going so I'll get us there faster. Plus you're a little distraught. If we crash and die, Mia is fucked."

Crude, but he made a good point. "Fine." Vincent unlocked his door and handed James his keys. He barely had time to climb in his passenger seat before James had the car moving. Lee still had the door to the backseat open, and quickly slammed it shut.

James drove fast through the city and even faster when he hit the highway. They were headed north, toward a remote area of wilderness that Vincent wasn't overly familiar with. The needle on the speedometer kept rising as James pushed the pedal down hard. The classic engine was purring loud and clear. If they were in a different situation, Vincent would have admired its beautiful sound.

Since the other guys weren't talking to distract him, Vincent tried to think of something else to stop him from freaking out. He tried to remain as emotionless as possible to roll back though the events of the day. It was almost impossible to do without mentally beating himself up for stopping to talk with Catherine. He tried to tell himself that anyone would have been surprised to see Catherine, that his reaction had been normal, and hopefully forgivable. Wait. Something bothered him a little. There was someone who wasn't so shocked that Catherine had been hiding in plain sight.

"You weren't surprised." Vincent's voice sounded too loud in the silent car.

"About what?" James didn't take his eyes off of the road.

"Catherine."

"No," James admitted.

"You knew she wasn't really missing." Vincent's mind spun as he started to put it together. "The photo. You recognized the guy at the airport, didn't you?" James's only answer was a shrug. Vincent had hit the nail on the head. "Of course you know him. Catherine told me that he was a member of the club. Why didn't you tell me?"

James shrugged again. "Not all missing people want to be found, Vin."

"You let Allison and Eve worry about her and…"

"No, *I* didn't do anything. Catherine did it. She made her own choices. Remember that."

"Still, you could have said something."

Lee cleared his throat from the backseat. "I'm sure when you've owned a club as long as James has, you learn to be discreet about certain matters." The comment hung in the air. Vincent didn't care about the intended meaning behind Lee's comment. He was still smarting from James not telling him that Catherine was safe. If he had known, perhaps he wouldn't have left Mia alone at the market. James looked at him. For just a second his eyes left the road. Long enough to give Vincent a cold, hard look. "I can feel your anger from here. Project it where it belongs, at Robert and not at me. I told you to drop it. I've never steered you wrong before."

Vincent slumped back into his seat. James was right. Vincent hadn't listened. He had been focused on his revenge and vengeance. Stupid.

The car fell back into quiet. That was fine with Vincent.

About forty minutes after they had left the club, James signaled for the next highway exit. They had made good time, but it was fully dark now. This far north, there weren't many streetlights to show them the way. Perhaps it was best. In the dark Robert couldn't see them. Unfortunately they couldn't see him either if he was lying in wait for them to arrive. That worried Vincent. James looked to be about the same. His hands were wrapped around the steering wheel so tightly that his knuckles had gone white.

They stayed silent until James pulled the car over onto the side of a narrow dirt road. They were so far off of the beaten path that surely no GPS would have found this address. It was clear that this road didn't see much traffic. Clearly the line Robert had fed Mia about just "happening" upon this cottage was bullshit. It was obvious to Vincent that he must have gone out of his way to specifically find a remote house where no one would hear her scream when he beat her.

Bile rose up in Vincent's throat but he choked it down. If Mia was here they didn't have a single second to waste.

Vincent unbuckled his seat belt at the same time James did and climbed out of the car. Lee followed, closing his door as the other men did, careful not to make a sound. They were parked off the side of the road on a large flat rock. The bushes that lined the cottage driveway were overgrown, but it was clear that at least one other car had traveled this road before them, breaking off branches and flattening down wild grasses.

James gestured that they would have to jump down off of the rock and walk into the woods. It was a good plan, probably better than waltzing right up the driveway and broadcasting to Robert that they were there.

So they walked into the woods toward the back of the cottage. It would be a long hike. They basically had to circle around the property to get close enough to see the cottage without being seen. The only sound in the darkness was their breath and the crunch of brush under their boots. He tried not to stumble over the uneven ground but it was impossible, especially as the overhead foliage blocked out the moon, their only light source. Brush scraped at his arms and clothes as he walked. He tried not to react to the sting of the cuts, he had far worse when he was younger and had camped with his parents. Back then he was a boy scout and new a thousand different things about wilderness survival. But that was so long ago and he had forgotten most of it. His hands curled into fists at his sides. He had never felt so useless and out of place.

He was a contradiction of emotions. He both wanted Mia to be inside Robert's cabin, and he didn't want her to be there. Maybe this was all just some big mistake and they could get back in his car and drive home.

Vincent almost tripped when James stopped abruptly before him and put up a hand. "See the light there?" James whispered, and pointed at a faint glimmering light in the distance. It was hard to see through the trees, but it couldn't be more than two hundred yards ahead of them. It had to be the cabin.

Without a second thought, Vincent took off running toward the building. Without James to guide him he was running blind. His heart was in his throat. No matter what he had wished or thought previously, he could only focus on running toward that light. His girl could be there and that creep could be inside doing unspeakable things to her. He had to get to her, save her.

"Careful," James hissed from behind him. He was running now too, trying to catch up to Vincent who was slowed by tripping over downed branches. Vincent's eyes were swimming with emotion so he could barely see the light ahead of him. The only things leading him right now were his ears and his heart.

His feet stopped moving when he reached the clearing. The line of trees fell away, as did any camouflage. This is where James had sat vigil last time while he waited to rescue Mia. Robert's modest cottage sat before them now, lit up brightly. Someone was there all right, and they were not afraid of being spotted.

James caught up to him, panting. Lee was right behind him. Both men looked ready to kill him.

Vincent didn't care. "What's the layout like inside?"

James pointed to the back door of the cabin. "That's how he comes and goes. It enters into a kitchen, and luckily the room he kept her in was just off of it. I didn't see much more than those two rooms. I went in a kitchen window last time." James frowned. "Vin, I know you love her, but we can't just go charging in there like a group of macho Doms. Who knows what he had rigged this time or what he'll do to Mia if he spots us."

Vincent nodded. He tried to calm down his racing heart and catch his breath. If this was going to work, he had to listen to what his friend knew about this creep and the best way to approach things. "Tell us what happened when you found her last time."

"You know that already."

"I know the summary but not the details."

James sighed quietly. "You couldn't have asked me back in the car?"

"Calm down, I doubt he can hear us. He might not even be here." Even as Vincent said the words he knew for certain that the creep was here. It wasn't intuition, it was common sense. The cabin couldn't be empty and have every light on. Clearly the creep was here, and he wasn't hiding it.

"Last time I camped out just about here. I waited for days, but then I got desperate..." He paused. "I couldn't stand waiting anymore, so I lit his car on fire."

"You what?" Lee had recovered from the run enough to pant out the question.

James shrugged. "Yeah. I never told anyone that, but you can see the outline of his car over there where the ground is still black. Lucky it didn't catch this whole forest on fire. It was the only thing I could think of to do to get him out of the cottage so I could get in. And it worked, it got him out of the house. While he was trying to put it out he was distanced long enough that I was able to get Mia out safely."

"Do you have any matches?"

James shook his head. "We're not going to get so lucky this time. Do you see a car around here?" The eyes of three men scanned the clearing. If Robert had driven a car here, it wasn't here now.

"He must have moved his car back and parked on the main road or hidden it someplace."

Shit. There was no easy way in this time. "What do we do?"

James considered the question for a minute then shook his head. "I don't know. We wait for him to leave on his own?"

"Fuck that." Vincent stood and began pacing. "Last time you waited because you didn't know what was going on in there. This time we know what he's probably doing to her."

Vincent looked across the clearing to the cabin. It was two basketball courts away or less. It had been a dozen years since he had played on game of pick up, but he knew he could still easily make that distance. He calculated how long it would take him. He wouldn't have sports shoes on, so that would slow him.

His thoughts where cut short by Lee's whisper. "Do you hear that?" he asked.

The men were silent as they listened hard to hear what Lee meant. It was a faint, yet unmistakable tempo of a cane smacking against flesh.

"Mia!"

"Vin, it might not be…"

Vincent ran across the clearing toward the house as quickly as he could. Now there was no way he could leave her in there one minute more with that fucking creep. He had one singular focus and only one thought. Save her.

He tried to listen as he ran to see if the sadist was still using the cane. Instead all he heard was the sound of his feet hitting the ground as he ran full out, with nothing left to lose. He didn't have a plan. If he was running into a trap, so be it. His life meant nothing to him without Mia in it. He would sacrifice himself if it allowed the others to save her.

He skidded to a stop outside the back door, the one that James said that the creep used. He remembered him saying that it opened onto a kitchen. The bedroom she was confined in last time was close to the kitchen. That's all he knew and all he had to go on.

He took a deep breath and took out his gun. *Five, four, three, two, one.* Then he turned the knob and pushed the door open. He could be walking in to his death. He hoped that wasn't true and that he would live to hold his beautiful girl again.

The place was old, but immaculately kept. It was also eerily quiet. The sound of the cane was gone and now there was absolutely no sound to cover his movements nor to help him distinguish where in the cabin the creep was holding Mia.

There was one door out of the kitchen. It led to a hallway that must have opened to the rest of the structure. He tried to keep his footsteps quiet but it was impossible. So instead he starting moving quickly, hoping that he would find Robert before the creep found him. It was like walking on water when all he wanted to do was run.

In the hallways the space opened up a bit. A huge hanging light fixture lit up the space brightly. It also fully illuminated him. There was no place to hide.

He inched toward the first bedroom. This must have been where James had found Mia last time. Vincent took a deep breath, and steeled himself for what he might see in the room. Then he chanced a look in around the door frame. The bedroom was empty.

So his pilgrimage down the hallway continued. The house was still very quiet. Vincent was starting to think that maybe he had just imagined the cane sound earlier. Maybe the lights were just left on and nobody was home. Maybe Mia was safe in his bed waiting for him. Maybe this was all a terrible mistake.

He peeked around the next door frame with hope that this room would be empty too. All strength left him. He would have fallen to his knees if he didn't have a mission at hand.

Mia.

Fuck.

His Mia was naked, lying out on a bed, bound and spread. Red welts marked her pale skin. She looked so impossibly fragile. Her eyes were closed. She made no movement to show if she had heard him arrive. There was sound in this room. It was low but unmistakable. It was the sound made by the difficult rise and fall of her chest as she struggled to breathe through the pain.

Oh, Mia. His beautiful girl was broken. She had been his smiling girl, who liked vegetables, and his dog, and watching the boats at the pier. She was the doctor who was in control at work, but otherwise gave him the gift of control and the reward of the sweet little sound she made when she came. No one who saw her now covered in blood and cane welts would believe those things applied to the slight creature restrained on the bed.

Putting one foot in front of the other and trying to choke back all emotion, Vincent went to her. He wanted to hold her, but first he had to free her. He put his gun on the side table and started unwrapping the rope that had been looped around her. It looked like Robert hadn't had enough time to gather chains to restrain her with.

Even when he freed her, she didn't open her eyes or move. Was she so deep in subspace that she didn't know that he was here? He sat down on the edge of the bed and carefully pulled her in his arms. This was the most important session of aftercare he had ever given her. He kissed her hands, her face, her hair. "I love you, Mia," he whispered as he gently rocked her back to consciousness.

Gradually she opened her eyes. "Vincent?" she asked as she rapidly blinked.

He smiled. "Yes."

"I knew you would come."

"James is here too, and Lee."

"Really?" Her eyes filled with tears. He wished he could take the time to kiss them away, but first he needed to get her out of here to safety.

He worked on her binds and soon the rope loosened. Vincent helped her sit up and she looked at the burns the ropes had made on her wrists, right over her red X tattoos.

Vincent sucked in a breath when he saw the cuts on her arms and shoulders caused by the cane.

"Is it bad?"

It took him a moment to respond. "Yes." He angrily barked through gritted teeth.

Mia's breathing was laboured because of the pain. The bed was covered with blood. When she saw this, she started hyperventilation.

"Shh, stay calm. I'm going to get you out of here." Vincent quickly grabbed a blanket to cover her naked body with. As he turned to open the blanket, he stopped dead in his tracks. There was a change in the room. They were no longer alone.

"Hello, Vincent."

His heart stopped. He hadn't heard Robert approach, but he did feel the cool metal of a gun barrel as it pressed against the back of his head.

"No!" Mia screamed.

Vincent couldn't see it, but he heard the smile in the creep's voice. "Quiet, Slave, he didn't come alone."

As if on cue, James appeared taking two large steps inside of the room. "Put down the gun, Robert." There was a brief second of horror and repulsion on his face when he looked past Robert to make eye contact with Mia. When that second was up a mask of indifference skid over his face.

"Nice to see you again." Robert turned toward James but didn't loosen his grip on the gun or Vincent. "Did you come for your whore again?"

"Yes." James's hands curled into fists. His gun was still in the waistband of his leathers. It was obviously that he was itching to grab the pistol, but couldn't risk it with Robert's gun against Vincent's head.

"Did you think I didn't know you'd come? Did you think I didn't hear you in the woods? I'm smarter now. I won't let her go this time."

"You have to." James paused. "Do you get off on the fact that she doesn't want to be here?"

A dry laugh came from Robert that turned Vincent's stomach. "She's mine."

"She has another Master now."

"This asshole?" Robert poked him with the gun. "Hardly. I had to step in when it looked like he was about to claim her. He can't give her what she needs."

Maybe that had been true once, but the critique now made Vincent want to smile. The lessons combined with the weeks he had spent with Mia had changed him from a man who couldn't please a woman into the Dom who could see his skill reflected on the satisfied face of his Sub. "Really? Then why is it my name that she screams out when she comes?"

"Shut up." Robert rammed the gun into his head harder. "A pain slut like her doesn't know what she wants unless I tell her."

James used the distraction to step further into the room. Vincent could see Lee just outside the door. They shared a look. Vincent knew he had to keep Robert talking. Then maybe they could distract him enough to end this standoff safely.

"I don't have to tell her. I give it to her so good that she comes on her own now."

"Don't worry, I can beat that back out of her." Robert laughed.

James shuffled a few more steps into the room. This time Robert noticed the movement. "Not so fast, Richie Rich." Quickly Robert raised the gun and fired at James. Mia screamed.

James saw the shot coming, and twisted out of the way as he raised his own gun. He was a second too late. He jerked back as the bullet hit him. The impact knocked the gun out of his hand. Robert had meant the shot to hit James square, but because James had been moving, it missed being a kill shot. Instead it had found purchase in his shoulder. A hole had been torn in his black T-shirt from where the bullet entered his body. If it had been a white shirt it would have turned bloodred with James's blood loss.

Cool, collected James was now in shock. He looked at his wound, then back to Vincent. When the shock lifted, a clear determination took its place. The following look he gave Vincent communicated everything they were now both thinking. This guy needed to be taken out.

"You can stay where you are too." Robert's gun now moved to land on Lee, who had been following James's lead and trying to sneak into the room. Lee's head snapped up as Robert's finger pushed the trigger.

Lee was hit. He fell back into the hallway. After he hit the floor there was silence. Shit, Vincent thought of his daughter Sage and hoped that her father wasn't dead. From behind him a low primal wail began, a sound clogged with tears and pain. Mia. She had seen it all.

Vincent was too close to Robert, and was at a disadvantage. Although Robert didn't have the gun against his head any more, he was still within range to end Vincent's life if he made the wrong move. He still would have made that move if he thought that the others could get out safely. With James hit he didn't know how slim that possibility was, but he had to try.

Vincent and James locked eyes. Now was the time. He had to do something. Vincent turned and reached for his gun. Except his gun wasn't there. Fuck, where was it?

Vincent's panicked gaze swung from James over to Mia. Mia saw it just as Vincent did. He had put down his gun in his hurry to free her. It sat just out of her reach. If he could distract Robert for a few minutes more, maybe she could get to it.

It was one of the most difficult things to do, but Vincent turned away from her and faced the creep again. He trusted that Mia still had enough strength left in her to take the window of opportunity he was making for her. She either had to get to the gun and use it or somehow get out of there and get help.

"So how did you do it?" Vincent asked Robert.

"Do what?"

"How did you make her fall in love with you? I can't get her to love me."

Robert smiled widely and it turned Vincent's stomach. "That was the easy part. Mia had been looking for someone to love for a long time, to fill the hole left in her heart after her mom killed herself. She always blamed herself for it and that made her vulnerable. An easy mark. You should be able to see that. Didn't she teach you that a Dom needs to be able to read their Sub and then give them what they need? She needed someone to take control over her completely. Once I did that, she was hooked. I could do literally anything to her, she loved me so much she'd let me do it."

"See, I disagree." Vincent chanced moving a step further away from Robert. It wasn't much, but hopefully it would be enough. "I think she was wounded before, but now she's healed."

Robert chuckled. "Hurts like that never heal."

"And that's just another lie you tried to tell me." Mia's voice was strong and firm. While Robert was distracted, she had managed to reach Vincent's gun. His beautiful girl had proved just how brave she really was. As tears poured down her face she stood on shaking legs and raised the gun toward Robert.

"As your true Master, I command you to put the gun down, Mia."

Mia shook her head. "Sorry, you're not my Master anymore."

Robert chuckled. "I can change that." He turned back to Vincent. "Baby Dom, my next bullet has your name on it."

The moment Robert moved to pull his trigger, Mia pulled hers. Vincent braced himself for impact, but Robert hadn't been quick enough. The first bullet out of Mia's gun hit Robert in the chest. Robert, stunned, looked down at the wound as the second bullet she fired hit him in the shoulder, knocking the gun out of his hand. Her third shot tore through him and brought him to his knees, his eyes now lifeless. She ran out of bullets the same time Robert ran out of breath.

The words she had kept locked inside of herself for the past year spilled out now. She needed to say them, even though it was too late for Robert to hear them. "You're a liar, a sadist and a criminal. You targeted me online and groomed me to trust you. You begged me to bring you to the club and to train you. But you never wanted me and you never wanted to be a real Dom. You just wanted someone to degrade and someone to keep as your prisoner. I fell for it then, but I'm not that girl anymore."

Mia stood over her captor.

"I belong to me," she whispered. Then she turned to Vincent and held out her arms. "Thank you for coming for me," she said, her voice shaking with emotion.

Gladly, Vincent held her tightly. "I should never have left you alone."

Mia shook her head. "No, it's not your fault. None of it. Sooner or later he would have come for me. I'm sure of it."

"Call 911." James barked from the floor. Even injured, he was still very much in control. Quickly Vincent punched the three-digit number of the emergency service into his cell phone. Signal was poor out here and his call wouldn't connect. He tried again while Mia checked on James.

"How bad is it?"

"Stings like a bitch. It'll be a while before I'll be able to do a whipping scene again." Mia helped James apply light pressure to his wound. "I'm fine, go check on Lee."

Mia scrambled to her feet and Vincent followed her out into the hall. Unfortunately Lee hadn't fared as well as James. The bullet Robert fired at him had hit his side. As a result Lee was wheezing for air.

"I'm sorry." Tears splashed down Mia's face.

Lee grimaced when he tried to move further. "God Mia, I'm the one who's hurt and you're the one who's crying."

"I can't help it."

"I was joking." Lee's features softened. Whatever bad feelings were between them were quickly fading. "I heard what he said in there, every ugly word. Mom's death had nothing to do with you."

Mia shrugged. "Maybe if I had just been a better daughter she wouldn't have—"

"No, you are not to blame."

"Just like I'm not to blame for you and James being hurt and for Robert being dead. I never meant to bring you all into this situation. It's because of me this happened."

Vincent closed his eyes against the pain of her words. He tried his cell phone again and finally it found service. He was relieved when an operator finally came on the line. He quickly relayed the address of the cabin and the details of their situation the best he could.

When the call was done and police and ambulance were on their way he turned back to Mia. She was standing over Robert's body now, just looking at him. Vincent joined her and carefully wrapped a blanket around her. "He was dead. You're finally free."

Mia nodded, but he could tell that she didn't believe him.

Chapter Fifteen

"Good morning, sleepyhead."

Mia opened her eyes and looked around the room. She stretched, and scowled, probably realizing that she had woken up once again in the hospital.

To Vincent even a scowl was a blessing. He was glad to be with her in this hospital room because it meant that she was safe and she was alive.

"I can't wait to get out of here!"

"Me neither." For the past two days Vincent had sat in a chair by her bedside, even slept there. He had only left at brief times to get food or to check on Gus. "The nurse said that your doctor should be in to see you around nine a.m. Hopefully he'll have some information on when you can come home."

"Great." The hospital had kept Mia so that she could heal. She was suffering from shock, and would need some therapy. Dr. Mia wholeheartedly agreed with the recommended course of treatment.

She also was kept because she needed to physically heal. The cuts on Mia's back made by Robert's cane were deep and required stitches.

Vincent stood and walked to the window to open the curtains. Maybe some natural light would improve Mia's mood. A display of flowers and cards filled the windowsill. There were also dozens of letters waiting for Mia to read. Robert's death had piqued the interest of the nightly news. Thank God the local reporter hadn't been able to find the connection between all of them that would have led back to Club Perfect. Instead she spun their story as a pair of lovers and a jealous ex. The storyline had been picked up by a few online sites and had even gotten a mention on the national news.

Vincent had found out when he received a call from his mother and sister to see if he was all right. Once his safety was confirmed they had demanded to know all the details. They also demanded to meet Mia, but that would have to wait for a while. Mia was in no shape to travel. His Mom hadn't liked that answer but she had been satisfied, for now.

Mia shifted in the bed to get more comfortable. "It's hard to believe that they're going to let me go home. I should be going to jail."

"Don't say that."

"It's true."

They had learned from Mark that police had searched the cottage and found evidence that corroborated their story that Mia had been held there against her will. Apparently Robert the creep had ended up incriminating himself by keeping photos of Mia he had taken last time he held her. He had also kept a written document of what he had planned to do to her this time as her slave training. Each item the police found was more horrific than the last. There was no official doubt that Robert's death was anything but self-defence. Case closed. Mark told them that Mia was thought of as a hero down at the precinct.

Mia fiddled with the hem of her blanket and wouldn't look Vincent in the eye. "Do you think his family will try to contact me?"

"No, why would they?"

Mia shrugged. "They must hate me." Mia turned back to face him, her eyes shining with tears. "I hate that I did that to him."

Bile rose in Vincent's throat. "Mia, he would have killed you. Maybe not that day, but eventually. He shot James and Lee…" Although Mia hadn't been able to visit their hospital rooms, Vincent had. Robert's bullets had hit them hard. James had a shattered shoulder and Lee a deep chest wound. An inch to the left and Lee's lung would have been punctured, an inch to the right his heart. Both men had been rushed into surgery and had luckily had a good prognosis for recovery.

Vincent closed his eyes. He couldn't believe that Mia had one moment of sympathy for the creep. It made him sick to his stomach, but he had to ask, "Do you still love him?"

"No." The word was said slowly.

"Is that the truth?"

"Yes." She cried, tears running down her face. "But I'm a human being, Vincent. I killed someone. So excuse me while I try to deal with that. I don't need your jealous macho bullshit right now."

"I thought you liked my macho bullshit, Sub."

"Not now, Vincent." She shook her head. She was right. This wasn't the time or place for any of that.

Vincent went to her and wrapped his arms around her the best he could. He didn't want to injure her or mess with any of the hospital's equipment.

She allowed herself to be held for a moment before she shrugged off his arms. "I don't need that right now either, Vincent."

"Then what do you want?" Vincent was getting frustrated.

Mia shook her head. "It's not what I want, it's what *you* want. Since the cabin you haven't told me that you loved me."

Vincent was shocked. Her words weren't loud enough to echo in the room but they echoed in his head. What she said was unbelievable. "That's not true. I do love you."

"No, you thought that you loved me because you were fucking me. You did the same thing that I used to do, you mixed up sex with love."

"That's not true."

"Isn't it?"

"No."

Mia looked away. "I'd appreciate it if you would pack the things I left at your house and drop them off at the club."

"Mia." Vincent sighed. "Don't be like this. My house is your house now."

"Vin, there's no reason for me to continue to live with you. I killed Robert. It's done. I don't need your protection anymore."

"You don't think you need me anymore." It wasn't a question, it was a statement. Robert had tried to drive a wedge between them when he was alive and it looked like he was succeeding now.

She slowly nodded. "You don't need me either, Vincent. Your training is over. Don't worry about your final exam. It was just something stupid James made up. James will still give you full membership to the club and you'll be able to bring Catherine there no problem."

Each thing that came out of Mia's mouth shocked him more than the one before it. "She has someone else now—"

"Then another Sub can—"

"No, another Sub *can't*. You're it for me, Mia. Why can't you see that? I'm sorry I didn't react the way you wanted me to back at the cabin, or here, but that doesn't mean that I don't love you and that we don't belong together."

"Vin, you deserve a life with someone that isn't fucked up in the head."

Vincent was so angry he had to turn away from her. "You don't think very highly of yourself, do you?"

Mia nodded and looked away. "I don't think you think very highly of me either. You just want to own me like the people at my father's charity auction wanted to win those expensive prizes. Helping the charity was secondary. I'm bragging rights to you. You never saw me as a real person. Well this is who I am, Vincent. How do you like it?" She held her arms open. The gown slipped down her shoulders revealing the bandages from her whip wounds. They would eventually heal, but would Mia ever heal from her emotional wounds?

Vincent felt gutted, wounded himself. "I love you, Mia."

Her smile was sad. "Both the club and my body were just a distraction for you."

"Why did you save my life if you were just going to throw me away like this?"

"I don't know." Mia's shrug broke his heart. The pain he felt when Catherine dumped him was nothing compared to this.

"Tell me what you need, Mia. Whatever it is, I'll do it or I'll be it. You can continue to train me and I'll learn how to be what you need. I'm not losing you without a fight."

"I was never yours to lose, Vincent." She took a deep breath. "I think you should go now."

Vincent felt defeated. His will, his strength was utterly deflated. "Is that what you really want?"

"Yes." Her face was a stone mask. She wasn't lying.

That verbal punch to the heart was his last lesson from her. A real Dom would probably argue. A Real Dom would probably punish her and then show her how much she was loved by him. A real Dom would have never let his Sub doubt how precious she was to him. A real Dom was something that Vincent wasn't. Maybe she was right. Maybe he had been pretending all along.

"Fine." Vincent stood. He didn't say anything else as he walked out of the room.

He held it together until he got home and closed the door to his bedroom. He sat down on the bed they had shared not long ago. The room still smelled like her. Her clothes were still here, her jewelry. She belonged here.

Tears dripped down his face. He had never felt so broken or so weak. Looks like you couldn't teach someone how to be a Dom after all.

Chapter Sixteen

Mia pulled her car to the curb and hit the button to unlock the doors. She had the air conditioning cranked to full blast, but when James opened the door, the heat of the day still forced its way into her car.

James groaned as he slid into the leather bucket seat and carefully buckled the seat belt. He was very protective of his arm in the sling, but the even the slight movement caused him pain. He leaned his head back and took a deep breath.

She felt like she should say something, maybe a joke, but instead just decided to pretend to ignore his injury until he was comfortable to talk about it. It was hard for Mia not to worry about her dearest friend, but she knew that he wouldn't want her fussing over him. Weakness was not part of who James was. Being seen as less than strong would be mortifying for him.

Door closed, she pulled away from the curb and into traffic.

"Thanks for the ride, doll."

Mia smiled. "No problem." She checked her mirrors and then eased out into traffic. "Do you mind if we make a stop before I take you home?"

"Of course not."

Mia didn't say anything. Of course James would know that she would come running right to this spot and the memory of her mother. But what would her mother think of her now that she had killed a person?

They pulled into the parking garage right around sunset. Perfect timing. Neither of them said a word as Mia piloted the car up and around the floors until they reached the top. She drove out toward her usual spot and turned off the engine. This wasn't the first time Mia had brought her best friend here and she was sure it wouldn't be the last either.

They unbuckled in silence. James used his free hand to open the car door. His movements were jerky and uncoordinated. "This cast is a bitch."

"I bet." They each took their time walking around to the front of the car. Mia helped James to sit on the hood before she hopped up beside him.

Today, as always, the view was remarkable. The sky was lit up in pinks and purples and the special kind of orange that shows when the sun sets after a particularly hot summer day. Lights were slowly being turned on in the buildings around them. The streetlights followed them, snapping on in a row, one-by-one illuminating the road below. The sidewalks held people hurrying to their destinations before night fell.

Mia and James just enjoyed the silence. She had a strange feeling. It was part relief and freedom, now that she no longer had to watch her back. Unfortunately it was also an equal mix of sorrow with a huge amount of guilt. She was free now, but she was alone.

"Do you remember the first time you brought me here?" James's voice broke the silence of the night.

"For sure. I had just met you."

James savoured that memory for a while and then slowly smiled. "You were a mess."

"I was a mess? You were a mess!"

"At least I didn't have pink hair."

Mia laughed and it felt good to be here again spending time with her best friend. It had been a while since they had really talked. They hadn't spent any real time alone together she had stayed at his house after she had been rescued the first time.

"Okay, okay, but which one of us was the bigger mess is still up for debate."

"Remember when I tried to kiss you?"

"Yes! How could I forget? That was so awkward!" They both laughed. James smiled, remembering the teenage version of himself who had been attached to the strange punk-rock girl who was trying to find her way in the world. Back then he had thought that a romance with him could have been a perfect fit. It didn't take them long to realize that they were much better as friends.

"I was some dumb, horny kid, what could you expect?"

She paused, sorry to sour their night with bad memories. "That was right after your dad went to jail, right?" Her tone was soft, but the words still made James's shoulders fall. His father had been set up, blackmailed into a no-win situation. He'd either take the fall for a crime he hadn't committed, and go to jail for a very long time, or he'd sacrifice his family, his company and his fortune. He had picked the jail time, feeling that it was the easier way out. That decision hadn't seemed so easy to James, who had a tumultuous almost nonexistent relationship with his father at the time.

"Yeah. That was right before he went in. I came to say good-bye and found out he had both a new wife *and* a mistress."

Mia rolled her eyes. James was always dramatic. "They had an open relationship. I was hardly his mistress." She hadn't thought about her relationship with James's father in quite some time. She had glossed over their brief relationship when she had told Vincent about it back at the club.

She had met James's dad after she discovered his name and address in his mother's papers. Less of a diary and more of a calendar of life events, really. At first she couldn't understand why when a young woman her mother had gone to this man's house almost every weekend. There was nothing to show that they had dated or had any other relationship that would have given her a reason to be there.

"I'm sure Thomas Stoyanovsky loved finding out that his little girl was corrupted by his former best friend." When she had searched for the man who ran the underground sex club her parents had met at, she hadn't expected to have any sort of relationship with him, let alone a sexual one. But through him she had discovered her submissive nature. And she had met his son who ended up being her rock and her partner as she explored the BDSM scene.

"There were plenty of other places that corrupted me far more." Mia let her shudder finish the sentence for her. "Thank God we have the club now, eh?"

When they had first opened Club Perfect, neither knew exactly what their roles should be. Mia knew she was a Sub, but it took more than her submitting to run a successful club. Thankfully James had a head for business and they had managed to survive their first year open. Slowly they had built a network of likeminded friends. Now many of those friends felt more like family then friends.

She was pretty sure her days as being the head Dom trainer were over. Although she loved helping to shape men into realizing their full dominant potential, it was time for a new role for her. She wasn't quite sure where she would fit into Club Perfect now, but she knew she wasn't done with the lifestyle yet. It was a part of her and always would be. She just couldn't let herself get attached to anyone ever again. She had made that mistake twice now and had paid dearly each time.

Although she hadn't paid anywhere near as dearly as Robert had.

"You were a mess then, doll, and you're a mess now."

James frank words didn't surprise her. He was never one to hold back. "You're right," she sighed.

"You need to deal with your survivor's guilt."

"Murderers should have guilt."

"Self-defence isn't murder."

Mia thought about that for a moment. Of course she knew, legally, that self-defence was different than murder, but inside her soul it felt the exact same. "I don't know if I can forgive myself, James. I made so many mistakes."

"You shot him because you had to. He could have killed me or Lee or Vincent. You didn't kill an innocent person."

She sighed. "No, but I killed someone who loved me once."

James smiled weakly. "We can argue later about if he loved you or not. Yes, it's a horrific thing to deal with, but you can't give up living just because he's dead."

"I don't know what to do."

"You said that a year ago when you were freed the first time. You got help, you moved forward, and you fell in love with someone."

"I don't—"

James put up a hand. "Stop. I can see right through you."

"Then you see a murderer, a sexual deviant, a weak—"

"No I see you. I love you too. You're my oldest and best friend. You're scared and making excuses. I can understand why you thought you had to tell Vin to beat it, but make no mistake, he loves you and you love him too."

"That's awful touchy feely for you." She sighed. "Vincent may love me, but he sees me as an object."

"No, it was Robert who did that. Don't put his shit on Vincent." And that right there was why James was her best friend. They were similar in so many ways, and equally as fucked up. "Are you sure you're not the psychiatrist?"

"Nope, remember I was busy out in the real world while you were buried in books." While he was opening the club with half of her inheritance as seed money, she had used the other half to put herself through medical school. It had been hard work but she loved it. To many it had seemed like an odd choice for a young woman who was so lost, but to Mia it had been inevitable that when she settled down she would go into the mental-health field.

"Maybe one day I'll be as good with giving out advice as you are."

She had seen her first psychiatrist long before her mom passed, and had gone back to therapy after, as a way of trying to make sense of why her mom decided to end her own life. She wanted to help people like that. Now she loved that she counseled others who felt as much despair as she had and was there to comfort others after tragedy hit. Besides her Doms, her professional work was what she was most proud of.

Maybe now she needed something else to be proud of. Something to counteract the guilt she felt. Maybe the thing that could save her would be her love for Vincent. Fully admitted, and given generously and constantly. Could she stop holding herself back, climb out from all her baggage and actually have a normal life?

"You deserve to be happy, doll. And don't give me any of that 'I'm not worthy' crap."

"But what if he doesn't want me back?" She had hurt him. She knew she wasn't an easy woman to love. Hell, she wasn't even an easy woman to take out to dinner. But James was right. Vincent did love her and she could have had a future with him. She had thrown all of that way, but now she wanted that future, damn it!

James rolled his eyes. "Mia, the man is crazy about you. You don't need to read people like I do to know that he's full-on crazy about his Sub."

Mia sighed. "Doesn't he deserve to be with a normal woman like Catherine?"

"Okay first, Catherine is not normal." James counted off on his fingers. "Second, this stopped being about Catherine and his revenge when you two went on your first date together. And third, he couldn't get Catherine back even if he still wanted her."

"Is that so?"

"Yes. And if she can find happiness then so can you." Mia took a minute to think about that. James's hand found hers. His long fingers threaded in between her short ones. His touch was different than

Vincent's but it still brought her a warm sense of comfort. Of coming home, if that could be possible.

A long time ago she had learned along with James that touch was the ultimate barometer of a person. There was much that you could hide or lie about, but your natural reaction to things couldn't be hidden by the physical connection between two people. Immediately they had both known there would never be romantic feelings between them. That didn't mean they didn't love each other in a different sort of way.

"I hope you're right. None of this was supposed to be about me. When we started the training it was simply about him and his girlfriend. If it helped me learn how to be a Sub again in the process, then that would just be a lucky bonus."

James nodded. "Yes, that's the line I sold you when I got you to agree to teach him."

"You knew this would happen." It was a statement. A fact. Mia knew it as well as she knew James. He always wanted the best for her and for her to be happy. He had set this up hoping that they would fall in love.

"Not all of it. If I could have saved you from Robert again, I would have. You know that. But I knew Vincent fairly well and I saw potential there."

Mia nodded. "It's not only that, he walked into the cottage not knowing if he would get back out alive. He was willing to sacrifice himself for me. That's a little overwhelming."

"No, that's love." It was true. There was a reverence to his words. She hoped that one day someone would love her friend as much as she was loved. "Do *you* want to be with Vincent?" He squeezed her hand. He was the one person who would never judge her. He also already knew what the answer was. She just needed the courage to admit it.

She sighed. "Yes. More than anything. But I'll never forget Robert."

"Nor should you. But it's time for you to take control of your life again." James got a mischievous look in his eye that she didn't exactly like. "You know, Vincent does need more training."

"Yeah. I was a little lax with him."

"And you both still owe me a final exam."

Mia raised an eyebrow. "*I* owe you a final exam?"

"Yup." James grinned. "I think I have exactly the plan to get old Vin boy back. And then you can live happily ever after."

Chapter Seventeen

I don't even know why I'm doing this.

He should have said no. This place wasn't home to him anymore if Mia wasn't by his side. He didn't need to be here and be reminded of how he had lost the one person who mattered the most to him.

Vincent walked up the steps to the club one last time. He wasn't wearing the boots, the black T-shirt, or those awful leather pants. Those clothes were balled up and shoved to the back of his closet. They'd probably meet a dumpster soon. He certainly didn't want to wear them anymore.

He tried not to think about the bag he was carrying, or that it contained everything that Mia had left at his house. Her work outfits, her sexy club clothes, her hair brush, her stupid canned beans. He would give the bag to James and then he wouldn't have any objects left in his home that reminded him of her.

He wished he could bag up and drop off his memories and his broken heart as well.

Heartbreak. That was something he was getting used to. Two girls in a row now had thrown him aside. Shouldn't it hurt less the more it happened, not more? This heartbreak had almost gutted him. There was no revenge he could take or vengeance he could plot to make him feel better. There was nothing he could do to get her back.

He showed his ID to the new bouncer and walked into the club. He would drop off her things as quickly as possible and get back home. He and Gus had a pizza to eat. Poor dog missed Mia as much as he did.

Inside the main room, Vincent stood, for the last time, and watched the people in the packed room. The floor pulsed with a living, breathing energy. People of all shapes and sizes were together, having fun, exploring their needs and helping others to find pleasure. He had once been one of those people, but not anymore. He would never come here again. He had no reason to. There would never be another Sub for him, ever.

That was the other reason why he was here. He needed to see James. Unfortunately his friend wasn't out on the floor or easily spotted. *Ugh.* Where was he? Vincent pushed his way through the crowd and past the bar area toward the stairs that led to James's office. Just like Vincent's first night at the club, the floor was packed. Had kinky Christmas come twice in one year? Maybe James and Terry were doing a scene again. Too bad he couldn't stick around to watch. It would be different now that he had the knowledge and experience to not run scared like a Baby Dom, who didn't know the difference between a monster and a Master.

Vincent stomped up the stairs. He fought for a minute to calm his emotions, before opening the door and walking inside.

"Hi, Vin." James sat behind his desk, clearly expecting him. The differences between this office and James's office at the warehouse were obvious. The office at the warehouse was cold and empty. This one was richly decorated like the rest of the club, but it wasn't the work of a decorator. James had clearly set up this space himself. There were personal touches everywhere, even framed photographs. Some showed friends while others displayed what must have been important nights at the club. Yes, Club Perfect was James's life.

His friend looked his usual self. Although Vincent had decided against the Dom club uniform tonight, James wore it well. The last time Vincent had seen James was when he was in the hospital. He felt a little guilty that he hadn't even thought about going back to visit him again or check on Lee. He had been too wrapped up in his sorrow to remember that he wasn't the only one hurting. With his friend's arm still in a cast, it was impossible to forget the danger they had all been in not long ago.

"Hello, James. I hope you're healing well."

"Yeah, I'll have to take it easily for a few more weeks, but I'll be okay eventually." James shrugged and winced when he moved his arm. Obviously it hurt a hell of a lot more than he let on.

"How's Lee?"

"He's doing really well. He's back home now. He had to hire some homecare to help him and his daughter. Every day he improves but it will still be a long recovery for him."

There was a silence and an awkwardness between them that was new. James and Mia were so close. Did it mean that if he'd lost Mia, he'd also lost James's friendship as well?

"So you said that you had some paperwork for me to sign?"

James nodded and pushed a stack of papers toward him. "Yes, to cancel your membership. Although it's not too late for you to reconsider."

"There's nothing to reconsider." Vincent grabbed a pen off the desk and signed each page without reading them over. There was no reason for him to keep his membership valid. As far as he was concerned this was one last formality. He needed this closure. Once things were final he could begin to try to move on. He needed to try to figure out how to live the rest of his life without having any connection to Mia, without ever holding her in his arms again or kissing her lips.

Vincent cursed. He would not cry. Not here anyway. He would save his emotions for home where there was only his dog to see him crumble.

He turned to go, and then remembered the heavy bag in his hands. The other purpose of his last visit to the club. "I have her things, can you give them to her?"

James nodded. "She hoped you would bring them. She asked you to leave them in her dungeon."

Fuck that. He wasn't going in there ever again. "Can't you do that for me?" Vincent whined. That was her place. Yes, it had also been his place for a short while, and it was where he had learned not only how to please her, but how to love her. Unfortunately Mia hadn't learnt any of the same lessons.

"Come on, Vin. It's just a room."

"No. Definitely not. It's not just a room, not to me." He growled. His fists curled at his sides.

James sighed. "I know, but you have to lose the anger. People make mistakes. Can't you accept that?"

Vincent didn't answer. He released his fists but not his bitterness. He didn't particularly care for being referred to as a mistake. Not one single minute of his time with Mia had felt like a mistake to him.

James stood. "I'll come with you. It will be the last thing we'll do and then you can go. I need to deactivate your key card anyway."

"Fine."

The two men left James's office and walked down the stairs to the dungeons. There was a silence that was almost alarming. As they rounded the bar the reason became evident. The main club floor was empty. Minutes ago it had been pulsing with life. Vincent had never seen it this empty. Even when James had performed his scene, and most of the members were by the stage, there were still plenty of people milling about the main club area or working their own demonstrations.

Look over at the alcoves showed that they and the audience area were both empty. Whatever had attracted the attention of the members wasn't in his line of sight. James didn't seem to notice the difference. Perhaps they were closing early tonight for whatever reason. Guess he hadn't gotten the membership newsletter.

He was an ex-member now. He didn't belong there anymore. He had this past of his life taken away from him six days, twelve hours, and fifty-two minutes ago.

They stopped outside of Mia's dungeon. Vincent took a deep breath. It was just a room.

James held out his hand for the key card. The look on his face was almost angry. "You know, Vin, I really expected you'd be different."

"What is that supposed to mean?" He was really starting to get tired of James's shit.

"I expected you to fight for her."

Vincent was incredulous. "I tried! But she wouldn't let me. Her mind was set on hating herself and getting rid of me."

"True." James nodded. "But a Dom is supposed to be able to read their Sub and give them what they need. You should have seen through what she was trying to do."

"So I guess I'm not the perfect Dom."

James shook his head. "Not yet, but remember, anything can be taught." He swiped the card and the door unlocked.

"Are you ready?"

"Yeah. Let's get this over with."

James gave him a hard look. "You know, acting like an asshole isn't a good fit for you."

Vincent sighed. James was right. Just because he was bitter about what Mia had done, didn't mean he had to take it out on James. "Look, I'm sorry."

"I know." James's face softened. "You're a good guy. Be the Vin I know instead of some jaded hurting piece of s—"

Vincent held up a hand. "Hey, I get it. I'm sorry." He tried to relax, to shake off the anger and hurt. Sure he still felt it, but he could bury it for a bit. He would drop off the bag, say good-bye to his friend and be home before the pizza got cold. "Let's do this."

James surveyed him for a moment. "Just remember what's in this room is the most precious thing to me in the world." He turned the door handle and pushed the door open. "Go ahead."

The room was pitch black. No, that wasn't right. As he stepped inside the dungeon and his eyes adjusted, he saw that there was some light. Candles were lined up in a circle in the middle of the room. They gave off just enough illumination to allow him to walk further inside the dungeon without stumbling. James followed him, leaving the door open. It was odd to not have that big door shut, but at least the light from the hallway helped him to see more.

What he was seeing didn't register initially. He was stunned that the room wasn't empty. In fact there must have been a hundred or so people crammed into this room. Mark and Terry were there, as were others that he recognized. They stood silent off to the side.

Vincent turned back to look at James. His friend smiled and nodded his encouragement. He gestured for Vincent to continue further into the room. Vincent wanted to ask questions, but it didn't seem right. A line of worry crossed his face. Was he walking into a scene already in progress? Was someone else using Mia's dungeon now?

The bag of her things slipped out of his hand when he realized that there was a person inside of the circle of candles. She was nude, with her long dark hair falling into her face as she knelt in the slave position. Her eyes were down. She was waiting.

Mia.

He must have said her name out loud, because her head snapped up. This wasn't the same Mia that he had seen the last time he was in this dungeon. This one seemed small and vulnerable. He went to stand before her.

When her eyes met his, he knew. He understood why he was here and why she was here and why they had all these witnesses. He understood in an instant, but she said it anyways. "I'm sorry."

"It's okay."

"No it's not," she whispered. "I love you, Vincent."

Vincent tried to memorize this moment. "I love you too."

"I couldn't say it earlier because I was scared. I think maybe I've loved you since the day at the pier."

Vincent smiled. "I think I've loved you since the day I first saw you."

James stood by his side. "Are you ready for your final exam?"

Vincent laughed. It broke the tension in the room, and several club members voiced their encouragement with cheers and whistles.

Mia smiled. "It's time."

"You know, you don't have to do this. You've been through so much."

"I know." Mia looked so pretty and so sure. There was no hesitation in her words or actions. If there had been, Vincent would have stopped this thing before it started. Yet, he felt the need to ask her again, to give her an out in case she needed it. "I'm not doing it because I have to do it. I'm doing it because I want to. I'm ready to give myself to you."

"Maybe we should talk about this first."

"Vincent." Mia raised an eyebrow with a look that showed there was no changing her mind. "I'm your Sub. Let me show you through my action and my body that I'm ready to submit to you."

"Last time. Are you sure?"

"Absolutely." She looked at him with warmth and with love. He hoped the love he felt for her also showed as clearly. She had his whole heart.

Vincent stretched and rolled his shoulders to prepare. He remembered every lesson she had taught him. He was ready for this. The things they had practiced came back to him. "Please stand, pet, and present yourself to me. I'd like to show everyone how pretty my Sub is."

Without hesitation, Mia rose gracefully from the floor. Even in the candlelight, he could see there were still some bruises on her body. She also had stitches. He would have to be careful with her so not to hurt her body more. Anger rose in his chest and he fought it back down. There was no one left to be angry with. Later when they were alone at his—their—home, he would lay her down on the bed and kiss every single bruise she had. For now, he would ignore them. They did not distract or take away from her loveliness.

"Sub, whose body is this?"

"Yours, Master."

"Do you give it to me willingly?"

"Oh yes." The smile she rewarded him with backed up her words. He had no doubt, she was his.

"Good. Because my Sub needs to be punished. Five swats for lying to me. Five more for making me think it was over. Five more for trying to break my heart, five more for…"

"That's a lot of swats, Master."

"…five more for being a brat and for trying to top from the bottom. I will not allow that. Who is in charge here?"

"You are, Master." Mia gracefully stepped outside of the ring of candles. Then she turned and walked toward the spanking bench.

"Stop right there, Pet. No bench today. I think your punishment should be a bit more personal. I would like you on my lap."

Mia returned to him. Soon they were inches apart. He didn't need to hold her hand to feel their connection. The space between them could have cracked from the electricity of their bodies. Still, he reached out and took her hand. He was startled when his fingers brushed dried flowers at her wrist. He held up her hand to get a better look. She wore the corsage he had given her at her father's party. Perfectly preserved, the red flowers still looked beautiful against her skin.

"Hi." She smiled.

"Hi. I missed you."

"Me too."

"You're not allowed to push me away again. If you get scared, we talk, if you get mad, we talk, if you—"

"I get it…we talk."

James moved a high-backed chair into position for them to use. Vincent nodded his thanks and sat down. He took a minute to look around the room. All eyes were on him. He felt powerful. He finally felt like a Dom. "Take your position, pet."

Without hesitation, Mia happily stretched her body over his lap. She braced herself with her hands against the floor. In position, her pussy was against his thigh, and her bare ass high in the air. The crowd could clearly see every part of her. She gave herself freely to him without a second thought for modesty. This was her Master's body to use as he saw fit.

"Are you ready to take your punishment?"

"Yes, Master."

Vincent caressed the smooth skin of her bottom. He enjoyed the moment and the feel of her. He had thought that he would never get to hold her again, never touch her again. He was willing to let her go before if it was what she had really wanted. Now he could never walk away from her again. She was his first real love and his last.

Having her on his lap was a lot different from the last time he had punished her. Before, he had used a variety of instruments from the wall. This time he would only use his hand to spank her. He needed the intimacy that only skin-to-skin touch could bring.

The first spank was soft. His hands barely tapped the fleshly part of her left cheek. "One." Mia's voice rang out against the silence in the room. The second and third spanks were harder. "Two, three. four, five." She counted as each blow landed.

"And what are those five for, pet?"

"For lying. I'm sorry, Master."

"I don't think of you as an object, Mia. You're smart and funny and the most precious person in the world to me."

"Thank you. I was wrong and I'm sorry for saying all of that before."

"You are forgiven." He took a moment to rub his hand over her ass. His caress meant that he accepted her sweet apology.

Next his hand came down on her with a little more force. He hit the back of her thighs first to surprise her. "One, two." She counted.

The next connection his hand made was with the top of her ass. It seemed to be a sensitive area for her. "Three, four, five. Five for making you think it was over."

"And is it over, Mia?"

"No. It's just beginning." He liked that answer. As a reward he bent and pressed his lips to the sensitive area he had just hit. A new beginning for them. He liked that. All the dreams that he had thought were lost were once again within reach.

The next spankings were harder to deliver. They represented everything that he felt when he realized she was gone, and when James and Lee had helped him find her. These blows represented how scared he had been when he found her strapped to that creep's bed. And lastly, they represented all the pain and anger he had felt when he had left her hospital room.

He wanted to get them over with quickly, so he hit her hard and fast on her left cheek. He tried not to be too hard on her, but he wanted her to remember, and to know that he would not accept her turning her back on him again. It was hard and fast enough that she couldn't count, and could merely yelp at every strike.

"What are those five for?"

Her voice was small and soft. "For trying to break your heart."

"Will you do it again?"

"No, Master, never. I promise."

Vincent softly caressed her skin, feeling the heat he had brought out. If there was enough light, her skin would probably be bright red. "Why should I believe you?"

"Because trust is the most important part of a relationship."

"Very good, Sub." The next words were a joy to say. "You are forgiven."

He had five final spanks to give her, and then her punishment would be over. These last five would be slow and soft. "One, two, three."

Perhaps it was because he was going slower, Mia reacted most to these gentle swats. Her body rocked across his lap. And each number was spoken a little breathier. "Four, five."

"Those are for being a brat, Sub."

"Thank you, Master. I'm sorry."

Vincent chuckled. "I have a feeling that won't be the last time you'll be punished for being a brat." Mia was quiet, but he could bet she was smiling.

He was about to let her up, when he felt her squirm on his lap. He felt her grind against him. He touched her pussy. He was a little surprised to find it soaking wet. Yes, those last swats sure had an effect on his girl. He decided to change his plan for how their scene would go. She had taken his punishment beautifully. Now for a little reward.

He dipped his finger inside of her, gathering some of her wetness. Then he gently touched her clit. Even that slight touch was enough to make her buck on his lap. He held her down with one hand as he continued to prod that little nub of pleasure.

"Do you like this, pet?"

"Yes. Please touch me more, Master," she begged.

He smiled. This was the most responsive he had ever seen her. This was his gift from her. He had her body, her soul, and her core wrapped up in a bundle of nerves, responding to him.

She groaned when he removed his finger from her clit. He didn't deny her his touch long. He inserted two fingers into her and began to massage her G-spot. This new stimulation made her go wild. She began trusting her body to meet his fingers as they moved inside of her.

"Oh yes, Master." She moaned.

Her movements rubbed against his hard cock. He couldn't wait to have her in private. He would love nothing more to sink his cock into her to the hilt and then fuck her fast until he came. The romance and making up would have to wait for a second round. He wanted her too badly to be gentle the first time. He wanted her so badly that he almost ripped off his jeans and had her now. But he knew he had to wait until they were alone and they could make love properly, without interruption and without an audience.

Mia sure didn't seem to mind the audience now. Vincent's fingers stroked inside her walls harder and faster. She was panting. He knew she was quickly approaching the point of no return. He wanted his Sub to come, then he wanted to kiss her while the pleasure was still flush on her face.

He stopped holding her down to reach under her and caress her breasts. He tugged on her piercings, but she was too far gone to register that slight pain. Instead he let go and grabbed a fistful of her hair. He pulled her head up gently so that he could see her expression, her scrunched-up eyes, her lips forming a gentle O. She was so close.

He was about to give the order for her to come, the command she always needed to find release, but instead he was pleasantly surprised to feel her walls clamp down on his fingers all by themselves. He stopped moving and let her muscles milk them as they gave her own release.

"Vincent!" she screamed.

Finally, she was able to let go and come on her own. That was another gift she gave him.

As her orgasm faded away, he removed his hands from her and instead used his arms to swing her around into a seated position. He held her tightly as she struggled to regain her breath.

"Thank you." She panted.

"You're welcome." He kissed her lips sweetly. What a perfect moment with his perfect girl. He would never stop loving this little spitfire and he would never let her go again.

"Looks like you passed your exam with flying colours." James's words startled them both.

"I agree." Mia face was a mixture of satisfaction and pride as she gently eased herself out of his arms and returned to the circle of candles and the slave position.

"There's only one thing left."

Vincent frowned. What had he forgotten? "What?"

"To collar your Sub. That is, I do assume that you want to collar her?"

Vincent looked at Mia, his teacher, his Sub. Slowly she nodded, encouraging him. His heart swelled. It was a gift that she would allow him to collar her. Collaring in this world meant that she was his.

The only problem is that he didn't have anything to collar her with. He had seen collars on the Subs here, and had dreamed about what kind of collar he would one day get for Mia. It would have to be something beautiful, unique and strong, just like her.

"I'm sorry, but I didn't come prepared."

"Allow me." James handed him a small box. It must have been in his pocket, this whole time. Vincent took the box from him. He felt the heavy weight in his palm. Whatever was inside was substantial.

He probably should have let Mia open it herself, but he wanted to see it first. He wanted to see what James had found worthy enough for him to use to collar the love of his life with. Opening the antique box, he saw a beautiful necklace nestled inside on a bed of silk. It wasn't quite the type of collar Vincent had envisioned, but it was very impressive.

"It's too much, James. I can't afford this. And I can't take it as a gift."

The silver chain was delicate but strong and its charm was a beautiful diamond lock. It was subtle enough to wear as regular jewelry, but its meaning wouldn't be lost on anyone in the club or those in the lifestyle. It was a collar and it was perfect. It was as beautiful as Mia, and just as precious.

"Take it." James smiled. "It was her mother's."

Vincent looked to Mia for confirmation and she smiled and nodded. "I've been waiting my whole life to wear that."

Vincent carefully picked up the chain and handed the box back to James. "Thank you," he said to his friend, meaning thank you for everything. For introducing him to Mia, helping to save her, bringing him back to her today, showing him this life could be possible and could be his. He owned his friend everything. His eyes swam with emotion. A simple thank you would never be enough.

James understood and patted him on the shoulder. "Go claim your Sub."

Vincent approached the circle and carefully stepped inside of it. Mia looked so beautiful as she knelt at his feet. "Pet?"

"Yes, Master."

Vincent hesitated for a moment. He didn't know the proper words he should say. Instead he spoke from his heart. "Will you wear my collar? Will you accept me as your one and only Master?"

"Yes."

"Will you share a home and life with me and Gus?"

"Yes, Master."

She had been so open and accepting. He decided to ask one more question. The only one he had left in his heart unanswered. "Will you marry me, Mia?"

"Yes, Vincent."

He held his hand out to her. She gladly took the connection and allowed him to help her stand. Gently he placed the collar around her neck and fastened the intricate clasp. It shone bright against her pale skin. It seemed designed to be unable to be removed without the help of a second person. He liked that feature and hoped that he would never have to help her remove it. The lock was shaped almost like a heart. Yes, this collar was perfect. "Gus will be jealous that your collar is nicer than his," he joked.

With the collar on, their scene was complete. The crowd cheered and applauded as he wrapped Mia up in his arms and kissed her. Sweet Mia. His forever.

"I love you." She looked up into his eyes. They glowed as bright as the diamonds in her collar. "I tried not to, but I couldn't help it."

"To make up for it, pet, I'm going to make you say it to me often."

"Deal. Are you ready to go home?"

Vincent gave her what he hoped was a stern, but loving, Dom look. "I was hoping we could play a little more before we leave. Or are you sick of me already?"

Mia smiled mischievously. "Let's play."

Vincent quickly kissed her lips. Play they would. He had a good idea of what he wanted to do with his love, but first the needed privacy.

"James?" he called out.

He had lost track of their friend, but Vincent spotted him ushering the last people out of the dungeon.

"Yeah, Vin?"

"Close the door."

"With pleasure."

Vincent waited until James had shut the heavy door to pull Mia to him.

"Thank you," he whispered.

"For what?"

"For everything. For the training, the dates." He chuckled. "And especially for loving me."

She gave him a saucy look. "I could say exactly the same thing."

Mia turned and walked away from him. He watched her walk around the equipment. She paused at each piece as if considering it. It was great foreplay and made his already-hungry cock ravenous for her. "Will you just pick one already!"

"Patience, Vincent. Good things come to those who wait."

"No, good things come to those who train for it."

She laughed. "Very true, Master."

He watched her change her mind and walk away from the equipment. He almost growled when she sat on the sofa instead. She patted the seat beside her, inviting him over.

"Do you want to play cards?" he asked, as he sauntered over.

She looked adorable with the mischievous glint in her eye. "Do I? You decide, Master. Tell me what to do."

He stopped when he stood in front of her. He had walked so close that his crotch was inches away from her face. She smiled and looked up at him, licking her lips. "I think I'm going to like this game. Sub, please pull down my zipper and take my cock out." Mia smiled as she did as her instructed. "And now wrap your hands around me." Again, she did exactly as he asked.

"Now what, Master?"

"Stroke me, show me how much you like my cock. You can give it a kiss if you want."

She grinned and started to stroke him as instructed. Her long fingers were very agile as they slipped up and down his shaft. A small kiss to the crown of his cock followed. "All done, Master."

Vincent growled. "Good job, Sub, but I'm far from done with you." He reached down and grabbed her under each arm. Picking her up like she weighed nothing, he held her high as he maneuvered himself into a seating position on the couch with her over him.

Mia hovered inches away from his cock. "Me on top?" she asked.

"Are you doubting me, Sub?"

"No, not at all." She lowered herself slowly. Each inch she slid down on him felt incredible. When she was fully seated on him, she claimed him just as much as he was claiming her.

She closed her eyes to enjoy the sensation. Vincent took the opportunity to lick one nipple and then the other. He teased first one tip and then the other into his mouth and pulled on her piercings.

Mia moaned. "Oh, Master, I think I like being on top."

"Yeah?" Vincent flexed his hips. This position limited his movement, but what range he had he used to his full advantage. He withdrew from her just slightly, then pushed his way back into her again. His cock dragged on her private muscles as he slowly moved back and forth.

"My turn," Mia declared. Then she took a deep breath and rocked her hips. Vincent hissed in a breath at the sensation. Having Mia in the driver's seat was a special treat. Watching her take her own pleasure was intoxicating. "Did you like that?"

"Oh, pet, I loved that."

Mia giggled and began moving faster on his cock. Her breath quickened and her eyes closed. She concentrated on the sensations.

She startled when Vincent touched her clit. He couldn't resist. As he watched her ride his shaft, her little button was pushing its way out of her hood begging for some attention. They made eye contact as he lightly stroked it. Her dark eyes were heavy with desire. Her movement increased to keep pace with his fingers. Soon she could barely keep pace as her hips jerked trying to keep in time. He loved seeing her like this.

He loved that he now had the opportunity to get to know her even better. He was going to spend that time learning her body and her mind. Learning how to read every emotion, every look, every reaction. It would be both an honour and a joy. He couldn't imagine ever tiring of being with her. She was his perfect Sub. She was his as much as he was hers.

She was close, and so was he. He started thrusting again, rising up to meet her. He was pushing back on her so hard she was almost standing. She held onto him tightly.

He could feel the exact moment when her orgasm started. It was a light flutter that built sharply to a crescendo inside of her. Mia stopped moving and threw her head back. Her nails dug into his arms as wave after wave of pleasure over took her. Although she had come just minutes before, this second orgasm was intense.

It was impossible for Vincent not to follow her lead. He thrust back into her as far as he could and held her hips down. He came just as hard as she did. The feeling was overwhelming.

A sweet smile played on her lips as they recovered from their orgasms. He watched it spread to light up her flushed face. "That was perfect," she whispered. "That was exactly what I needed. You're exactly what I needed." She paused. "I love you, Vincent."

"I love you too, Mia."

She smiled and wrapped her arms around him. "You're the perfect Dom for me."

"I should be. You trained me."

She laughed. Her joy was contagious. He loved seeing her so open and so free. "Just because you passed your final exam doesn't mean you're done training."

"I'm not?"

"Nope." She shook her head. "I have just created a new extra final exam for you."

"Oh really, you just created it?"

"Yup. And it's extra hard to pass."

Vincent frowned. "How long will I have to study for it?"

Mia pretended to consider his question. "Probably the rest of your life."

"I don't think I'll have that amount of time available. I'm going to be pretty busy with your training."

She raised an eyebrow. "My training?"

He nodded. "Yup. I have a few things I need to train you on."

She groaned. "Please no more lessons on the history of kung fu movies!"

Vincent pretended to be heartbroken. "I thought you liked those!"

"I was being polite."

"Fine."

Mia tried to struggle out of his arms but Vincent held tight. "Can we go home now?"

"Absolutely." He smiled, but before he let her up, he gave her a deep, soulful kiss. It held all of his love and all of his promises to her for their future.

It would be fun training the trainer to love and build a life with him.

"Let's go."

Her lessons would begin immediately.

THE END

WWW.JADEBELFRY.COM

ABOUT THE AUTHOR

Jade Belfry has always been a writer. Even in grade school she wrote long chapter books, often with a suspenseful or comedic story line. Now as an adult, her books still showcase suspense or comedy, but she prefers to write stories that also have a healthy amount of spice!

She inherited her love of reading from both her grandmother and mother. She definitely shares her writing talent with her mother, Dale Cadeau, who also pens erotic romances. It's a unique situation having two authors in the family, but it makes for fun family meals with plenty of after-dinner shop talk.

Jade was originally born in the Georgian Bay area, but now lives just west of Toronto in Ontario, Canada. Although she will admit that some days she wishes she lived somewhere much warmer! She shares her life and her home with her very supportive husband John and their cute kitties, who love to keep her company as she writes.

Siren Publishing, Inc.
www.SirenPublishing.com

CPSIA information can be obtained
at www.ICGtesting.com
Printed in the USA
LVHW081330190619
621723LV00008B/61/P